Previously Engaged

Previously Engaged

Elodia Strain

CFI
Springville, Utah

ISBN 13: 978-1-59955-251-4

Published by CFI, an imprint of Cedar Fort, Inc., 2373 W. 700 S., Springville, UT, 84663
Distributed by Cedar Fort, Inc., www.cedarfort.com

LIBRARY OF CONGRESS CATALOGING-IN-PUBLICATION DATA

Strain, Elodia Kay, 1979-
  Previously engaged / Elodia Strain.
    p. cm.
  ISBN 978-1-59955-251-4 (acid-free paper)
  1. Young women—Fiction. 2. Weddings—Planning—Fiction. 3. Chick lit.
  I. Title.

  PS3619.T724P27 2008
  813'.6—dc22

                          2008043662

Cover design by Nicole Williams
Cover design © 2009 by Lyle Mortimer
Typeset by Kammi Rencher
Edited by Allison Kartchner and Heidi Doxey

Printed in the United States of America

10 9 8 7 6 5 4 3 2 1

Printed on acid-free paper

Dedication

To Miranda.

Two of the greatest blessings in my life have been one, to call you my sister, and two, to call you my friend.

Acknowledgments

A hundred thanks to:

Heidi Doxey—awesome editor and friend, Jennifer Fielding, Nicole Williams, Allison Kartchner, and the rest of the great team at CFI.

Mom and Dad. You have been so amazing during this writing journey, and I appreciate all your help, advice, and support.

My wonderful and encouraging siblings and siblings-in-law: Brett Saavedra, Theresa Saavedra, Brian Saavedra, Miranda Bergevin, Eli Bergevin, Jenny Wappett, Kerry Wappett, Tracy Bergeson, Brett Bergeson, and Wyatt Strain.

Jack and Nancy and Blake and Brielle for making the last month and a half of the process so great.

Dan and Kimberly Black and Brianna Monson and clan for being such great friends.

Dr. Keith Willmore and Sarah Greer for helping me be healhty enough to write.

As always, Jacob. For listening to my brainstorms, reading my many drafts, and hugging me when I just didn't think I could do it.

And most of all, thanks to all the readers who enjoyed my first book and wrote to me about it. Without you, this book probably never would have happened. Thank you!

Chapter 1

*A*pparently, weddings are breeding grounds for disaster. Did you know that?

Well, I certainly didn't.

Maybe it's because I've only been to two weddings in my life—those of my two sisters—and with Mom as master organizer, they turned out pretty much perfect.

Even when my sister Cammie insisted she wanted a "Winter Wonderland" theme for her December wedding, Mom did not look at her and say, "You're so spoiled. It's just like you to insist we turn our home in Monterey, California, where the average December temperature is 65 degrees, into a 'Winter Wonderland' for you and the guy who can't seem to eat cereal without making that awful slurping noise and who seriously should not sing along with rap music."

No. Mom gave a scolding look to the person who said that—who may or may not have been me—and then made the "Winter Wonderland" wedding happen. She brought in enough fake snow to make me think we were in Vail, Colorado, not Monterey, California. She dipped dainty faux snowflakes into glitter and strung twinkle lights everywhere. And she made it look so easy.

So when my best friend Carrie asked me to be her Maid of

Honor, I thought my job was going to be fun and simple, and I spent the months leading up to the wedding doing what I thought a Maid of Honor was supposed to do.

I helped Carrie pick out a gorgeous pair of organic-satin shoes to go with her wedding gown. I tasted way too many "I promise the carob tastes just like chocolate!" wedding cake samples and then discreetly spat those "Um, no, this tastes nothing like chocolate!" samples into napkins. I helped her stuff the off-white recycled-paper invitations. And when the big day came, I thought I had my bases covered.

But then, the night before the wedding, I was painting Carrie's toenails in her living room—celebrating our last ever Paint and Popcorn night as two single gals—when a show called *Wedding Disasters* came onto the TV, and I realized I had been very, very wrong.

"Change it," Carrie said in her soft, yoga-instructor-esque voice. She twisted her wavy blonde hair into a bun, being careful not to mess up her manicure.

"Wait," I said, my eyes glued to the screen, remote clutched in my hand.

"I'm not watching this," Carrie said. "I need to be calm tomorrow."

"Okay. Fine." I turned the TV to a movie channel and we watched an old black-and-white until Carrie said she was going to bed.

"You're getting married to Miles tomorrow," I said as I hugged her goodnight.

She smiled a giddy smile and spun around before heading for her bedroom. I listened for the sound of her door closing and then turned *Wedding Disasters* back on.

I spent the next hour glued to the TV with my mouth wide open as women told stories and showed video clips of their wedding disasters.

Josie Starbuck of Tulsa, Oklahoma, had her couture dress stolen by a staff member at the hotel she stayed in the night before the wedding.

Lucy Wabble of San Antonio, Texas, had to watch from the aisle as her groom was taken away in handcuffs for something he had done at his bachelor party.

And Frenchie Marmel of Kirkland, Washington was eyebrow-less in all of her reception pictures because her groom singed her $300, perfectly sculpted brows off with a candle during the ceremony.

I watched the whole show and when I clicked off the TV, I was a changed woman. I was not the naïve little Maid of Honor I had once been. No, I was ready for disaster.

I immediately and frantically began to assemble the Wedding Disaster Prevention Case—or WDPC—one of Carrie's rolling suitcases, which I filled with all the things I might need the next day.

I had the stick of paraben-free eyebrow pencil I stole from Carrie's bathroom in case her brows got burned off somehow the next day. As far as I knew, Carrie wasn't having candles at the wedding, but really, you never know who might be walking around with burning objects these days. It's a weird world we live in. And I wasn't taking any chances.

I had the number of a place where I could get a vintage wedding dress at a moment's notice.

I had the number for a bail bond guy.

And I had the small things I thought might be needed: stain-remover wipes, sewing kit, and lots and lots of duct tape.

So when morning came, I was ready.

I kept Carrie out of the kitchen, away from knives, burners, and the toaster.

I made sure she didn't walk near any objects that could fall and hit her head.

And when Carrie's uncle came to pick up the wedding dress to transport, I let him know I was watching him. I did that little move where you use your first and second fingers to point to your eyes and then to the person as if you're saying, "I've got my eyes on you." He looked at me like I was crazy, but he definitely got the message.

When I tried to make Carrie wear a pair of non-slip water shoes into the shower, though, she wouldn't do it. "Please, Annabelle," she said. "You're going crazy. It's making me nervous."

"All right. But if you end up in the ER with a broken femur instead of at your wedding ceremony, don't blame me."

"Do you even know what a femur is?"

"Not *exactly*. But Maxine Dover of Madison, Wisconsin, does."

"I told you not to watch that show," Carrie said as she closed the bathroom door on me.

Much to my relief, the wedding day seemed to go perfectly. No one choked during the wedding breakfast, no one took a wrong turn in Oakland and got carjacked, and Carrie looked gorgeous in her organic silk dress, holding onto Miles's arm tightly and smiling the biggest smile I have ever seen.

But the thing with disaster is it comes when you let your guard down. And I, my friend, let my guard down.

I was standing on the bamboo dance floor that had been set up on the lawn in Carrie's—and soon to be the happy couple's—backyard for the wedding reception. The sun had gone down, and the Monterey Bay in the distance was inky blue and lit by the lights of the city and those of a few tiny boats. The oblong tables were decorated with linens and flowers in vibrant pinks, yellows, and oranges, and round Chinese lanterns hung above the tables and dance floor. Everything was perfect.

Well. I should have knocked on wood. Or bamboo. Is bamboo considered wood? I don't know.

I was pulled away from my reflection on how beautiful everything was when the DJ, Carrie's cousin Joey—a lanky honors student/aspiring hip-hop DJ—put on the song Carrie decided to play during the bouquet toss: "Girls Just Wanna Have Fun."

"What's up Monterey!" Joey said into the microphone, trying to make his voice sound deeper than it was. It cracked slightly in the process. "J-Dog here, spindle for your funindle."

I tried not to laugh. Carrie had explained to me that as his "trademark" Joey decided to form his own language, "Like Snoop did." So when he's DJ-ing all of Joey's words end in "indle."

"Let's get all the ladindles on the florindle for the tossindle of the bouquindle!"

Several versions of "What?" sounded throughout the yard.

"Time for the bouquet toss!" someone yelled.

The single ladies giggled and gabbed as they formed a big clump on the floor.

I rushed over to my seat at the head table and reached into the WDPC for the one thing I had brought for myself: Isaac's baseball glove. And what was I doing with my boyfriend's baseball glove you ask? Well, I was making sure I caught that bouquet.

And not at all because I'd been dating Isaac for an amazing nine months and wanted to catch that bouquet and harbor the fantasy that I would be getting married next. No. According to more than one wedding disaster story, the bouquet toss can lead to broken bones, bloody noses, and cat fights. So basically I was just performing my Maid of Honorly duties by making sure I caught the thing.

The other single ladies looked at me like I was a bit of a nut standing there in the pretty yellow organic cotton sundress Carrie had picked out and a dirty baseball glove with "Crush 'Em" written on it in faded black writing. But it was probably just because they wished they had thought of bringing a glove themselves.

Squeals filled the air as Carrie asked us if we were all ready and then tossed the lilies over her shoulder with her trademark grace. I watched the flowers' trajectory and moved my body to follow it, my dark hair swishing around my face. Soon the flowers were soaring directly toward me. I reached my glove up and out, just as Isaac had showed me.

My smile grew very wide as I watched the bouquet move closer and closer. My glove was mere inches from the lilies and then . . . Boom! Someone smacked me in the head from behind. Really hard. So hard I was positive the hit couldn't have come from another female.

"Hey!" I hollered as the ground got kind of swirly and my legs felt like jelly atop the cute Italian designer sandals I'd found at a garage sale in Carmel. "No guys allowed on the—" Plop.

Yep. That was the sound of me hitting the floor.

With my last second of clarity, I saw Miles' cousin Greta—the former Olympic hockey player who I had heard Carrie refer to as "215 pounds of pure muscle"—holding the bouquet of lilies triumphantly, and heard the faint sounds of Carrie's mom gasping and DJ J-Dog putting on the song, "Another One Bites the Dust."

The next few moments were filled with alternating blackness and blurriness, and I'm not quite sure how long it took me to come to full awareness. But when I did, I noticed a large group had formed around me.

"I know CPR," Carrie's grandpa said, looking down at me.

"No!" I said quickly. "I'm fine." I tried to sit up and the world turned very, very kaleidoscopy. I felt someone put a hand behind my head and hold it up. From the strength of the arm, I thought it must be Isaac.

"Thanks," I said, letting the strong arm hold me up as I blinked and tried to orient myself.

Carrie rushed to my side and bent down next to me, not at all concerned about getting dance floor dirt on her dress. "Annabelle! Are you okay?"

I nodded my head and immediately discovered that head movement equaled throbbing pain.

"Yeah, sure," I said, alternately opening and closing my eyes.

"Do you think you need a doctor?" Carrie asked. "Maybe I should get someone. Like your mom. I think she's in the kitchen."

"And another one, and another one, and another one bites the dust," Joey sang into the microphone. Carrie glared over at him.

"I'll take care of her," I heard a male voice say.

My entire body suddenly turned icy cold. I knew that voice. I knew that voice well. And it did not belong to Isaac.

No. It belonged to Alex Mikels. Alex Mikels who I hadn't seen in nearly seven years.

"Okay," Carrie said. "But I'm still going to find her mom." With that, Carrie rushed off and the crowd around me began to break up a little.

Alex helped me up from the ground and led me to a nearby table. I looked around for Isaac.

Once I was seated, I caught a quick glimpse of Alex.

I had pictured this moment many times. The first time he saw me after, well, let's just call it The Incident.

And the way I pictured it was this: We'd see each other somewhere like a supermarket. I would be buying something cool like two bottles of Pellegrino for a date with a handsome someone, and I'd be looking great in a cute outfit and would be having an unbelievably good hair day. Alex, on the other hand, would be buying something embarrassing like athlete's foot powder, and he would have gone bald, grown a potbelly, and maybe even started to get unsightly ear hair.

He would then proceed to stare at me and wonder why he had been so stupid.

But we were not at a supermarket. And Alex Mikels was not a balding potbelly. In fact, he looked pretty much the same as I remembered. Same sandy blond hair. Same strong jaw. Same blue eyes. He did look a little older, though. And a little fuzzier.

Within seconds, my brain—which has started to sound a lot like my mom lately—started asking me all kinds of questions.

What in the world is Alex Mikels doing at Carrie's wedding reception?

I didn't know. Last I heard Alex was living in New York City doing something in publishing.

But was he invited?

I didn't think so. I had helped with the invitations, and I was sure I would have remembered if Carrie had invited him. But, now that I thought about it, Carrie didn't seem too surprised to see him . . .

After Alex made sure I was comfortable, he turned behind him and instructed someone to get a cold pack for my head.

"You okay?" As the question came from Alex's mouth, our eyes met for the first time.

And I, like a kid afraid of a roller coaster, quickly snapped my lids shut. "I'm fine," I said, my head facing his. "Just fine."

"You sure?"

"Yes, of course," I said as if it was completely normal for me to be talking to him with my eyes closed.

"Is your vision blurred or something? Because that's not a good sign."

"Nope," I said. "Vision's fine. Hunky-dory."

Hunky-dory? Okay. That's the first time I've ever said that. And hopefully the last.

"Then why aren't you looking at me?"

I slowly opened my eyes, and saw that Alex was staring at me, flashing that smile that had been voted the best at Monterey High.

I shifted uncomfortably. "What?"

"I always did love your eyes. The color reminds me of maple syrup."

I pretended I hadn't heard the comment. "What are you doing here? I thought you lived in New York."

"I couldn't miss Carrie Berry's wedding," Alex said.

Carrie Berry. That had been Carrie's high school nickname.

"Plus," Alex continued. "My company has me out here

for . . . a project."

"In Monterey?"

Alex nodded. "Yep. It's so good to be back. And so good to see you."

I stared at him. The way he was acting, you'd think we were still great friends. You'd think he hadn't done what he had done.

"How long are you in town for?" I asked.

"As long as it takes."

"As long as what takes?"

Alex looked at me in that boyish I-have-a-secret way he used to look at me back in high school.

"Annabelle!" Isaac was suddenly at my side, kneeling beside me and inspecting the damage. "Oh, sweetie, are you okay?" He placed a pack of ice wrapped in a towel against my head. "Carrie told me what happened. Your mom was bringing this out, but I told her I'd take care of you. You poor thing." Isaac kissed the top of my head ever so softly. Then, as if noticing him for the first time, he looked at Alex with a "who's he?" expression on his face.

I cleared my throat. "Isaac, this is . . . Alex Mikels. And Alex, this is my . . . this is . . . Isaac."

Isaac nodded over at Alex in that "What's up man?" way guys nod. Alex returned the gesture.

"Where have you been?" I asked Isaac, my voice soft and, I'll admit it, a little pitiful.

"I was outside photographing the getaway car—Miles' brothers trashed the thing." Isaac set his Nikon on the table with much less care than he usually takes with his camera, and rolled his white dress shirt up to his elbows, revealing his gorgeous basketball-toned forearms. "I'm so sorry I wasn't here to help you, sweetheart."

"It's okay."

"Well I guess my job here is done," Alex said abruptly. "It's probably time for me to say good-bye to the bride and groom and head home, anyway."

"Thanks for, um . . . helping me," I said.

"Yeah, thanks," Isaac added.

"No problem." Alex smiled at me, stood up from the table, and walked away.

Isaac took the newly vacated seat at the orange, cloth-covered table. "How do you know that guy?"

"He's just a guy Carrie and I used to hang out with in high school," I said vaguely.

Isaac nodded his head, his messy-in-a-good-way brown hair catching the light. "Oh."

Chapter 2

Alex Mikels broke my heart.

Not just an oh-he's-a-cool-guy-but-it's-nothing-a-few-pints-of-Cold-Stone-ice-cream-won't-fix kind of heartbreak. No, with Alex it was much more. And suddenly, as Isaac left the table to take a few final pictures of the reception, I was thinking about it all over again.

Alex transferred to Monterey High from a fancy prep school in New York. On January 11—I remember because it was the day after my eighteenth birthday and I was wearing a new pair of earrings from Dad—he walked into my first period English class, and I lost my place in the Shakespeare play I was reading.

I don't think I'm the only girl who did.

After English, I tried to muster up the courage to talk to him, but by the time I got to the door, he was gone.

When he strolled into my second period science class, I couldn't believe my luck that the girl who used to sit by me had mono and would be gone for the rest of the year.

"Hey," Alex said as he sat down on the stool beside me.

I stared at his designer sweater, perfectly cut blond hair, and azure blue eyes. "Hi."

After the new guy and I quickly exchanged names,

Mrs. Lynch started her lecture, and I took detailed notes of everything she said.

Oh, wait, I can tell you the truth, can't I? Okay. Mrs. Lynch started her lecture, and I snuck glances at Alex the whole time. One time I think he caught me, but I recovered by pretending I was reading the "Musculoskeletal System of the Human Body" chart behind him.

What? Maybe he'd think I was into muscles. He sure had some nice ones.

After lecture Mrs. Lynch instructed us to look at some slides under a microscope with the person next to us. I quickly put a piece of gum in my mouth, smothered my lips in lip gloss, and tried to buff my nails on my sweater.

"So do you like sports?" Alex asked as he secured a slide with a leaf on it under the little clips on the microscope.

"Oh, yeah, totally."

"Which ones?"

"Um . . . Tag?"

Yep. I said tag. What can I say? Back then I hadn't quite become the cool, confident woman I am today.

Oops. Just spilled organic wedding punch on my dress.

Anyway, back to the story.

Alex smiled the kind of smile that makes boy bands famous. "Cool. I like crew. I was on the team back at Chase."

I had no idea what crew was. "That sounds enjoyable," I said. Yep. Enjoyable.

Alex laughed. "You're kind of cute."

And that's all it took. I was on my way to falling 100 percent head over heels.

No guy had ever called me cute before. I had gotten plenty of: "Hey aren't you the girl who fell off the stage during the school play?" And, "Hey aren't you the girl who doesn't know the pledge of allegiance?" (What can I say? I honestly thought it was "one nation *individual*" when I volunteered to lead the school in the pledge at an assembly.) But never had I heard a guy describe me using the word *cute*.

Hence my quick trip to Head-over-Heels-Ville. And once I was there, I became a full-fledged resident. Oh, yeah. I immediately began doing anything and everything I thought would make me irresistible to Alex.

I got a bunch of fashion magazines and found pictures from fashion shows in New York. I asked Carrie to cut my hair into a shoulder-length razor-cut style I saw on one of the models at the Calvin Klein show. It was a lot edgier than anything I had ever done, but I thought maybe it would remind Alex of his homeland.

I debuted my new cut in English class the next day. Alex responded with: "Wow. You look like that hedgehog thing on my little brother's video game."

Mortified, I wore a San Francisco Giants hat the rest of the day. A hat which, since I'm going for full disclosure here, I'll tell you I found in the class lost and found. Not the best idea I've ever had, but hey, I was desperate.

Ick. It makes my head itch just thinking about it.

At lunch, Carrie asked me what was wrong. I pointed to my hair and told her I'd never be able to show my hedgehog-y self around Alex again.

My best friend rolled her eyes. "Whatever Annabelle, Alex doesn't care about your hair. He totally likes you. Joe told me."

Joe was a cute drummer who flirted with Carrie all the time and a friend of Alex's. Joe knew.

I threw my arms around Carrie in joy.

After that, Alex and I began that crazy journey from hanging out to talking on the phone to dating. Alex had a whole pack of girls who liked him, but for some reason he was interested in me. I felt pretty and cool for the first time in my life.

Then, during the senior trip to Santa Cruz, Alex and I somehow ended up alone on the beach eating hot dogs.

"It's been so fun hanging out with you today," Alex said. "Sorry Mitch spit his gum in your hair from the gondola."

I fingered the spot in my hair where Bethany—my sort-of friend who never went anywhere without her full makeup bag—had used eyebrow scissors to cut the gum out. "It's all right. It was kind of worth it to be walking with you."

"You're sweet," Alex said. "Sweet and cute and fun. Pretty much the perfect girl."

My insides bubbled.

"When I first moved here, I hated it," Alex said, looking out at Bruce Winter who was showing off his surfing skills to a bunch of girls. "But then I started hanging out with you. Maybe you're the reason I moved here."

"Well, I'm glad you did," I said in my best flirty voice.

"Why is that?" Alex asked, his eyes on me.

I looked away. "I think you know why."

"I've liked you since the first day I saw you in science class, wearing those cool silver earrings," Alex said.

I made a mental note to give Dad a huge hug when I got home. "I've liked you too."

"But now it's more," Alex said. "Now I think I might love you."

I responded to the beautiful words the way any eighteen-year-old girl would: I dropped my hot dog on the guy.

Alex laughed, and before I could do anything about de-dogging him, he leaned over and kissed me. My very first kiss. It was everything I had dreamed it would be. My stomach did flips.

That night, I told Mom the whole story over sundaes made with her secret homemade vanilla ice cream recipe.

"Didn't Grandma Joy meet Grandpa Earl in high school?" I asked, popping a maraschino cherry into my mouth.

Mom smiled at my knowledge of family history facts. "She did."

"Maybe Alex is my Earl," I said dreamily.

"Maybe," Mom said.

And right then and there I decided the high-school sweetheart thing must run in the family. Like a dislike of the color lime green and a fear of waffle irons. Don't laugh. Do you know how hot those things get?

I fell completely in love with Alex over the next few months. He made me feel so amazing. The only guy who had ever shown interest in me before Alex was Marty, the kid who thought it would be funny to run across the gymnasium floor during a pep rally dressed in a Speedo and a cape. But Alex was this good-looking, well-spoken, East Coast guy, and for some reason he loved me.

Then one night when we were at the beach in Carmel, Alex gave me a heart pendant necklace.

"I've decided I'm going to go to Cal Poly with you."

"But what about Columbia?" I asked. Alex had been accepted to Columbia, his top choice. I, however, hadn't applied to a single school east of Lake Tahoe.

"I don't want to go without you."

Alex put the necklace on me and I immediately began imagining us in matching Cal Poly sweatshirts.

Alex asked me to the prom by baking me a Boston cream pie, a New York cheesecake, and a Pennsylvania Dutch apple pie. Each had a plastic bag inside containing one word, adding up to the phrase: "You . . . me . . . prom?"

I responded by asking Alex's dentist to give him a toothbrush with a note on it that said "Yes!" after his annual exam. Apparently, the dentist had to explain why he was handing Alex a toothbrush with a pink glittery "Yes" attached to it, which kind of ruined the whole thing. But oh well.

Then, just before the prom, things changed. Alex listened to Joe talk about New York—he was going to some music school over there—with a bit of sadness in his eyes, and he seemed to get annoyed with me a lot.

Then came the thing that changed it all.

This gorgeous new girl with an accent sort of similar to Alex's moved to Monterey. Rona Bircheck.

She went to church with us and naturally sort of became a member of our group. I noticed right away that Alex seemed different around her.

One day as we hung out on Cannery Row, I asked him, "Do you think the new girl's cute?"

Alex laughed. But he didn't answer my question.

Then the night of the prom finally came. My hair and makeup were done to perfection by Mom's beautician Antonio, and Mom had even paid for me to get a manicure. I was sitting on my parents' couch in my black sequined dress, looking at the boutonniere I had picked for Alex—the florist had followed my "Make it look as manly as you can" directions well—when the phone rang.

"Hey." It was Alex. "I know I'm supposed to pick you up for dinner in a few minutes, but something came up. I can't make it for a while. I think we'll still be able to make it to the dance though. At least the end."

"Okay," I said, feeling a sudden ache. "Is everything all right?"

"Yeah," Alex said. "It's just . . . a thing. I'll call you when I'm done."

"All right, call me."

I hung up the phone and tried to convince myself it wasn't a big deal. So we didn't go out to a fancy dinner. We would still go to the dance. And take the picture. That was all our kids would really care about.

Feeling antsy, I decided to occupy myself so the time would pass more quickly. I did need a couple pairs of spare pantyhose to take to the dance just in case—I don't have great luck with the things. So I got into the Toyota that Cammie and I had to share, feeling kind of like a celebrity in my fancy clothes, and drove to the drugstore.

I felt a little envious as I saw a row of limos in front of the great Italian restaurant nearby. But it was okay, I was going to the dance with someone I loved.

I bought the pantyhose and a couple boxes of Milk Duds and was exiting the store when I saw Rona Bircheck through the window of the restaurant. I stared at her for a minute because it was hard not to. Her auburn hair looked red-carpet ready and her blue chiffon gown was amazing.

Weird, I thought, *last I heard Rona didn't have a date for the prom.*

And that's when I saw him, sitting right next to her in the booth, but behind her in my view.

I felt like I was in the last moments of a horrible dream where you can feel yourself wanting to wake up. Suddenly I got hot all over and was overcome by a rage I had never, ever experienced before. I marched in the restaurant, past the *maître d',* who asked how many were in my party, and right to the red vinyl booth.

"How could you!" I hollered.

He looked up and I saw . . . not Alex, but this kid from my history class, Jeffrey.

Oops. Wrong table.

"Sorry," I said. "Carry on."

I took only a few steps before I was facing Alex and Rona. His arm was around her, his fingers playing with her hair. I felt ill.

His eyes met mine, and his face was like those guys on COPS when they know they're caught and they have no where to run. Usually on COPS they still try to get away, but Alex didn't.

I approached the booth. "You lying, two-timing, jerk!"

"Annabelle," Rona Bircheck said, looking up at me, "I'm . . . um . . . we're . . ."

"You're . . . um . . . you're . . . what?" I said, mimicking Rona in an icy voice I didn't know I had.

"Don't be mean to her," Alex said.

And that, my friend, is when I turned into a psychopath.

I suddenly wanted nothing more than to throw something. Anything. So, before I knew what was happening, I was removing the little boxes of pantyhose from the pharmacy bag and chucking them as hard as I could at Alex. Nude, sandle-toe, control-top weapons aimed right at his head. And as I threw I yelled, "I can't believe I ever thought you were my grandpa!"

Alex winced as one of the boxes hit him right in the eye, and just about everyone in the restaurant turned to watch the scene. I think I even saw a few people whip out their cameras.

My eyes began to fill with tears, and I knew I had to get out of there fast. "Don't you ever speak to me again," I said, looking into Alex's stunned face. Then I turned and walked away, ignoring the whispers and references to PMS behind my back.

Alex tried to call me all weekend, but I didn't take any of his calls. I was too busy destroying the letterman jacket he had left in my car, shoving Pop Tarts into the new Nintendo game system he had brought to my house the weekend before, and trying to use my pull with the yearbook committee to get them to superimpose a zit onto Rona Bircheck's senior portrait.

Okay, fine, a zit *and* a chin hair. But still, they didn't do it, so what does it matter.

The calls eventually stopped, and Alex and I never did speak. He ended up going to Columbia, and I never saw him again. Not until that night when he showed up at Carrie's reception, acting like nothing had ever happened.

I felt someone bump into the back of my chair, snapping me back to the present. I shoved thoughts of Alex Mikels out of my head. It wasn't very hard as I had had many years of practice. This was Carrie's wedding. I had been looking forward to this for months.

I was not going to let Alex ruin things.

Chapter 3

"Hey peepindles!" DJ J-Dog hollered into the microphone. "Time for the lastindle danceindle of the eveindle!"

"Speak English, young man!" Carrie's grandma Ruby shouted.

I laughed into my yellow napkin and took another bite of Carrie's organic lemon wedding cake. Mom—who's been doing a lot of wedding cake baking since I mentioned her and her amazing recipes in an article I wrote a while back—baked and decorated it for Carrie's wedding gift. The cake was gorgeous—three tiers decorated with yellow, orange, and pink flowers—and absolutely delicious. In fact, I'd already had two pieces.

Okay, fine, three. But the first one was really small.

Joey hunched his shoulders and got back onto the microphone. "This is the last dance of the night," he mumbled.

Joey put on, "Someone to Watch Over Me," and I observed from my seat as Carrie and Miles broke away from the wedding guests and moved to the center of the bamboo dance floor.

I stared at them as they glided across the light wood. Carrie looked so beautiful and so joyful. And the way Miles held onto her, I knew he loved her. I knew he would take care of her. He'd go shopping at the Farmers Market with her and watch movies with her and . . .

Wait a minute.

Suddenly the inside of my mouth felt very dry. For the first time it really hit me: My best friend was married. Married!

My mind raced with questions. Would we still grab seafood at Shrimpy's? Would we still have our weekly Paint and Popcorn Night? Or would Carrie and Miles fade away into married people land? It seemed all the singles I knew from church faded into married people land after the big day.

A second later, Isaac was behind my chair, his hand on my shoulder. "You feeling better?"

"Yes. Thank you."

"Do you want to dance?"

I nodded. "Let's go dance by Carrie and Miles, so I can give Carrie her gift." *And show her that I am a good, un-ditchable friend who she really, really needs.*

I reached into my bright-orange, satin clutch—my friend Katrina from work got it at a sample sale in L.A. and sold it to me for $10 after she stained the inside with lipstick—and retrieved the pale blue envelope that held my wedding gift to Carrie.

Isaac eyed the envelope. "She's going to love it."

I stood up from my chair. "I hope so. Let's go."

Isaac held my hand as we walked onto the dance floor together. "I know no one is supposed to look more beautiful than the bride," he said, "but you look absolutely gorgeous tonight."

"Thanks." I twisted my lips in thought. "Could you tell Carrie that? Tell her that I obviously know a lot about clothes and shoes and hair and makeup and that while Miles is cool and all, she is very lucky to have me to help with those girl subjects."

"All right," Isaac said, looking confused.

"Great. Thanks." I pulled Isaac toward Carrie and Miles. Once we reached them, I tapped Carrie on the shoulder. "Hi."

Carrie and Miles greeted us, and Isaac and I danced next to them. I love dancing with Isaac. He moves so well and smells so good.

"Are you two having an enjoyable time?" Miles asked in that funny always-proper English of his.

For the longest time I had no idea how a guy from Idaho ended up with an almost-British accent. But recently, Carrie told me she thinks it's because when Miles was growing up the only television he was allowed to watch was the BBC. I guess it makes sense. I used to talk like the kids from *Saved by the Bell.*

Not that I ever watched *Saved by the Bell.* My, um, friends did.

"It's a great reception," Isaac said.

"And I can't get over how pretty you look," I said to Carrie.

Miles looked at her adoringly. "She does look most lovely."

I nodded toward Carrie's feet. "You know, I did her toenails last night. They look great, if I do say so myself. I bet you don't know how to do toenails?"

"I suppose I don't," Miles said.

"I bet you also don't know how to do hair. And I bet you don't know anything about clothes."

"He actually has pretty good taste in clothes," Carrie said, looking at her new husband like he was the only thing she needed in the whole world.

"What does D&G stand for?" I asked swiftly, my eye on Miles.

The group looked at me like I was crazy.

"Perhaps," Miles ventured, "it stands for . . . Dockers and G—"

"Not even close!" I said, cutting him off. "Guess Carrie should always come shopping with me."

Isaac cleared his throat. "Oh, yeah, you definitely should, Carrie. Especially since Annabelle knows so much about clothes and shoes and . . . what was it again?" he lowered his head toward mine.

"Hair and makeup . . ." I whispered.

Isaac raised his head. "Oh yeah, and hair and makeup. And, in fact, all of the girl subjects."

Carrie laughed and rolled her eyes at me. "Thanks, Isaac."

"So," I said, grinning at my best friend excitedly. "I have your gift."

"I have something for you too," Carrie said.

"Huh?"

"A Maid of Honor gift. It's in my room. I'll go grab it."

"I'll come with you!" I stopped moving my feet, and pulled away from my handsome dance partner.

Carrie let go of Miles. "Here, honey, dance with Isaac for a second."

Miles looked at Isaac awkwardly. He obviously wanted to make his new bride happy, so he started moving toward Isaac with his arms kind of out in front of him.

Isaac looked mortified.

"I don't think she meant that," I said with a laugh. "We'll be right back. Talk about sports. Or blowing stuff up."

Carrie and I giggled and linked arms as we headed in the direction of the house.

Once in her room, Carrie plucked a lavender box from her dresser. It was weird seeing my friend in her room in a wedding gown.

"Here," she said.

I opened the box and inside found a shiny silver frame. Inside was a picture of Carrie and me the night we met. We looked so young and happy, our arms around each other's shoulders. As the memory rushed back to me, I felt tears beginning to form in my eyes.

"Where did you get this?" I asked.

"I remembered that Ally Nichols had a camera that night. So I called her."

"Didn't Ally move away a long time ago?"

Carrie nodded. "I had to track her down. I finally got her number by Googling her and asking if I could be her friend on MySpace."

"Seriously?"

"Yep. Look at us." Carrie peered at the picture in my hands. "Thank you for being my friend, Annabelle. There is no way I can tell you how grateful I am to know you."

"I'm grateful I know you!" I hugged my best friend, tears escaping from my eyes.

"Love you," she said as she squeezed me.

"Love you too."

Carrie smiled as she retrieved each of us a tissue from the box on the dresser.

"You were trying to make me cry, weren't you?" I asked as I wiped my eyes and checked for mascara smears in the mirror on the wall.

"I wasn't. I promise." Carrie dabbed at her eyes, careful not to mess up her wedding makeup.

"Well, I guess that brings us to my gift." I bounced excitedly as I handed Carrie the pale blue envelope.

She ripped it open and after a second looked up at me in shock. "Are you kidding me?"

"I got the whole package!" I squealed. "It has everything! A honeymoon suite right on the beach. A full-service spa with massages, facials, pedicures, and manicures. All you can eat buffets with organic selections; I checked to make sure. Couples yoga. A private dinner on the beach on Friday. And you get to stay for two weeks!"

"But we're going camping in San Diego," Carrie said.

I shook my head. "You're the most organic girl I've ever met, but I know you hate camping. You are not going camping on your honeymoon."

Miles and Carrie were originally going to get married back in August. But when a fire broke out at Fresh Food Fanatics—Carrie's health food café located on Monterey's famous Cannery Row— they postponed the wedding until January, and she and Miles had to say good-bye to a lot of things I knew they had hoped for. Carrie said the money was better spent on the café, but I knew she was disappointed.

"You leave tomorrow afternoon," I said. "Since you guys are staying at the Fairmont in San Francisco tonight, I got a flight out from the San Francisco airport. You're going to The Bahamas!!"

Carrie frowned slightly. "But . . ."

"I packed for you. Everything you need is in your car. And Miles knows; I kept him in the loop."

"How did you afford—"

"I wrote a few freelance pieces. Look for my upcoming article in *Bay Area Bowling.*"

Carrie threw her arms around me and I saw a mental montage of all our wonderful memories. I saw the night the picture she had given me was taken; the night she saved me from a boy-related super-crisis at a youth conference and I knew I had a friend for life.

I saw our Paint and Popcorn Nights, with us sitting on the floor eating popcorn and painting our nails while watching chick flicks. The floors changed from teen bedroom floors, to dorm room floors, to grown-up home floors, but the feeling of friendship remained the same.

I saw the road trip to Las Vegas Carrie organized when I finally stuck with a major long enough to follow in her footsteps and actually graduate from Cal Poly. I saw the "You're in Business" party I threw when she opened the café, and the bridal shower I threw when she got engaged to Miles.

And now here she was: Married. No longer Carrie Fields, but Mrs. Miles Newton.

"Carrie," Miles' voice sounded in the doorway, "your father has just pulled the car into the drive. Are you ready to depart?"

"No!" I said.

Miles knitted his eyebrows together as if to say, "What's

up with you?" Although in Miles language it would have been something like, "What the devil? Tallyho!"

Carrie squeezed my hand. "I'll see you in two weeks."

"Have fun in The Bahamas," I said as I reluctantly let go of Carrie's hand and hugged Miles. "Take care of my best friend," I whispered.

"I will," Miles promised.

And I knew he would.

Outside I watched as Carrie and Miles said good-bye to their reception guests and made their way out the back gate.

I found Isaac near the buffet table and the two of us followed the couple and crowd onto Carrie's front driveway, blowing biodegradable bubbles as they got into Carrie's barely recognizable—man, Isaac was right, Miles' brothers really went to town on the thing—hybrid car. Isaac snapped what seemed like a hundred pictures, and I waved to my best friend one last time as she drove off with her new husband.

While Isaac continued to snap photos, I ducked into a quiet corner of the yard and reached into my handbag, clutching the pink notebook I carry with me everywhere. The notebook where I write what I call my "Pink Notes:" Little entries on people who inspire me or have an impact on me. The tradition actually started when I was fourteen. My first ever "Pink Note" was Carrie.

I opened the notebook, removed the cap from my pen, and began to write.

Pink Note #133
Name: Miles Newton

Why He's Noteworthy: Today Miles married my best friend. As I watched them dance their first dance as a couple, it was unmistakable that they were in love. He makes her so happy. And for that he belongs in this book.

I was just finishing the entry when Isaac came up beside me.

I closed and put away my notebook. "I can't believe she's married."

"I know," Isaac said. "And to think, we've been together about as long as they were when they got engaged."

I stared at him in complete and utter disbelief. Did he really just say that? Did he really just leave a perfect moment for me to start the "So . . . we've been together for a while now, when might we start thinking about getting engaged?" conversation?

I believe he did!

"Well . . ." I said, treading carefully. "Speaking of that, I know we've talked about us and the future, but it's always been kind of vague. Do you see us . . . I mean do you think about us . . . I mean do you . . ."

Isaac smiled, his gorgeous eyes twinkling. "Yes."

I opened my mouth to speak, but before I could, Carrie's mom, Marian,—who looks more like Carrie's older sister than her mom—sidled up to us. "Hi, you two," she said. "Isaac, we're about to move all the presents from the gift table, and I was wondering if you could take a couple more photos."

"Sure." Isaac kissed me on the cheek before disappearing, camera slung over his shoulder.

I watched him go, wondering how I would bring the subject back up again.

Mind reeling, I headed back to my seat, listening as DJ J-Dog put on the song "Closing Time"—I think in an effort to get people to leave. I plopped down in my chair, and rested my chin in my hands.

And that's when I saw it.

Sitting right beside the bright orange place card with my name on it, was Carrie's bouquet.

I looked at it for a second and noticed there was a note attached, which was folded into thirds. I unfolded the top third.

You were definitely the rightful bouquet catcher.
Hope this will bring a smile to your pretty face.

I looked around for Isaac. How had he convinced Greta to give up the bouquet? And better yet, what exactly was he saying in his note? Was he saying I was the rightful winner because I was going to get married next?! Maybe he was!

Maybe there was a ring hidden inside the bouquet!

I quickly began searching the flowers for any sign of a ring. But I found nothing. I unfolded the rest of the note, in search of clues. And what I found will shock you. Yes, at the bottom of the page was . . .

Hope to see you around.
Alex

I stared at the name. Alex? What in this crazy world?

What was Alex doing getting the bouquet from the hockey player who nearly killed me and then attaching a note in which he called me pretty?

I'll tell you what he was doing. He was trying to get on my good side. Trying to make nice after all these years. But it wasn't going to work.

I quickly wadded up the note and shoved it into an empty cup on the table. I would keep the flowers—only because, in all fairness, I *was* the rightful bouquet catcher—but I wanted nothing to do with Alex Mikels. Not again. Not ever.

Chapter 4

The Monday after the wedding, I was sitting up nice and tall at my desk at *Central Coast Living* magazine, working hard and dutifully on my next piece for my Soul Food column.

Okay, okay. I was slumped in front of my computer, staring at the blinking cursor on the flat screen, daydreaming about Isaac.

I imagined we were back at Carrie's reception dancing to Red House Painters. Isaac was holding onto me in that perfect way between tightly and tenderly as we swayed to the music.

Then, just as the last few bars of the song played, he took my hand and led me to the edge of the dance floor where he got down on one knee. My heart raced as I watched him retrieve a ring that looked exactly like the one in the advertisement I ripped out of Carrie's bridal magazine two weeks ago and inserted into his February issue of *Photography Today*.

Hey, a little hint never hurt anyone.

"Annabelle," he said. "You are the most wonderful and beautiful woman I have ever met. You look perfect even without makeup and smell lovely after a long jog. Will you marry me and buy a house with me in Monterey with a gourmet kitchen where your mom can make her famous *crème caramel* and a bedroom I'll let you paint whatever color you want?"

"Yes!" dream-me exclaimed.

"Yes what?" a female voice came into my ears, bringing me back to reality.

I turned my head as Katrina, my closest friend at *CCL*, entered my office. Her smooth, $275-every-six-weeks blonde hair was styled pin-straight and she had shimmery shadow on her eyes.

I tapped on my computer keys. "Oh, um, I was just excited because I finally spelled *hors d'oeuvres* right on the first try."

Katrina nodded her head and set a cup of cocoa on my desk. "I got you a Wipe Out."

I picked up the yellow cup decorated with Bean There Bun That's trademark surfboard logo. "Thanks."

Arvin—aspiring professional surfer, former *CCL* employee, and friend I know from church—opened Bean There Bun That, the trendy gourmet cocoa and cinnamon bun shop down the street from the office, about three months ago. And true to his surfer ways he named all the menu selections using surfing terms. The Wipe Out is hot cocoa with caramel and whipped cream.

"I got us a box of mini Rip Curls too."

Ahh Rip Curls; the most delicious cinnamon buns on earth.

Katrina sat down in the spare chair in my office, kicked off her stillettos, and folded her legs underneath her. She removed the yellow bag from her huge red designer tote and passed it to me.

"Thank you!" I removed one of the still-warm treats and took a bite. It was beyond delicious. The gooey cream cheese icing dripped down the buttery, cinnamony sides, and the flavors danced together in my mouth.

Katrina took a sip of her bottled water. "So tell me all about the wedding."

I filled Katrina in on the highlights: The dress. The cake. The knockout. I was just about to get to the part about the heartbreaker turned bouquet-giver when the phone in my office rang.

I mouthed "just a sec," to Katrina and picked up the receiver. "Hello?"

"Pleasanton, it's George. I've moved our editorial meeting up to 9:30. I have an important announcement to make. And if Groberg is in there, tell her too."

I smiled. Overall, George was a very good boss, but the way he referred to me and everyone at *CCL* by our last names made me feel like I was in a football huddle. I always felt like the next words out of his mouth might be, "Now get out on the field and show no mercy!"

"I'll be right there," I said. "And I'll tell Katrina if I see her."

"I bet he wants to talk to us about the typo problem," Katrina said after I filled her in on the meeting time change. "Did you see Becca's article last month?"

I nodded and tried not to smile. Becca Tyler had joined the magazine last month to take the place of Patty, *CCL*'s former associate food editor, who had recently met her soul mate on MatureMatch.com and moved to his private island in the Caribbean.

Becca's first article was on a new bakery in Downtown Monterey. Well, when the magazine came out, right there on page seven was: "Monterey's Best Belly Doughnuts," by Becca Tyler.

She blamed it on the copy editors.

Katrina applied some cream blush to her cheeks as we walked to the conference room. We took our usual seats and talked to the other writers and editors who trickled in as we waited for George to arrive.

George ambled in with the same semi-intimidating presence he always had. But after nearly two years working at the magazine, nine months of those as a full-fledged food writer, I was totally comfortable.

"Good morning," George said.

"Good morning." I raised my hand to wave, and sent the pen I was holding flying behind me.

Okay, so I'm not *totally* comfortable.

"All right everyone," George said as he took his seat. "I moved up the meeting today because I have an important announcement to make."

The chatter in the room began to die down.

George leaned back in his chair. "I suppose some of you have heard the rumors."

Um. The rumors?

There were tons of rumors going around the office: Vivian in copy editing is related to that kid from Silver Spoons. Andrea in marketing did not meet her wealthy stock broker husband at the library but on a reality show called "Yes I Would Sell Out My Best Friend for a Chance to Date a Wealthy Investment Banker with an English Accent." George's tan is not from his "Christmas trip to Hawaii," but from a spray-tan machine he makes his wife wield on him bi-weekly.

Everyone looked around and uttered various forms of "I don't pay attention to office gossip because I am much too good an employee."

George cleared his throat. "Well, they're true."

The room suddenly grew dead silent.

"But before we get into the specifics, I want you to know it's been terrible keeping this a secret. I finally have the ability to tell you, and it's a relief."

"Someone's getting fired," Katrina whispered to me.

"Shh."

George looked over at me. "Pleasanton, is there something you want to say?"

I gulped. "No."

"I heard you talking to Groberg."

"I wasn't . . . I was just . . . Wow, you look really tan."

George frowned at me and reached into his briefcase, retrieving a glossy magazine with a pink cover. "Many of you probably already know, but I'm going to make it official: As of today, our magazine is owned by Pearson Publishing, a company based in New York. The company has also acquired

Beautiful Bay Weddings. In two months our magazine will
merge with *Bay Weddings* to form a single publication, still
called *Central Coast Living,* which will put out twelve issues a
year plus four seasonal wedding issues under the title *Central
Coast Weddings.*

"Most of you are probably wondering what this means for
your jobs. The truth is: I have no idea. But I do know there is
an opening for editor-in-chief of *Central Coast Weddings* and
the new publisher wants to fill the position from our staff."

All eyes in the room got as big as Oreos. An editor-in-
chief job?

George continued, and the pens in the room scrambled
furiously as he spoke. "If you are interested, you have four weeks
to put together a portfolio. As part of your portfolio you should
include a sample letter from the editor that features a theme
or subject idea for a future issue of *Central Coast Weddings,* a
letter of intent, an updated resume, and five writing samples
including *at least* one wedding-related writing sample. Any
questions?"

Five hands went up.

George frowned. "All right then. Let's move on."

George moved on to other orders of business, but I wasn't
really listening. This was just too huge.

To be completely honest, the thought of working for a
wedding magazine had never really crossed my mind. But now
that I thought about it, it seemed so right. I was finally coming
into my own as a writer, finally writing what I cared about.

I loved writing the real, true, inspiring stories of the food
world. Stories that went beyond which restaurants were the
best in town to the good those restaurants and the people who
worked in them were doing in the world. But maybe it was
time to stretch myself a little. Maybe it was time to explore the
stories of the wedding world.

The wedding world!

I looked around the table, to check out my competition.

1. Becca Tyler.

She had at least six weeks before she recovered from her typo, so I wasn't too worried about her.

2. Andrew Broderik.

Let's face it, what does a guy know about weddings? I would definitely get the job over him.

3. Nadine Johns.

She was a good editor, but since she was on some kind of special diet, she always smelled a little like cabbage. I'd just have to write in my letter of intent, "In addition to my many qualifications, I do not smell of pungent vegetables."

4. Katrina.

Great. I hate competing against friends.

I was in mid-thought when Katrina scrawled me a note. "You'd be so perfect for that job."

"You'd be good too," I scribbled back.

Katrina made a face before writing back. "Come on. I've worked here for five months. I'm not even going to bother applying. No big deal. I like my job."

I spent the rest of the meeting only half-listening as I jotted down ideas for my portfolio and practiced my signature.

Just in case.

After all, the editor-in-chief's electronic signature is one of the first things magazine readers see.

Before I knew it, people were exiting the room, grabbing stale cookies from the food cart in the back as they left.

George stood up from his seat and regarded me. "Pleasanton, I need to speak with you for a moment."

I gulped. "Okay."

George ushered me toward the back corner of the conference room. "I've been asked to send you to the annual Dream Wedding bridal fair sponsored by *Beautiful Bay Weddings*. It's the fair's final year since the magazine will no longer be in existence after next month."

"Oh, okay. Am I supposed to write something about the fair?"

George shook his head. "No. Our new publisher needs help

with a project, and he requested that I send you to the fair so you two can discuss it."

My throat suddenly felt like it was stuffed with cotton candy. "Who's the new publisher? What project?"

George rubbed his temples. "I'm completely blanking on his first name, but his last name's Pearson. He's the son of the publishing company's founder, Clive Pearson. Darn nepotists. I don't know the specifics of the project either. I got all of my information from my assistant. You know how that goes."

"But he said he wants me specifically to help?"

"That's what I understood."

"Did he say *why* he wants my help?"

Oops. That came out a little bit like I think I'm a loser who no one should ask for help, didn't it?

"I believe he said he knows you," George answered.

Pearson? I did a quick mental check, but I didn't think I knew a single person named Pearson. Hehe. A person named Pearson.

Come on, it's kind of funny.

"Okay, well, I guess I'll . . . meet him at the bridal fair."

"Great." George reached into his suit pocket. "Here are two tickets. You can take someone if you'd like. Just make sure you meet Pearson at 7:30 at the Furry Friends Formal booth."

"The what?"

"They sell formal outfits so your pets can be in the wedding."

I looked down at the fancy white tickets embossed with silver writing. "So it's tonight? That's weird, a bridal fair on Monday?"

"Apparently Monday is the new Saturday in weddings," George said with a roll of his eyes.

"All right. Well, thanks."

My heart was pounding as I left the conference room and made my way to Katrina's cubicle.

When Katrina heard me approaching, she quickly minimized the website she had been perusing and pretended to be typing. I knew she couldn't type that fast.

"Just me," I said.

Katrina reopened her online shopping. "I'm just going to buy these jeans really fast." She did some pointing and clicking and then turned to face me. "You got the job didn't you? That's why George wanted to talk to you afterwards. He just had to tell all of us it was open for legal reasons, but you got it, right?"

"No. It's weirder than that." I plopped down on the plush red chair Katrina had made the guys in tech support carry up to her cubicle.

Katrina blinked. "Well, tell me."

"Not here," I said, sounding too much like a shady criminal in a cop movie. "Let's go to The Marble."

The Marble was the name Katrina and I gave to the executive bathroom because of its marble floor. We weren't technically supposed to use the executive bathroom, but it was such a nice place to talk with its comfy couches, non-florescent lighting, and fancy toiletries.

Once inside The Marble, we sunk into the beige couch in the little lounge area.

"The new publisher wants me to meet him at a bridal fair tonight. Do you want to come with me?"

"Totally! For what?"

"I just thought you might like to go."

"No," Katrina said. "Why does the publisher want you to meet him?"

"Apparently he wants my help on some project."

"Seriously? You're so lucky! Nadine Googled him after our meeting and found out his vital stats: Single. Rich. Gorgeous."

"Did Nadine mention his name?" I asked.

"Yeah, but I don't remember it." Katrina got up from the couch and began pumping some of the vanilla lotion sitting on the counter into her hands. "But she did email me a picture and all I can say is, Yum-my. I definitely need to go home and get out of this suit before the fair."

"Okay. I'll pick you up around . . . 6:30?"

"Sounds good," Katrina said. Then she scrunched up her nose. "I pumped way too much of this lotion. Do you want some?"

I shook my head. "Whenever I put lotion on my hands at work, I get this gross sticky film all over my computer."

"Well put it on your feet then."

"Fine." I slipped out of my shoes—a pair of black rounded-toe pumps I found on Piperlime.com for a price that made everyone in the office jealous—and smoothed the lotion onto my feet.

I was standing, putting my shoes back on and getting ready to leave, when the door opened and in walked Ingrid Chandler, editor-in-chief of *Central Coast Living.*

And I was standing in the wrong bathroom with no shoes on.

"Hi," I said, stepping forward to, I don't know, shake her hand, I guess. But the problem was the lotion on my feet made them very slick. And slick feet + a marble floor = a sliding me.

I slid my way right into what can only be described as an awkward hug with Ingrid, a woman who shakes her husband's hand when she says good-bye to him.

Ingrid looked appalled. "What are you doing?"

"Uh . . ." My feet were still sliding around. I held onto Ingrid like some kind of anchor. "I . . . I just wanted to say thank you for . . . letting me use your spoon last month when I forgot mine. I really wanted to eat that yogurt. And it was all possible because of you."

"All right." Ingrid made a perturbed face and moved quickly away from me.

I slipped around like a deranged ice skater as I picked up my shoes and headed for the door, listening to Katrina giggle from behind me.

Nice. It had been just twenty minutes since I'd received

the news that I might have a chance at a big, life-changing promotion, and I was off to a great start.

Chapter 5

Have you ever been to a bridal fair?

Well, let me just say, I think the name should be changed to bridal un-fair.

Why, you ask? Well, I'll tell you why.

Because brides already get to be in love, use the words "my fiancé" in every sentence, have an excuse to taste inordinate amounts of cake, and spend hours staring at their left ring-fingers because there's something sparkly on them. And then, on top of all that, they get to go to huge extravaganzas like the Dream Wedding bridal fair and get free stuff.

Lots and lots of free stuff.

And it's not the kind of free stuff we non-brides get like XXXL T-shirts from the bank. No, it's really, really good stuff.

"Would you like a free sample of our Glowing Bride moisturizer?" a heavily made-up woman just inside the doors of the fair asked me and Katrina. "It's a $100 value."

See what I mean.

"Yes, please," I said. "Thanks."

The woman handed Katrina and I tiny pink pots of moisturizer and tote bags with the Sephora logo printed on them.

"I've heard this stuff is amazing," Katrina said as she dabbed some under her eyes.

I removed the product's lid and inhaled the fruity scent as I gazed starry-eyed around the room.

The fair was incredible. It was being held in the Sand Dollar Room at the Princeton at Pebble Beach, the hotel known for its rich and famous clientele. The room looked gorgeous. Decorated in chocolate brown and hot pink, the wedding colors of the moment according to all the bridal magazines, it was made to look like a wedding reception—except instead of accommodating wedding guests, the square tables that lined the floor were vendor booths. There was a DJ playing soft tunes, waiters serving *hors d'oeuvres*, and the tinkling sound of very happy brides.

"Can you believe this?" I asked Katrina.

"I know. Like brides don't have enough already."

Good. I wasn't the only one suffering from a case of bridevy (definition: bride envy.)

"So, where are you supposed to meet Mr. Yummy?"

I looked at the clock on my cell: 7:03. "I'm not supposed to meet him for another 27 minutes. We got here a lot faster than I expected. Maybe we can look around while we wait."

And get some more free stuff. If they were giving away $100 face cream inside the doors, who knew what other treasures were waiting.

"All right," Katrina said. "You go ahead and look around. I'm going to go freshen up in the ladies'. I'll meet you back here in twenty."

"Okay."

Katrina took off for the restroom, and I wandered around the booths. After collecting a free CD of wedding songs performed by the Big Band Boys, and a sample bottle of "Wedding Cake" perfume that smelled good enough to eat, I stopped in front of a booth marked "Pre-wedding Legal Consultations."

"Would you like a free fifteen minute consultation?" The

man behind the table asked. "It's a $200 value."

A $200 value! "Okay," I said, my weakness for a good bargain kicking in.

The man led me into a quiet little area behind a blue curtain.

"My name is Jonathan Lawson with Law and Lawson Attorneys at Law," he said as he slid a business card across the round table.

"Wow. That worked out pretty well didn't it," I said with a smile.

Jonathan Lawson gave me a look that said "Listen lady, I'm a serious lawyer, please don't bother me with that joke I hear all the time" and removed an expensive-looking pen from the pocket of his expensive-looking suit. "Now, I'm going to ask you a few simple questions before we get into the hard stuff."

I nodded. "Okay."

"Do you possess any considerable holdings or earning capacity that the aforementioned party, your intended, may wish to procure subsequent to any action resulting in the dissolution of your marital agreement, and thus wish to protect the rights and privileges you shall have in the property of the other in the event of death, divorce, or other circumstance which results in the termination of the agreement?"

That was a simple question? "Uh. Sure."

"All right. Why don't we go through a list of your most valuable assets?"

"Well . . . I think I'd say I'm a pretty loyal person. Hardworking. Good taste in shoes. And— "

"Your material assets," Jonathan Lawson interrupted.

"Oh, um . . ."

"About how much money is currently in your bank account?"

About $18. "I don't think I feel comfortable telling you that."

"That much, huh? In that case I would most definitely recommend that you sign a prenuptial agreement."

"Don't all the celebrities get those?"

Jonathan Lawson closed his eyes and shook his head in a way that said, "Oh, you poor little girl who knows not the ways of the long arm of the law."

"A prenuptial agreement is not only for celebrities," he said. "It's for anyone who has substantial assets or earning power. It can be drafted in such a way as to provide both parties with the assurance that the marriage is about love and not money. But then when he cheats, it can be all about money."

"Isaac would never!"

This got a "You don't even want to know the things I've seen in my lawyer days" head shake.

"You know what," I said, standing up, "I should probably be going." I tossed Jonathan Lawson's card back onto the table.

He obviously didn't know anything.

I was headed toward a booth that was giving away free shoe insoles, when I was stopped by a man in a doctor's coat who was standing behind a table covered in pictures of bare legs.

"Would you like a free 3X magnification mirror?" he asked me.

I approached the table. "Sure."

The doctor man handed me a bright yellow mirror that made my face look huge.

"Thanks," I said.

"Does the groom-to-be have a beard?" he asked me.

"Um . . . no."

"Well then you shouldn't either."

"What?"

"Call us," the man said with a sympathetic nod as he handed me a card: Joey's Laser Center.

I covered my face with my hand and slowly backed away.

My eyes searched the room for Katrina, and I saw her with a fresh face of makeup, standing in the place we were supposed to meet. I rushed to her side.

"Katrina," I whispered, the sound muffled beneath my

possible-beard shielding hand.

"Yeah?"

I leaned in toward her. Man she was wearing a lot of makeup. "Do I have . . . facial hair?"

Katrina shot me a weird look. "What?"

"The guy over there told me I have a beard."

Katrina rolled her eyes. "Let me guess, the laser hair removal booth."

"Uh huh."

"I walked past that booth and the guy told me I have toe hair. I know he was lying because I had my toes waxed during my pedicure on Saturday. Don't listen to him. He's just using scare tactics."

"You promise?"

"You don't have facial hair, Annabelle," Katrina said pretty loudly. A couple people walking by turned to look. I instantly turned the color of a cinnamon bear.

"She's right," I heard a male voice say from behind me.

I spun around and saw Alex Mikels standing there in a really nice suit and what I think was an Hermès tie.

He gave me a half smile. "I thought we were supposed to meet by the Furry Friends Formal booth."

"Excuse me?" I stared at Alex for a moment. "No . . . you're not . . ."

"*Central Coast Living's* new publisher."

No. No. No. No. Of all the people to be the new man in charge. Donald Trump would have been better. He'd probably have made me cry, but at least he wasn't . . . Alex. This was not good.

"Annabelle, are you all right?" Alex's voice came into my ears.

I looked at him with a stunned expression. "But . . . your name's not Pearson."

"Clive Pearson is my stepfather. My mom married him about four years ago."

"She sounds like a fabulous woman," a husky voice said

from behind me. I turned around to see who it was. Katrina. Why was she talking like that? "Looks like she raised you very well." Katrina moved close to Alex like a cheerleader drawn to the captain of the football team.

"Well, thank you," Alex said, smiling at her. "You should tell that to my stepfather. He won't think I've made anything of myself until I make the cover of *Forbes*."

Katrina laughed a little too loudly for a little too long.

I didn't even think that was funny.

"Maybe you haven't made *Forbes* yet," she cooed. "But I hear you made the cover of *New York Life's* Most Eligible Bachelor issue."

What? I didn't know that?

Alex responded with a nonchalant nod that said he didn't put much stock into his cover-guy status.

"Still a bachelor?" Katrina asked.

"I guess you could say that," Alex said charmingly.

"You're hilarious!" Katrina hit Alex playfully with her $100-manicure hand.

"So," I said, breaking into the nauseating PDF (public display of flirting). "George said you have a project for me."

Alex tore his gaze away from Katrina. "Yes. It's more of a favor than a project. The company bought me a great house on 17 Mile Drive. But the problem is, I just found out I have a few things to take care of back in New York and won't be moving in for a couple months. So, I was hoping that maybe you could help me find a house sitter. The company wants the place to stay occupied."

Wait a minute. "You're . . . moving to Monterey?"

Alex grinned. "Clive wants me to oversee the new magazine for at least two years. I get to move back. Cool, huh?"

Um, no. Go away. I don't want you living here.

"So, what do you think? Can you help me find a house sitter?"

"I'll do it," Katrina said. She smiled coquettishly at Alex. "And I won't even ask for anything in return."

"Thanks," Alex said. "But I think it's a good job for Annabelle. She knows me pretty well and knows what kind of individual I would feel comfortable with."

Was it just me, or did Katrina's eyes shoot daggers at me?

"That's fine," she said. "I can help with another project. I'm very multi-talented."

Oh, brother.

"I can do it," I heard myself say.

Alex looked pleased. "Great. I'll email you the details."

"Okay. So is that everything?" I asked, my voice short.

Alex seemed confused by my tone. "Yes. I guess that's everything."

"Great, well, I'll watch for your email. Kat, I'll meet you in the car."

Katrina barely nodded before beginning to talk to/giggle at/touch Alex.

My mind was reeling as I headed for the nearest exit. So, Alex was back. Alex was back and was *CCL*'s new publisher. Alex was back, was *CCL*'s new publisher, and wanted my help finding a house sitter.

I released a long yoga breath á la Carrie. I could do this. I could find Alex a house sitter. I could set aside the weird jumble of feelings he seemed to bring up inside me and get the job done. In fact, I needed to. I needed to earn all the points I could with the higher-ups for when it came time to fill the editor-in-chief position.

"Would you like a free slice of cake?" I heard a voice ask when I was a few yards away from the door.

Yes, cake. I could definitely use some cake.

I walked toward the table where a brunette-bobbed woman who looked like the quintessential "soccer mom" was handing out free samples. She held out a clear plastic plate with a tiny sliver of a delicious-looking white wedding confection on it.

"Thank you." I took a small bite. "Wow. This is amazing."

The woman smiled. "Please think of Food Fight catering company for your wedding."

I swallowed my bite. "Food Fight. That's an interesting name."

"Don't look at me," the woman said. "The kids came up with it."

"The kids?"

The woman nodded her head and handed me a brochure. The cover had a photo of what appeared to be parents standing with their children. The copy read, "100 percent of Food Fight's proceeds are used to lighten the financial burdens on families who have children with autism."

I looked up from the brochure. "Wow, 100 percent of proceeds. You don't see that a lot."

The woman smiled. "I'm Hope Bergevin." She offered me her hand to shake.

"Annabelle Pleasanton. Nice to meet you."

"My friend Liz started the company," Hope explained, pointing to the brochure. "That's her in the red. Her son was diagnosed with autism when he was almost four. The myriad of therapies he needed weren't paid for by insurance, so it all came out of the family's savings. Liz didn't want other families to feel that frustration. The company just celebrated its third anniversary. This year the kids are saving for a trip to Cabo San Lucas for a Surfers Healing camp. The camp is free, but we wanted to make a whole trip of it."

"Surfers Healing?" I said. "I think I heard something about them on the news."

Hope handed a few passersby cake samples. "Probably. It's an awesome organization—started by a former competitive surfer and his wife. Their son was diagnosed with autism, and they found that being out on a surfboard with his dad was very therapeutic. The ocean seemed to have a calming effect. The family thought the therapy might be helpful to other children with autism, so they organized surfing camps. We can't wait to go."

"That's so exciting. I—"

Before I could say more, a pair of giggling women

approached the table and started asking Hope questions about price per slice and icing options.

As I finished my piece of cake, my mind wandered to the boy who holds the record for my longest Pink Note ever: Baxter.

During my senior year of college, I worked as a substitute school secretary for the elementary schools in San Luis Obispo on days when I didn't have class. In addition to being on the secretary sub list, I was also on the classroom aide sub list. One day in mid-September I took my first classroom aide job. I was to spend three days working with Baxter, an eight-year-old boy with autism, in his classroom.

I'll admit I took the job initially thinking it would be a good way to give, to teach. To be around someone who could use my help.

But soon I learned how far off I was. Because as Baxter and I worked together, I realized he was the one doing the giving and teaching.

I remember during our first day together, I sat in a chair next to Baxter's desk as he worked on his writing exercises. Often, Baxter's focus would go from the assignment to the clasp on his belt or the trinkets on his desk. He inspected these objects with such focus, such wonder. I gently guided Baxter back to the task at hand, but his amazement at what I had come to think of as everyday things reminded me to find the wonder in the world around me.

I don't know why some people are born with or develop impairments that the rest of us can't understand. But I do know that I spent just three days with Baxter, and I am forever better because of it. I wonder if that isn't part of the answer.

I got out my Pink Notes and scrawled a quick entry.

Pink Note # 134
Name: Food Fight Catering Company

Why They're Noteworthy: I'm standing in a room filled with companies who offer services and products for brides and weddings. This one is unique, though. 100 percent of proceeds are used to help families who have children with autism. It's such a remarkable idea, and it reminds me that when possible, it's important in a world full of material things to find ways to give and to serve.

As I read over my note, my pulse quickened a bit—the way it does when I get a story idea. This idea would be perfect for the sample wedding article I needed to include in my portfolio for the editor-in-chief position!

Oh, it was so meant to be!

I paced excitedly in front of the booth as I waited for a moment when Hope was free. When she was, I approached her. "I'm a writer for *Central Coast Living*, and I was just thinking Food Fight's story is a really amazing one. Maybe I could call you for an interview."

"Oh, wow, sure, that would be great." Hope's smile was wide as she handed me her card. "The number on here is for our main shop in the L.A. area. Our satellite shop in the Monterey Bay area is only open on an as-needed basis."

I took the card and turned toward the exit. "All right. I'll be in touch."

"Wait," Hope said. "Don't forget to enter the drawing."

"Drawing?"

"Yes, it's for a free wedding cake from Food Fight. And free mini-replicas for every monthly anniversary for a year."

"That sounds great. But I'm not—"

Hope ignored me. "I'm writing your name down."

"Okay," I relented.

She was just being nice. Plus, I knew I wouldn't win the drawing—I never win anything—so it wasn't a big deal.

Of course, it didn't cross my mind that cake . . . Well, cake has a history of getting me into trouble.

Chapter 6

Do you think a girl can tell when her boyfriend is going to propose?

Because it was Isaac's and my nine-month anniversary, and I had a funny feeling he might be getting ready to.

At first I thought maybe I was just suffering from a bad case of wedding brain. After all, I had just attended my best friend's wedding, gone to a huge bridal fair where I got to see just how charmed the life of a bride is, and spent hours doing research and interviews for my wedding-related portfolio piece.

But something told me it wasn't just wedding brain.

And here's why: There were clues. A whole bunch of can't-just-be-coincidences that occurred in the week leading up to our anniversary that made me think there might be a ring and a knee and a poem entitled "Annabelle" in my future.

Maybe you can read over the clues and tell me if you think they point to an imminent popping of the question.

Okay. Here goes.

1. After the bridal fair, Isaac came over to my parents' house for family night. After a game of Scrabble, Isaac showed us some of the pictures he had taken at Carrie's wedding. When

we looked at the photos he had taken of the cake Isaac asked Mom if she planned on making *my* wedding cake and if she had any ideas about what it would be like. Mom practically nudged a hole in my side when Isaac wasn't looking.

2. On Tuesday, when I told Isaac about the interviews I was doing for my article, he asked me if Food Fight was a caterer I might like to use. When I asked him what I would need a caterer for he said, "I don't know . . . Easter."

3. When I wore a white dress to church on Sunday, Isaac stared at me a little more than usual.

4. And this one is the real biggie: On Sunday night, after dinner at my parents' house, Isaac asked me my *ring size*. He tried to play it off like he was comparing his hand to mine, but whatever . . . What else does a guy need a ring size for? Huh?

So what do you think? A proposal in the works?

I was almost afraid to hope. My luck in the guy department has never been great, and with Isaac everything was just so wonderful it almost scared me.

I tucked the thoughts into the back of my mind as I swung open the door at Bean There Bun That.

I had just endured yet another unsuccessful lunch-break interview with a potential house sitter for Alex, and I needed a little pick-me-up—a Billabong (raspberry lemonade) and a Rip Curl, okay, fine, three Rip Curls—before heading back to work.

Arvin was working the counter. "Hey, dude. How's life at *CCL?*"

I shrugged. "Fine. We just found out last week that we've been bought by a New York publisher." I handed Arvin my cash and placed my order.

"Whoa dude. Are they gonna start laying people off?"

"Who knows? I've actually decided to go for a position at a new magazine the company's putting out called *Central Coast Weddings*. It's an editor-in-chief position."

Arvin's eyes got wide as he used a piece of wax paper to put my Rip Curls into a bag for me. "Wow. That's cool. Good luck."

"Thanks. Hey, Arvin, you wouldn't happen to know anyone who's looking for a place to stay would you? I'm looking for a house sitter, but my advertising efforts have only turned up, 'Now, you won't be coming in to check if I'm, like, growing anything illegal outside will you?' and 'What happens if somehow some of the valuables end up missing?' kind of people."

"I can't think of anyone right now," Arvin said with a laugh. "But I'll let you know if I do."

"That would be great."

Arvin handed me my lemonade, and I dropped two dollars into the tip jar. Then with a wave over my shoulder, I headed back to work.

When I arrived at my office, Isaac was standing in the doorway. He looked a-ma-zing in a dark blue dress shirt, striped tie, and square-toed leather shoes. There's just something about a man in a shirt and tie.

Are you with me on this one?

Isaac kissed me on the cheek and followed me into the office, sitting down in the spare chair. "Happy Anniversary," he said with a smile.

"What are you doing here?" I set my handbag and food on my desk. "We're meeting for dinner in a couple hours."

Dinner at La Bonne Violette: Monterey Bay area's fanciest, most exclusive restaurant. I should have added that to my list of things that made me think Isaac was going to propose.

Isaac gave me The Look. The one that said he was about to tell me something I didn't want to hear. The one he'd been giving me way too much lately.

You see, Isaac is a freelance photographer. Right after we started dating, his family moved back to L.A., where they lived from the time Isaac was ten until he graduated from high school. Isaac took this as an opportunity to get more jobs.

It works out well because he stays with his parents when he's down there, so he doesn't have to pay for a hotel. Plus, his dad racks up tons of frequent-flyer miles traveling for his job, and Isaac gets to use them.

The only problem is he usually goes to L.A. on weekends.

"I'm so sorry, sweetie, but Chloe said she's on to something big."

Okay. I take that back. The *other* only problem is that when he goes to L.A. on weekends he spends his time with Chloe Payne—his childhood friend/former fashion model/ photography agent who now represents him.

If you want to know a secret, I Googled her the second Isaac told me about his "new representation." No, I wasn't just looking to see what she looks like. I wanted to know about her, you know, credentials. And those credentials are smooth blonde hair, porcelain-like ivory skin, and blue-green eyes that had to be contacts.

Not that it bothers me that Isaac spends his time with a former model. Oh, no. Maybe at first I was, you know, a teeny bit uncomfortable. But that's only because when Isaac and I first got together little jealousies and insecurities just about ruined things.

But then Carrie recommended this book written by her yoga teacher, who is also a famous and sought-after lecturer and life coach—apparently she coaches a lot of the stars in Hollywood. The book is called, *Dr. Harmony's Guide to Earth Sister Love: How to Strengthen Sisterhood and Banish Envy*, and it has changed my life. Just like all the testimonials on the back cover said it would.

When I first started the book I had to take a test to see how much Envious Energy I had toward my Earth Sisters. The book said I had Seven Black Clouds—the highest possible number—which I know was completely wrong.

But nevertheless, I started practicing the breathing and mental exercises and now whenever I hear about Chloe I'm Seven White Hearts—the best you can get—cool with it.

Okay. Maybe more like five white hearts.

All right, all right, since we're friends, I guess it's more like . . . four white hearts and a couple grayish clouds. Really little ones though.

I sunk into my chair. "When are you leaving?"

"In about an hour."

I glanced at the bouquet of tulips on my desk, an anniversary surprise from Isaac I'd received earlier in the day, and my face fell. "Before our dinner."

Isaac looked apologetic. "I'm so sorry, sweetheart."

"How long will you be gone?"

"A week," Isaac said. "But I'll be back next Wednesday. Valentine's Day. We'll celebrate then. It will be even more romantic because we'll be celebrating our anniversary *and* Valentine's Day."

Yeah. That's the same logic those poor kids who have birthdays near Christmas get fed.

I tried not to pout. "I'm going to miss you."

"I'm going to miss you too. But I thought maybe this would cheer you up a little."

Isaac set a shoebox-sized baby blue package on my desk.

I stared at the box.

This is it. The ring is in the package. He's going to ask me.

He's going to ask me and then when he works with Chloe this week he'll say things like, "Sorry I slammed your hair in that door and chopped it all off, but I was just daydreaming about my beautiful, funny, smart, sweet fiancée, Annabelle, and wasn't really paying attention to what I was doing."

I smiled as I ripped into the package. The first thing I saw were two DVDs. My two favorite chick-flicks: *While You Were Sleeping* and *Return to Me*. I had the movies on recorded-from-television VHS tapes, but had always meant to get the DVDs. I couldn't believe he did that for me!

I kept searching the box and found Milk Duds, my favorite candy; Red Vines, my favorite movie candy; and a pair of cute designer slippers with the tag still on so I could see that Isaac had gotten them for 75 percent off.

"Bargain slippers!" I shouted as I hugged him.

"There's more," Isaac said.

I gulped and my hands kind of shook as I removed the tissue paper from the bottom of the package.

But under the paper was not a small velvet ring box from John Wilfred jewelers. No, under the paper was a . . . picture.

I surveyed the photo and saw that it was Isaac, probably about fifteen years old, dressed in his Boy Scout uniform. He was standing with a group of boys. I recognized one as Ethan, his brother. It was odd to see him standing and not sitting in his wheelchair, but this would have been before the accident.

"So you can have me with you," Isaac said. "I know it's kind of old. But I don't have many pictures of myself. I'm always on the other side of the camera."

I stared at the picture. It was kind of weird to see Isaac as a teenager with a younger face, longer hair, and a look in his eyes that was . . . almost mischievous.

"What were you doing before this picture was taken?" I asked.

Isaac smiled. "The question is not what we were doing before the picture was taken. The question is what we were about to do."

"What were you about to do?"

"Scout camp secret," Isaac said, lifting his hands in apology. "It's between us and the woods. Let's just say it involved batteries, fire, and someone's tighty whities."

Oh brother.

I set down the picture and took one last look at my gift. I even put my hands in the slippers to see if maybe Isaac had hidden something inside them. "So is that . . . everything?"

Isaac looked a little worried. "Why? Did you want something else?"

"No."

"You sure? You seem disappointed."

"I just don't want you to leave."

Isaac put an arm around me. "I know sweetie. But, I have a very big surprise for you when I come back."

"Really . . . what kind of surprise?"

"Well . . ." Before Isaac could say more, his phone rang. He checked the caller ID. "Sorry, it's Chloe. I need to take this."

Isaac answered the call, and I could hear Chloe's voice on the other end.

My first thought was, "Nice timing, Chloe. Did you plan ahead to interrupt the only anniversary time Isaac and I are going to have today?" but I quickly stopped myself.

I channeled the sense of calm. I released the envy through my right nostril and breathed the sisterly harmony in through the left. I repeated softly in my mind, "I must not mentally magnify this woman's perceived faults in order to diminish her qualities, because her qualities do not detract from my own. I am loved for who I am, and I can have white hearts of love for all my Earth Sisters."

When Isaac was through with the call he looked gleeful. "She got me a meeting with the publicity people for a new TV series. They're looking for someone to take some still shots, and I'm one of three who has a meeting."

"That's so awesome honey!" I threw my arms around Isaac's neck and hugged him. He so deserved this.

Isaac's smile grew. "Chloe sounded really excited."

"Yeah I bet she did," I said. "She probably can't wait for you to tell her how much you *appreciate* her doing this," I added under my breath.

Isaac gave me a sideways look.

Oops. My envy releasing nostril must have been a little clogged.

Chapter 7

It had to be a mistake.

The yellow "Eviction Notice: Must Vacate the Premises within 48 Hours" on the door of my condo had to be a mistake.

I ripped the notice off the door and went inside, tossing my keys on the dining room table. I picked up the phone and called Gus, the owner of my condo. I heard the phone ring in his unit, which was right next to mine.

It was 11:00 at night. Since my plans with Isaac had been cancelled, I had decided to try the new "Hip Hop for Everybody" class at the gym after work. But after a "Hey, that was my nose," and an "I think you might have just broken my rib," from my fellow dancers, I think the instructor wanted to change the name of the class to: "Hip Hop for Everybody—except you, Annabelle Pleasanton."

Afterward, I drowned my sorrows in a chocolate soy smoothie because it's good for building lean muscle mass. Okay, because I wanted chocolate.

On the third ring, Gus picked up the phone. "This better be one of the three maintenance emergencies: Stopped toilet, flood, or no heat."

"Gus," I yelled through the wall and into the phone. "I

think someone made a mistake."

"What are you talking about?"

"There's an eviction notice on my front door. But that makes no sense. I paid my rent on time. I've paid my rent on time for three years. I'm a good tenant. I've seen what's out there. You aren't going to find anyone—"

"I have to sell," Gus interrupted.

"What?"

"I don't want your pretty little ears to hear the ugly details. I took a trip to Reno, talked to some guys, watched that boxer move around like a little sissy for three rounds and *Blamo!* I'm going to have to sell."

My forehead felt suddenly hot with worry. "What? Why? I'm sure you can get out of it. I'm sure someone can . . ."

"Not unless you want to see me lose a couple fingers; or possibly an ear. It's a done deal."

I scanned the notice in my hand, and with a few mental calculations figured I would have to be out of my condo by Friday evening.

"Gus, there is no way I can be out by Friday."

"Unless you want to be living with a guy named Crusher, there's not much I can do for you."

"Where am I supposed to go?"

"You can always stay with me for a while."

I pictured Gus in his preferred uniform of stained white tank top and boxer shorts, setting up an air mattress for me. "No thanks."

Gus yawned into the phone. "Sorry, kid."

I released a breath. "Okay. Bye, Gus."

I kicked off my work heels and walked barefoot on the wood floor. I opened the refrigerator, retrieved a pint of Ben and Jerry's—I'm-getting-kicked-out-of-my-house–and-need-some-comfort food fudge—and picked up the phone.

Isaac answered on the first ring. "Hi, beautiful."

Have you ever noticed no matter how many times you hear the word *beautiful*, it never gets old? Everything else does. Or takes on a weird sound. Try saying hiccup a few times in your head and you'll see what I mean.

"Hi," I said into the phone. "What are you up to?"

"Watching ESPN. I just got back to my parents' place. You won't believe the day I had."

Isaac told me about his day. He sat next to a, how should I put this, hygienically challenged, man on the plane who fell asleep and laid his head on Isaac's shoulder, and when Isaac tried to get him off, the man yelled out, "Come on, Trudi, we never cuddle anymore." Then he and his dad got a flat tire on the way home from the airport. Then he found out he has to add ten action shots to his book for his meeting with the TV people.

"I've got you beat," I said. "I just got evicted."

I couldn't see it, but I could almost hear Isaac wrinkling his brow in concern. "What?"

"Yep. Gus is selling the condo, and I have until Friday to get out. Why do homeowners have all the power and renters have none?"

"I don't know." Isaac was silent for a minute. "But maybe this is a good thing. Now you can get out of your lease and find a more temporary place."

"Why would I want to do that? Short leases are so much more expensive."

Isaac cleared his throat. "Yeah . . . But you never know."

Wait a minute. Why was Isaac suddenly interested in me having a short lease? Was he telling me without telling me that I wasn't going to be living alone for much longer? Was he?!

Well, if I played this right, I might be able to get him to tell me what I think he was telling me without meaning to tell me.

"I guess you're right," I said. "But I still think I should get at *least* a twelve-month lease. I mean, rent prices go up practically every day around here."

"Don't do that," Isaac said quickly. "I mean . . . I'd say go with three months, six at the most."

"Why?" I prodded.

"Because. Just . . . because."

I was so right! I could feel it! Isaac was going to come home and propose and since it was still early February we'd get to have a summer wedding! I smiled widely and picked up a napkin and put it on my head veil-style.

Oops. That was a used napkin.

"Okay," I said, stifling a gleeful giggle. "I'll get a short lease."

"Good," Isaac said. "I'll look online and ask around to see if we can find you a place. And I'll talk to Dirk Bag. I think his company has some rentals in Monterey."

"Dirk Bag"—as he is referred to by his friends and family—is Isaac's childhood friend, Dirk Bagley. He still lives in the L.A. area and he and Isaac hang out a lot when Isaac's down there for business.

"Or, you know," Isaac said, like he had just had a stroke of inspiration, "you could always stay with your parents."

"Probably not a good idea," I said.

I was almost twenty-five years old and it had taken me a while to . . . fully leave the nest. I blame Mom. She was far too good of a mother. I never went through the "I can't wait to leave home" stages that most of my friends did.

But now that I was on my own, I should stay that way.

"Okay," Isaac said. "Well, I'd better get to bed. Sleep good, pretty girl. I love you."

"I love you too."

I hung up the phone, changed into my pink silky pajamas, and plopped down on my homemade-quilt comforter with my laptop. As I was scouring the online For Rent ads, a thought came to my mind like a lightning bolt: Maybe I could housesit for Alex.

The idea percolated a bit. It would solve two of my current problems: finding a house sitter for him and finding a house for me. But it would also mean housesitting for Alex. Alex: the guy who I spent my first two years of college trying to hate, my second two years of college trying to forget, and, finally, the years since, not thinking about. No. Having contact with Alex was not a good idea. I would come up with something else.

I'd find something. How hard could it be?

Chapter 8

Not hard at all.

I found an awesome place within an hour and paid a group of kids to move my stuff in while I sat on the couch and drank a Fresca.

Um, no I didn't. The house hunt actually went like this:

The "One Bedroom Unit above Fish Restaurant" was already rented.

The "Stylishly Furnished Two Bedroom" was decorated with green frog wallpaper; a green waterbed with a frog eye headboard; a wall of frog artwork including a frog at the piano, a frog taking a bubble bath, and a frog doing yoga; and, here was the real clincher, a clock with a little pop-out frog that said "It's twelve o'croak, it's twelve o'croak."

The "Enchanted Cottage near Downtown Monterey," turned out to be a dank basement whose owner said, "There have been some complaints of an otherworldly presence, but I haven't noticed anything more than a howling sound at night."

By Thursday evening I was starting to get pretty worried. So I drove to my parents' house to steal their newspaper. I was sitting at the kitchen table, scouring the rentals section as Mom peeled potatoes, when I heard a familiar voice calling my name from the entryway.

"Annabelle?"

"In here!" I called.

Carrie glided into the kitchen. Her pretty blonde waves were a little more blonde than usual, and she was dressed in a flowing turquoise sundress with a white T-shirt underneath and a pair of wooden sandals.

"Oh Carrie, you look great," I said, taking her into a hug. "So relaxed. So vacation-y."

"I *feel* great," Carrie said. "The trip was so incredible. I know I sent you a lot of thank you postcards, but I just have to say it again. Thank you, thank you."

"Welcome home, hon," Mom said, giving Carrie a hug with her non potato-peeler-wielding hand.

"So did you bring pictures?" I asked.

Carrie nodded. "Yes, but first let me see your hand!"

I frowned in confusion. My hand? Why did Carrie want to see my hand? Well, I guess she just really missed me.

I held out my right hand for Carrie to . . . look at, I guess. I wiggled my fingers awkwardly.

"Not that one, silly," Carrie said, reaching for my left hand.

"Why aren't you wearing your engagement ring?" she asked, sounding shocked.

Mom dropped the potato she was holding and faced Carrie straight on.

"What did you just say?" Mom and I asked in unison.

Carrie searched our expressions for a moment and a look of realization mixed with horror came onto her face. "Nothing."

Without a word, Mom and I grabbed onto Carrie and pulled her to the kitchen table, forcing her into a seat like it was a chair in one of those interrogation rooms in the police station. We sat down and scooted our chairs very close to her.

"Carrie Lynn Fields," Mom said, "you tell us what you just said."

"Um . . ." Carrie stammered. "I . . ."

"Come on," I said. "I heard you. You asked me why I wasn't wearing my engagement ring."

"No I didn't," Carrie said. "I asked why you weren't wearing your . . . arrangement thing."

"My arrangement thing? That doesn't even make sense."

"I know. Sorry. I guess being out of the country made me a little rusty on my English."

"They speak English in The Bahamas," Mom said.

I leaned in close to my friend. "Carrie, do you know something I don't know?"

"Well. I know a lot of things you don't know. Did you know that San Francisco was the first city to ban the use of plastic grocery bags?"

"Come on Carrie. Tell me!"

Carrie pulled two pretty sundresses out of the straw bag that was sliding down her shoulder. "Look! Cotton sundresses! I got one for each of you!"

"We'll look at those later Carrie," I said. "You tell me right now!"

Carrie bit her lip. "I would . . . But first: Pictures!" she retrieved an envelope of prints out of her bag.

"That's it!" I said, and with determination to get Carrie to talk I stomped into the kitchen and threw open the refrigerator door. Time for a little whipped cream torture.

I retrieved a can of whipped cream and immediately began putting the creamy whip right into my mouth.

Carrie reacted just like I knew she would. She jumped up from her chair and tried to rip the can from my hand. "Annabelle, stop! That stuff is pure cream and sugar! No nutritional value! Here." She reached for a banana out of the fruit bowl on the counter and began to unpeel it. "At least put the cream on the banana."

I shook my head and continued to fill my mouth with shots of whipped cream.

"Okay!" Carrie shouted, like a criminal who had just been broken. "I'll tell you."

I put the can back in the fridge and returned to the table with a victorious swagger. Mom gave me a high-five.

"All right," I said. "Tell us."

Carrie released a long breath. "Isaac told me at the wedding that he was going to ask you to marry him."

"I knew it!" I exclaimed. "Mom, didn't I tell you I knew it!"

Mom nodded, her smile humungous. "Yes, you did."

Carrie looked concerned. "But I don't understand. He told me he was going to propose on your anniversary."

"He went out of town!" I shouted. Because, let's face it, when you hear your guy has plans to propose, everything kind of comes out in a shout. "He went to L.A.! And he gets back on Wednesday! And we're going to celebrate our anniversary and Valentine's Day then!"

"A proposal on Valentine's Day," Carrie said. "How romantic is that?"

"So!" I shouted.

"Oh, honey." Mom gave me a look of pure excitement.

I danced in my chair. "I can't believe it!"

Carrie, Mom, and I celebrated the big news over leftover slices of Mom's amazing key lime pie.

We sat at the table eating, talking, and brainstorming wedding ideas.

We were in the middle of fashioning a bouquet out of aluminum foil when I heard the sound of my cell ringing on the coffee table in the living room.

"I'll be right back," I said, raising my eyebrows in an I-hope-that's-Isaac-whose-secret-I-now-know manner.

The caller ID said out of area.

"Hello?" I answered

"Hi, it's Alex."

"Hi," I said flatly. Leave it to him to ruin the moment I found out about Isaac's upcoming proposal.

"So, any luck finding a house sitter?"

I cleared my throat. "No. I'm sorry. Things have been

really crazy lately. I had to move out of my condo. In fact, for a minute I thought maybe I should take the job and—" I stopped myself. Why in the world was I telling him this?

"Really?" Alex sounded pleased. "That would be great."

"Yeah, but I think I've come up with another plan."

I could just stay with my parents while I planned my summer wedding and then move in with my wonderful Isaac. I didn't need Alex's house. And I definitely didn't need to have any more contact with him than necessary.

"Okay, well, call me if anything changes."

I shook my head even though he couldn't see me. "Nothing will."

Chapter 9

For a split second, I thought I was in the wrong house.

I heard a crying baby, something coming from the TV that sounded an awful lot like those adults who dress up in primary colors and sing and dance around, and then a voice that sounded like it belonged to my sister . . .

"Cammie?"

I dropped my gym bag in the entryway and walked into my parents' living room. There stood my one-year-younger-than-me sister Cammie dancing around with her baby girl on her hip and her four-year-old son twirling around her in circles.

"Are you wearing my hoodie?" I asked without preamble.

"Camille threw up on my sweater," Cammie answered. "I found this one in your old room. Why do you have so many clothes in there? If I didn't know any better I'd say it was because you subconsciously feel conflicted about letting go of your childhood."

"Uh huh," I said, monotone.

Cammie is a licensed therapist, but since she works full time as a mom, she likes to practice her therapy skills on me.

I kissed my baby niece Camille on her little blonde head, sniffing in the scent of her baby shampoo. "What are you guys doing here?"

"Cameron's applying for a job in Salinas. Didn't Mom tell you?"

"What? No! Are you serious?"

"Yeah. We were going to stay with his sister over there, but they had a flood, so we're bunking here. If Cam gets the offer, we might be staying for a while."

"Really?"

"Uh huh," Cammie went to the kitchen to get a bottle for Camille, and I said a quick hello to my nephew.

"Hi, Camden."

Camden stopped twirling and looked to see where his mom was. "Hi Aunty Anna*smell*."

I tickled the little rugrat. "Did you hear what your son just called me?" I called to Cammie.

Cammie came into the living room and sat down to feed the baby. "What?"

I plopped down next to my sister. "Never mind. Where are Mom and Dad?"

"Mom went to the store to get some diapers and some ingredients for tomorrow's breakfast since she wants to make Camden's favorite, and Dad tagged along so they could make a 'quick' stop at the hardware store on the way home."

"So . . . where's everyone sleeping?" I asked, the worry evident in my voice.

"Mom said we need to work that out. I think Cameron and I should sleep in my old room and Camille and Camden can have your old room."

My head spun at all the Cam names. Note to you, dear reader, it may seem like a very cute idea to have a family full of alliterations, but it's terribly confusing. And can be embarrassing.

Like for instance if someone calls her brother-in-law by his baby daughter's name. Not that I ever did that. At a Christmas party in front of said brother-in-law's whole accounting firm.

"Great," I said in response to Cammie. "So I guess that

means I'm in with the food storage." The food storage room use to be the bedroom of our youngest sister, Sarah, who lives in Pennsylvania with her dental-school-student husband.

"I guess so," Cammie said.

My sister and I talked about the job Cameron was applying for and what she thought of moving to Salinas. Soon Camden had wiggled himself to sleep and Cammie put him and the baby, who was ready for a nap too, in my room. Cammie collapsed on the couch, and I offered to make her a homemade Italian soda, a treat we used to make all the time back in high school. I made Cammie's drink and sat down next to her.

"So," I said. "I think I might have some big news too."

Cammie took one look at my face, and knew. "No!" she said, her brown eyes huge. "Are you and Isaac?!"

I nodded and squealed a bit loudly.

Cammie hit me. "Shh. You'll wake up the kids."

"Sorry, I'm just so . . ." I made an exaggerated happy face that probably looked more like a psychopath face.

Cammie took a sip of her drink. "This is even more of a reason for Cam to get that job. I've always wanted my kids to be able to have cousins nearby."

I couldn't help it, I squealed again.

"If you wake them up, they're yours," Cammie said.

Just then, we heard the sound of the front door opening and the rustling of grocery bags. I jumped up to help Mom and Dad.

"I picked up a couple bridal magazines at the store," Mom said with a smile. "I dog-eared a few pages in the Martha Stewart while your dad was looking at racket wenches."

"Ratchet wrenches," Dad corrected.

"Whatever."

After the groceries were put away, Dad busied himself playing with his wrench in the garage and the three of us girls sat around the table looking through the couple—translation: five—bridal magazines Mom bought.

After some oohs and aahs over dresses and flowers, I

showed Mom a picture of a wedding cake fashioned out of Krispy Kreme doughnuts. "Isn't this cool?"

"Why on earth would you want to have doughnuts instead of cake," Mom said as if I had just told her I wanted to wear a death rocker T-shirt instead of a wedding dress. "I already have a few ideas in mind for your cake."

I couldn't help smiling.

Cammie closed the magazine she had been flipping through and looked at me. "You know, Annabelle, I would strongly suggest getting some premarital counseling. Not all couples need it, but I think you definitely will. It's good to work through some of your issues before you get married. It can help you deal with the inevitable disputes that arise during that difficult first year of marriage. I could do a four week course with you and Isaac if you'd like."

Before Cammie could finish, the house phone rang. *Thank you, phone.*

"Not it!" Cammie and I both yelled as if we were back in junior high.

Luckily, my "it" came out a little sooner than Cammie's, and she got up to answer the call.

It was Cameron. Mom and I eavesdropped as Cammie talked. It sounded like very good news.

"He got the job!!" Cammie shouted the second she hung up. "He's going to go back to Reno and pack up the house, and we'll store everything until we find a place here. He got the job!"

Mom broke out the sparkling cider and called Dad in from the garage. One of her daughters was getting engaged and the other was bringing her grandchildren closer to her—definitely cause to celebrate!

I smiled as we all clanked our glasses together. Cammie was moving to Monterey! She could help with the wedding plans, and I could spend more time with her and my niece and nephew.

I could just see it now, me and Isaac in our new house,

having my sister's family over for dinner. It would be so awesome!

Of course, what I didn't think of, was that in the meantime, my parents' house was about to get very small, very fast.

Chapter 10

Sunday morning, I woke up to the taste of graham crackers.

It took me a second to realize that Camden was standing beside me, still dressed in his race car pajamas, shoving teddy bear–shaped graham crackers into my mouth. I spit out the crackers, and Camden laughed his cute little laugh and ran away.

As I slowly sat up, I felt an awful pain in my back. I looked down at the air mattress and saw that nearly all of the air had escaped. Great.

A delicious smell wafted in through the open door, signaling that Mom was in the kitchen cooking her famous chocolate chip pancakes for pre-church breakfast. I got up to walk to the kitchen and noticed that someone had colored each of my toes a different color with markers.

Hmm. I guess that described the dream I had about Isaac giving me a foot massage.

The rest of the day went pretty much as expected:

Camden found his mom's long-wearing mascara and "painted" all over my favorite brand-name handbag—which was a gift from one of *CCL*'s advertisers—while I was singing the opening hymn at church.

Camden poured salt into my apple juice at lunch.

Camden cut off a chunk of my hair while I took a nap.

And finally, Camden put the leftovers of his chocolate cake dessert on my chair after dinner so when I sat down . . . Well, you can see where I'm going with this.

After that, Mom went to bathe the two chocolate-covered kids in the master bedroom, and I changed out of my pants and returned to the kitchen to cut myself a consolatory slice of cake.

I was sitting at the table when Cammie joined me, a glass of water in her hand.

"Well," I said. "Looks like I lost my favorite handbag and my best pants in one day."

Cammie rolled her eyes. "You and your clothes."

"So you don't think it's a big deal that my things are now ruined?"

"They're just clothes!"

"Fine. See how you like it." And with this, I turned four years old, and threw a chunk of my cake right at Cammie's USC sweatshirt.

In my defense, it was her raggedy old one that had a big grape juice stain on the sleeve.

Cammie shook her head slowly. "Annabelle, there's no need to get aggressive. I can see that you have some issues with using material things as a means to feel love. But I don't need *stuff* like you do."

"Oh really. So this doesn't bother you at all." I don't know why, really I don't, but I unscrewed the top of the salt shaker and poured its contents into my sister's water glass.

Her face quickly turned from calm therapist to angry sister. "Oh, you are so going to regret that." And with that she poured the water on my head and ran away.

Soon we were running around the kitchen throwing things at each other.

Cammie threw Camille's bib—which was covered in who knows what—at me.

"Gross!" I picked up an over-ripe banana and squeezed it all over her.

We struggled for a minute as Cammie tried to grab the banana. Finally she gave up and poured Mom's entire canister of flour on me. I looked like Flour Thing.

"That's it!" I yelled as I dipped my hand into the leftover chocolate icing on the counter and started finger painting all over my sister.

"Too far, Annabelle," Cammie hollered. "Too far!"

She grabbed onto my arms and held them behind my back. *Man. When did Cammie get so strong?* As she did this, she started shoving Dad's prunes into my mouth. Ick. I tried to spit them out at her, but I couldn't get enough power behind them.

Finally I broke free from Cammie's grip and was about to find my next culinary weapon when Dad came into the kitchen.

Cammie and I froze in place and stared at him.

Without a word Dad went to the utility closet and returned with a mop and a broom. "When your mom is done bathing the kids, this kitchen will be back in order," he said.

"Okay Daddy," we said in unison.

Dad handed me the broom and Cammie the mop and turned and left the kitchen.

"Nice going," Cammie said under her breath.

"You started it."

After cleaning up the kitchen, I was in the laundry room using Mom's homemade stain removal mixture on—yet another pair of pants—and my top, when I heard my cell ringing from the pocket of the pants.

I retrieved the phone and answered it. "Hello?"

"Hey. It's Alex."

"Hi," I said. "How did you get this number?"

"I saved it on my phone. Listen, I was just checking in to see how the house sitter hunt is going."

"I haven't found anyone. But—" I stopped short when I looked down at my multi-colored toes. Maybe now that the

situation at my parents' house had changed, it would be better
for everyone if . . . "What do you think about me doing it?" I
heard myself say.

Not a good idea, my brain spoke up quickly.

But Alex had a different reaction. "I think that would be
great. How long are you looking to stay?"

"I'm not sure. So . . . on second thought, maybe I'm not the
best option. You probably want someone who can stay as long
as you need, huh?"

"Not necessarily," Alex said. "No one's there right now,
and it's kind of a security pain for the company. Even if you
only stay for a few days, that's a few extra days we have to find
someone permanent. This will work out so well. Why don't
you stop by and take a look at the place tomorrow and then
you can make a decision."

I opened my mouth to respond and almost took it all back.
Almost said, "Yeah right I'm housesitting for you. There are
a million reasons that's a bad idea. One of them being that I
think you're a rotten heartbreaker who . . ."

But just as my mind was filled with second thoughts, a
naked little Camden streaked by the laundry room and threw a
hard plastic bath-toy submarine right at my head before being
caught by Mom who wrapped him in a towel.

"What time should I be there?"

Chapter 11

"Here. I think you should read this before you go over there." Carrie slid a book with a buttery yellow cover across the table we were eating lunch at in Shrimpy's, our favorite restaurant.

I picked up the book and read the title aloud: *Dr. Harmony's Guide to Self-strength: How to Maintain Your Strength When Dealing with a Former Love.*

I shot Carrie a what-in-the-world-is-this look across the table.

"Turn to chapter six," Carrie instructed.

I flipped to chapter six, which was all marked up with orange highlighter.

"Six Rules for Maintaining Your Self-strength When You and Your Former Love Share a Workplace," I moved my lips as I read the chapter's title to myself.

"Isn't it great?" Carrie took a sip of her lemon water. "It's her new release, and I thought it would be a good thing for you to look over before going to Alex's house this afternoon."

I ripped a piece of sourdough bread from the loaf on the table. "Why?"

Carrie shrugged. "There are some pretty good things in there. Dr. Harmony says it's only natural to want our exes to think we're beautiful and successful. But she explains this can lead to us relinquishing portions of our Self-strength. It took you a really long time to get over Alex. I don't want you to get sucked back in."

I shook my head vehemently. "That is not going to happen."

"Just read the chapter before you go over there, okay? At least the highlighted parts?"

"Fine," I agreed.

Carrie took a dainty bite of her grilled fish. "So what does Isaac think about this whole thing?"

"He's totally cool with it," I said, spearing a steamed broccoli floret and putting it into my mouth.

As I chewed, I thought back to the conversation I'd had with Isaac the night before.

He'd called for our nightly phone date, and near the end of the conversation I told him that Cammie's brood was now staying at the house and filled him in on all the details— including how Cammie picked a fight and threw food at me while I innocently told her I just wanted peace.

"You sound like you're thinking about finding another place," Isaac had said.

"Actually . . . I am. I'm thinking about housesitting. Remember how I told you that guy I went to high school with, Alex, the one we saw at Carrie's wedding, is *CCL's* new publisher and asked me to find a house sitter for him?"

"Yeah."

"Well I thought maybe I'd do it. It seems like the perfect solution."

"Wait a second," Isaac said. "Alex Mikels."

"Yes. Why are you saying his name?"

"Because I just realized how I know the guy. Didn't you used to date him?"

"I guess."

Isaac made a weird noise with his throat. "And you think it's a good idea to live with him?"

"I'm not going to be living with him. I'm housesitting for him. Watching his house because he won't be in it."

"But won't that be really awkward?" Isaac asked.

"I don't think so. We're both mature adults. Plus, our Monterey community isn't that big. I was bound to run into some old . . . you know, guys. Not *old* guys, but, you know what I mean. If it wasn't this, it would probably be something else."

"I guess you're right," Isaac said.

"Plus, it sounds like it's kind of a flexible thing, which is good."

"That does sound like a plus."

"Look," I said sincerely, "if you don't think it's a good idea—"

"No, no. It sounds fine."

"All right, well, I'll give you a call tomorrow after I go take a look at the place and let you know how everything went. I love you, Isaac. And I miss you so much."

"I love you too, sweetie. I'll see you soon."

And that's pretty much how it went down.

But, as I enjoyed my chicken and shrimp combo with steamed veggies at Shrimpy's, I had absolutely no idea that Isaac's "I'll see you soon" would be much sooner than I thought.

Because apparently, when you tell your boyfriend of nine months—who is planning to propose soon—that you are going to be having any kind of contact with a guy who you dated, liked, or smiled at anytime after first grade, and he says he's fine with it . . .

Well, chances are he's not all that fine with it.

Carrie and I finished lunch and hugged good-bye at a few minutes past 1:00.

I headed back to work and finished up my projects by 4:00, so I had a little time to kill before I had to meet Alex at the house. And since I had told Carrie I would, I decided to look over Dr. Harmony's "Six Rules for Maintaining Your Self-strength When You and Your Former Love Share a Workplace."

I opened the book and skimmed.

Rule 1: When at work, do not call your former love by his first name. And certainly do not call him by any nickname you once shared.

Rule 2: Do not dress up for his benefit. I know it's tempting. But do not do it.

Rule 3: Do not flatter him. Maintain your position of strength by avoiding any stroking of his ego. Do not comment on his car. Do not comment on his house. Do not comment on his tie. And most of the time, do not comment on his work.

Rule 4: If you must do any type of work for him, do not let him believe you are actually doing it for *him*. Let him know you are working for the company. Working for your own integrity. Working for the greater good. *Never* working for *him*.

Rule 5: Do not talk about your past.

(For some reason, Carrie had that one super-highlighted.)

Rule 6: Do keep contact with your former love to a minimum at work. This will send a very powerful message: You don't have a lot of time for him. You are a busy woman who has completely moved on.

I closed the book and tapped my fingers on my desk.

Dr. Harmony did have some good, if not a bit extreme, ideas. And, obviously, I did need a new approach. Up until then, being around Alex had made me feel all weird. So maybe taking Dr. Harmony's advice would help. She was a doctor, after all.

I shoved the book into my handbag, shut off the lights, and headed to my appointment with Alex.

Thirty minutes later, I pulled in behind a sporty BMW convertible parked in a horseshoe-shaped brick driveway and stared at the most amazing house I have ever seen in real life.

It looked like a picture out of an architectural magazine with its meticulously landscaped lawn, wraparound deck, and huge windows. I had never been so close to such an amazing house.

I double-checked the directions Alex had given me. I was in the right place, but I just couldn't believe it. The house looked like it belonged to a millionaire investment banker or celebrity.

I slowly approached the massive front door and rang the bell. Within seconds, a tiny, dark-haired woman dressed in a maid's uniform answered. "Hello," she said in an English accent.

"Cheerio," I said, because for some reason I decided she would understand me better if I talked like Mary Poppins.

The maid made a face.

"I mean, hello. I'm Annabelle Pleasanton. I'm here for—"

"Lovely. Please come in."

I stepped inside and couldn't stop my mouth from dropping open. The place was even more celebrity-worthy on the inside. After walking through a gorgeous entryway, we landed in an incredible gourmet kitchen with fancy chrome appliances and granite countertops.

Alex was sitting at the six-seat breakfast bar, looking through some paperwork. His feet were bare and he was dressed in jeans and a black cashmere shirt pushed up at the sleeves.

"Miss Pleasanton is here," the maid presented me.

Alex looked up and flashed me a smile. "Hi, Annabelle."

Do not use his first name, Dr. Harmony's first rule came to my mind.

"Hello Mr. Mikels. Um . . . Sir. Mr. Vice President."

Alex frowned. "Come sit by me for a second. I'm just finishing up some paperwork."

I eyed the barstool next to Alex and moved it about a foot and a half away from him before sitting down. But even from there I could still smell Alex's cologne.

I breathed out of my mouth.

After a couple minutes, Alex turned to face me. "Sorry. Just had to get that done. Wow. You look great."

I shifted in my seat and looked down at my favorite wide-leg trouser jeans—which I bought on BlueFly.com for just 35 bucks—button down shirt and waist-cinching belt. "Uh, thanks. I thought I'd wear something nice for you. I mean . . . for *this*. For our meeting." I paused. "Not for you."

Alex grinned. "You want something to drink?"

"Sure."

Alex retrieved two crystal glasses from a custom-built cabinet and used a small set of silver tongs to place ice into them. As he moved around the fancy kitchen I couldn't help thinking: *Who is this guy?*

Up until then I had thought of him as Alex Mikels, the guy I knew seven years ago. Just, you know, a little more stubble on his chin. But now . . . he was Alex Mikels Vice President/ Publisher of *Central Coast Living*, owner of a mansion, and guy who uses tiny tongs for ice.

He wasn't the Alex I knew at all.

"Annabelle?" Alex's voice came into my ears.

I blinked. "Yes."

"I just asked you what you wanted to drink. I have everything."

"What's everything?"

Alex peered into the refrigerator. "I have Icelandic water, Perrier, apple juice, coconut . . . Hey, I know what you want. Here." Alex set a bottle of Jones Soda on the bar in front of me.

He remembered.

Dr. Harmony's words shot into my mind. *Do not talk about your past.*

"Actually," I said quickly. "I don't like Jones Soda anymore. In fact, I don't like anything I liked in high school. Nothing. I'll just, uh, have some juice." I pointed to a reddish juice bottle in the fridge.

"That's tomato-onion-garlic juice," Alex said. "It's a detox drink."

"Sounds good to me."

Alex looked amused as he poured me a glass of the detox juice and him a glass of Jones Soda root beer. "Here you go."

"Thank you."

Alex watched with a bit of a grin on his face as I took a swig of the juice and immediately started to gag. It tasted like onion-flavored vomit with a hint of garlic. "Mmm."

"You hate it," Alex said.

"Do not."

"Yes you do. Just have the soda." Alex pushed the bottle of root beer toward me and I gave in and took a swig. By the time the bottle was gone, the taste of onion was almost out of my mouth.

"So," Alex said. "Should we start the tour now?"

"Sounds good."

Alex was charming and funny as he led me through the expansive two-story house. The place really was breathtaking—with its custom furnishings, sleek décor, and every electronic luxury imaginable including, get this, automatic toilet paper dispensers in all the bathrooms.

After touring seemingly endless rooms, Alex turned to me. "And here's the guest suite where you'll be sleeping."

I followed him through a set of double doors into what can only be described as my very own five-star hotel suite. I tried not to show how giddy I was as we entered the sitting area complete with an overstuffed couch, chaise lounge, fireplace, and table covered with fashion magazines.

Next we moved into the bedroom where I saw the whitest, fluffiest, most comfortable-looking bed I have ever seen, a TV about the size of my car, and a second fireplace that was also visible from the . . . *Oh my goodness, a Jacuzzi bath!*

I rushed into the marble-tiled bathroom and instantly felt like I was in a swanky spa. The tub was just the beginning. There was also a steam shower, a counter topped with Kiehl's beauty products, and a plush robe and slippers just waiting for me.

Alex must have noticed the look on my face. "What do you think?"

"It's . . ."

Amazing. Incredible. Breathtaking. I had a million words to describe the place. But Dr. Harmony was in my head. *Do not comment on his car. Do not comment on his house . . .*

"It's happenstance," I said with a weird shrug.

Alex furrowed his brow. "Pardon me?"

"Nothing." I plucked a tube of Kiehl's hand moisturizer from the counter. "May I?"

Alex smiled. "Of course. I got that especially for you. I remembered how much you like the stuff."

I abruptly set the tube back on the counter. "On second thought, my hands are fine. It's good for them to be a little rough."

"Okay . . ." Alex said. Then he paused for a minute and looked at me. "Is something wrong, Annabelle?"

"Nope. Everything's fine."

"All right."

Alex and I returned to the guest suite's sitting area, and I quickly claimed the single-person chaise.

Alex took a seat on the couch. "Well, that's pretty much the tour. Any questions about the place?"

I pursed my lips in thought. "Actually, yes. Besides staying here, what am I supposed to do?"

Alex laced his fingers behind his head. "Basically you'll be in charge of keeping the place maintained. You'll be in charge of the housekeeper, landscaper, and the pool guy. It shouldn't be too much work." Alex looked over at me. "I really appreciate you doing this for me, Annabelle."

The words of Dr. Harmony's third rule flashed in my mind: *Do not let him think you're actually working for him.*

I cleared my throat. "Actually, you know, I'm not really doing it for you, per se. I'm doing it for my own . . ." How did

Dr. Harmony put it? " . . . Integrity. You know, for the greater good. Of the universe."

Alex frowned. "All . . . right. So are you saying you'll take the job?"

Hmm. A mansion with a fully stocked fridge, a Jacuzzi tub, and luxury beauty products, or a leaky air mattress, flying submarines, and waiting in line for the bathroom? Was there really any contest?

"I think I will," I said.

"Awesome. Here's a set of keys for you." Alex removed a Tiffany key ring from his pocket and handed it to me.

I felt a weird churning in my stomach the second the keys were in my hand, but I chalked it up to the detox drink that was still swimming around in there.

"So," I said, playing with the key chain. "Anything else I need to know?"

"I just have one last thing I need to show you."

"What is it?"

Alex shook his head and motioned for me to follow him. We walked downstairs and into a side yard where he opened the door of a pool house. The second I stepped inside, my mind grasped a memory.

It was the day Alex told me he loved me. We were sitting on the beach after our first kiss, and I was looking out at the ocean. My mind was filled with thoughts of the future and I said, "You know what I want someday?"

Alex shifted to face me. "What?"

"I want to have a house with a pool you can see the ocean from."

"Why not just swim in the ocean?" Alex asked.

"It's usually too cold around here," I said. "Wouldn't that be awesome though? To have one of those infinity pool things that looks like it goes right into the sea."

"Then you'll have one," Alex said confidently.

And I kissed him.

"An infinity pool," a seven-years-older Alex said as

he opened the French doors that lead out to the pool of my teenage dreams.

"I . . ." I couldn't find words. Did Alex remember our conversation in Santa Cruz? I mean, he had remembered Jones Soda and Kiehl's products. Did he remember this too? The thought made me feel like I had pineapples prickling my skin.

"You know what," I said. "I just realized I'm pretty tired. I should probably get to bed."

"It's seven o'clock," Alex said.

"Yes. Well. Touring the house really took it out of me. So I guess I'll see you in what . . . a couple months?"

Alex shook his head. "I'll see you next weekend."

I raised my eyebrows. "Oh. Are you going to do some work at *CCL*?"

"That, and I'm going to check in on the house. I probably will every weekend. See if anything needs attention."

Keep contact with you ex at work to a minimum. Dr. Harmony's sixth rule was loud and clear in my mind.

"But . . ." I stammered. "Isn't that the point of me housesitting, so you don't need to check in?"

"It sounds like you don't want to see me," Alex said with a slight smile.

I don't! How am I supposed to keep my contact with you to a minimum if you're coming to my place of residence every weekend! This is not what I signed up for at all!

"It's not that I . . . it's just . . ."

"Do you want some Godiva chocolates?" Alex retrieved a box from a fridge in the kitchen area of the pool house and set them on the countertop. "I remember you like them."

I did like them. And Alex had been the only guy who ever splurged on them for me. "Um, sure."

I selected a chocolate and placed it in my mouth. Maybe I should have pulled another, "I don't like those anymore" line. But we're talking about Godiva chocolates here.

"Do you remember the first time I gave you these?" Alex asked, a glint in his blue eyes.

"Why are you acting like nothing ever happened?" The second the words came out of my mouth I looked around the room as if to see who had said them.

Alex held out a hand innocently. "What do you mean?"

"I mean, I see you at Carrie's wedding and you act all nice and friendly. Then you ask me to help you find a house sitter. Then you have me come over here and give me Jones Soda and Godiva chocolates like you're a nice guy or something."

Alex half grinned. "You don't think I'm a nice guy?"

"Come on Alex."

Alex exhaled. "I guess maybe I'm trying to make up for things. I'm sorry about what happened between us, Annabelle. I'm especially sorry that I just left. That I didn't try to fix it. I told myself I didn't deserve for you to forgive me, but the truth is, I should have tried. And when Clive told me we were buying a magazine in Monterey and I saw your name and photo on the employee list I—"

Before Alex could finish, the pool house door swung open and in stepped the maid with a very familiar man beside her.

"Isaac," I said, my voice all weird and squeaky.

"Hello, Annabelle."

Chapter 12

"What . . . what are you doing here?"

Isaac came to my side and hugged me. "I came home early. I went to your parents' house, and they said you were here." Isaac nodded in Alex's direction. "Hey."

Alex nodded back. "What's up, Ivan."

"It's Isaac."

"Oh." Alex moved toward the fridge. "Want a soda or something?"

Isaac nodded. "Sure. Root beer if you have it."

"That's exactly what Annabelle had."

Isaac looked over at me.

"Let's sit down," I suggested, my voice still on the squeaky side.

Alex handed Isaac his soda and the three of us settled into the pool house's cozy living space. But, I have to tell you, the vibe in the room was far from cozy.

Isaac looked around. "Nice digs. Must be your parents' place, huh?"

"Actually, no," Alex said. "Being Vice President of a publishing company is a pretty good gig. This isn't my only house. I have a loft in Manhattan, and a summer home in Key West."

Isaac nodded. "I have an ocean view place near Downtown Monterey."

Hmm. That was pretty funny. The view of the ocean from Isaac's house could only be seen if you stood on top of the counter in the bathroom and used a pair of binoculars. But, okay, I guess *technically* it was an ocean view.

Isaac smiled at me. "Annabelle and I have had lots of really great memories there. *Lots* of great memories."

Alex picked up the Godiva chocolate box—which he had dropped on the coffee table when we all sat down—and selected a chocolate. "Either of you want one?"

I shook my head. "Um—"

"Annabelle doesn't like chocolate that costs $30 a pound," Isaac said. "She's more of a Milk Dud girl."

Alex raised his eyebrows. "Really? She's already had five of these."

Isaac glanced at me.

"Not five," I said, biting my lip.

"So, Isaac," Alex said. "Annabelle tells me you work as a freelance photographer. It must be nice to turn a hobby into a profession."

I noticed Isaac's jaw tighten. "I enjoy it."

"And it must be great to only have yourself to worry about. It's hard keeping track of hundreds of employees. So how did you two meet?"

I opened my mouth to answer, but Isaac beat me to it. Funny how it almost seemed like I wasn't even in the room. "We worked together on an award-winning magazine article. We've been together for nine months now. Nine great months."

Alex nodded and looked out the front window, which had a view of the driveway. "That your car?"

Isaac nodded. "Yes."

"Hope it doesn't leak oil on my driveway. Old cars like that sometimes do."

I saw Isaac flinch. His classic Firebird was his pride and joy. "It'll be fine. The gaskets are in good shape, and I just replaced the front main engine oil seal. I work on it myself. I definitely prefer a good, solid classic to some girly sports car you need to put on a computer to know what's wrong with it."

Alex shrugged. "Give me all leather interior, a top of the line navigational device, and a jack for my iPod any day."

Okay. Was Alex quoting directly from his BMW owner's manual? This had to stop.

"So," I said, quickly. "Why don't we go in the house and have a snack or something?"

"Actually," Alex said, "it's getting late. I should go. I'll see you this weekend Annabelle."

Isaac's brow wrinkled. "What's this weekend?"

I opened my mouth to reply, and this time it was Alex who beat me to it. "I'm just going to stop by the place and make sure everything's in order."

"Well, Annabelle won't be here," Isaac said quickly. "We have plans for this weekend."

"Okay. Then I'll see you next weekend, Annabelle."

"You probably won't see her then, either," Isaac said. "We have very busy weekends. Out early and home late. She'll probably never see you at all."

"I'm sure we'll run into each other," Alex said. "Take care, you guys."

Alex left and Isaac and I watched as he got into his "girly sports car" and drove away.

"So that's Alex," Isaac said.

"That's him," I said as neutrally as I could manage.

"Does he always act that way around you?"

"Act what way?"

"Like he still knows you or something."

I shrugged. "I don't know what his deal is. He's . . ." I shook my head. "I honestly don't know. I could tell you were . . . I mean . . . it doesn't bother you that . . . you know . . ."

"It's okay." Isaac hugged me. "You need a place to live, and you'll be comfortable here. And that's what matters to me. I guess it was about time for me to meet someone you dated.

You had to last Christmas."

I remembered that well. Last Christmas a girl Isaac dated in college came to Monterey for vacation. This was before I started reading Dr. Harmony's sisterly harmony book, so when we ran into her on Cannery Row and she and Isaac were "catching up" I faked a mild case of food poisoning—conveniently cutting short their "Oh, yeah, I totally remember that!" walk down memory lane.

"But enough about the past," Isaac said. "Let's talk about the future. I have something for you."

He reached into his pocket and my heart jumped like a kid on a trampoline. Could this be it?

"Close your eyes," Isaac instructed.

"Okay." I snapped my eyes shut.

"I've been thinking a lot about us lately. I know we've been talking about where we're going and what we're doing. Well, I think this is the perfect next step for us to take. Are you ready?"

I held up my left hand. "I'm ready."

Isaac took my hand, and my heart pounded like crazy as I anticipated the cool feeling of a ring sliding onto my finger.

But wait a minute? Why was Isaac turning my hand palm up? And putting into it some kind of envelope?

"Okay. Open your eyes."

I opened my eyes to see a Delta Airlines envelope. What? Who puts a ring in a Delta Airlines envelope? That's why they give you the pretty velvet box.

"I want you to come to L.A. to meet my family," Isaac said.

Wordlessly I opened the envelope and found a ticket to Los Angeles leaving Thursday February 15th and returning Sunday the 18th.

"They've been wanting to meet you forever. I know you've met Ethan, but I want you to meet everyone else and see the house I grew up in. It'll be Valentine's Day weekend and . . . I just thought it would be a good time for you to meet them."

Isaac smiled at me, and his smile said it all: He was going to propose on Valentine's Day! And then he was going to take me, his new fiancée, down to L.A. to meet his family!

I threw my arms around him. "I can't wait!"

Chapter 13

The phone in my office rang, causing me to jump and minimize the "Designer Wedding Gowns at Discount Prices" website I had been looking at.

"Hello?"

"Is this Annabelle Pleasanton?" a voice that sounded slightly familiar came onto the line.

"Yes."

"Well, congratulations! You are the lucky winner of the 'Dream Wedding Sweepstakes' brought to you by John Wilfred jewelers!"

"Very funny Katrina," I said.

She was always calling to mess with me. Last week she called to tell me I won a lifetime supply of pork 'n beans. And since I had made the mistake of telling her about my upcoming Valentine's Day proposal, she was obviously having fun with it.

"Excuse me?" the voice on the phone said.

I rolled my eyes. "The drawing wasn't even for a 'Dream Wedding.' It was for free cake for a year. Shows what you know."

"Yes, but when you entered that drawing, you checked the box on the bottom of the card that said you wanted to be automatically entered into the drawing for the Dream Wedding."

"Is that so," I said sarcastically. "Wow. You really thought this one through, didn't you?"

Just then Katrina walked into the office carrying a box of chocolate chip sticky buns, aka Pipelines.

Wait a minute.

"Um, hello," I said into the phone.

"Hello."

"You aren't Katrina!" I hollered, causing Katrina to jump.

"Well, no, I'm not."

"So I really did win something?"

"Yes," the woman said, sounding exasperated. "You won the Dream Wedding brought to you by John Wilfred jewelers, valued at fifty thousand dollars."

My jaw dropped and my Big Red gum went plop on my computer keyboard. "What?"

"Out of over twenty thousand entries, you were randomly selected as the winner. Congratulations Miss Pleasanton!"

Instantly, my heart started pounding and my skin felt tingly from head to toe.

I've never won anything in my life. I mean, one time I tried to win N*SYNC tickets on the radio and ended up winning a gym sock signed by Lance. But that's the extent of it.

"I can't believe this!" I hollered, so excited the room started to get starry, and I felt a little lightheaded.

It must have shown on my face because I suddenly heard Katrina shout, "Put your head between your knees!"

I did as I was told as Katrina took the phone from me.

"Could you hold on for a minute?" she said before pushing the phone's hold button. "Who is it? What's going on?"

"I won the Dream Wedding brought to me by John Wilfred jewelers," I said, my voice muffled due to my awkward position.

"The one they were advertising at the bridal fair?"

"How did you know about that?"

"There were signs all over the place. I even entered the thing, just for fun. You won?! This is unbelievable!"

I lifted my head. "I know! I'm freaking out!"

"You should be! I read an article about the bride who won it last year. She walked down the aisle in—" Katrina paused for effect "—Reem Acra. I'm so trying not to hate you right now. You are one lucky bride."

Katrina's words made my jaw feel suddenly tight.

I wasn't a bride yet, was I?

"I'm so dumb," I said, shaking my head. "Here I was getting all excited about winning this prize. But I can't accept it."

Katrina looked at me like I just told her I was considering putting a diamond necklace out with the trash. "What are you talking about?"

"I'm not even technically engaged yet," I said, hands in the air. "I can't accept a wedding prize."

Katrina kneeled down in front of me. "Do people wait until they pop to accept gifts for the baby? No! Your boyfriend is proposing on Valentine's Day! You're as engaged as anyone else. Plus, I bet a quarter of the brides who entered that drawing won't even make it to the altar. You're fine, Annabelle."

"I don't know . . ." I said.

"Hello! We're talking a fifty thousand dollar wedding here!"

I bit my lip. "But . . ."

Katrina raised her eyebrows and then picked up the phone. "Hello," she said. "This is Katrina Groberg. I'm a colleague of Annabelle Pleasanton's. What does she need to do next to claim this prize?"

"Katrina!"

Katrina put her left hand over my mouth to shush me. She cradled the phone between her head and shoulder and scribbled something onto the Hello Kitty notepad in my office with her right.

After a minute she hung up the phone and ripped the top page from the pad. "You have a meeting with a wedding planner tonight at six. At this point, you're under no obligation to accept the prize. The planner will go over the details with you."

"But . . ."

"It's just a meeting," Katrina said. "What can it hurt?"

How many good things do you know, reader, that start with someone asking the question, "What can it hurt?"

That's what I thought.

Chapter 14

"Why are you jumping around like that? Do you need to use the bathroom? You know where the key is." Carrie cleared an empty Fresh Food Fanatics cup off the table she was cleaning and tossed it into the trash.

"I don't need to use the bathroom," I said. "I'm just so . . . excited!" I did a weird little hop for effect, and hit my foot on the stool in front of me.

"Have you been eating that Brazilian chocolate again?" Carrie asked.

"No."

Once, just once, I bought chocolate from an infomercial. It was late, I was tired, it was two pounds for the price of one, and I got a free Frisbee. Plus, it was a Brazilian chocolate that was 100 percent guaranteed to give me lots of energy.

Well, it turned out it was loaded with caffeine, and I couldn't sleep for two days.

"Well then what's up?" my friend asked in that kind, I-actually-want-to-know way of hers.

"What's the coolest thing that could happen?" I asked.

Carrie thought for a minute. "Yogini Rita Mashanta is coming into town and I get a private lesson with her."

"No. What's the coolest thing that could happen to *me*?"

"Isaac proposed!"

I scrunched up my lips. "Not quite. But that's close."

"How is that close?"

"I just got a call from John Wilfred jewelers, and I won a drawing for a free Dream Wedding!" By the end of my declaration my voice was, I'll admit it, a little loud. A few of Carrie's customers glared at me over their health food. I must have been messing up their chi or whatever it's called.

"How about we go to the back," Carrie suggested.

We walked into the back of the store and stood next to a stack of organic carrot juice palettes.

"I'm going to meet my potential wedding planner in twenty minutes," I said, smiling giddily. "The address is right down the street from here, and I thought maybe you'd like to come with me."

"But I thought you just said Isaac didn't propose. How are you planning a wedding?"

"Do people wait until their babies pop to give them gifts?" I asked.

Carrie frowned. "What?"

"Okay. Remember that bridal fair I went to a couple weeks ago?"

"Yes."

"Well, at the fair, this lady I met at a booth entered me into a drawing. And I have no idea how, because I never win anything, but I won the grand prize. A Dream Wedding! I don't know exactly what that means, or how it all works, but I do know that it's a fifty thousand dollar value. And I know that in just a few days I'm going to start officially planning my wedding, and fifty thousand dollars might come in handy."

"But what if Isaac doesn't—"

"What?" I asked, my eyes on Carrie. "What if he doesn't propose?"

"I wasn't going to say 'What if he doesn't propose?' I was going to say, 'What if he doesn't want a fifty thousand dollar wedding?' "

Huh? Since when did the groom get any say?

"Why wouldn't he want it?" I asked. "It's a free wedding! Everything paid for. Isaac and I can put the money we would have spent on the wedding toward something important. Like an investment in futures."

"Do you even know what futures are?"

"No. But we can definitely get some now! It's just so perfect. Isaac gets to surprise me with a proposal, and I get to surprise him with this!"

Carrie looked at me and shook her head. "I guess if there was a time to win something, this was it," she said. "Much better than that Backstreet Boys gym sock you won from the radio station."

"It was N*SYNC. And true."

"I can't believe you won a free wedding!" Carrie grabbed onto my arms, and we jumped up and down like we did when we were kids.

After our mini-celebration, Carrie asked Moonbeam to cover the shop while she and I went to meet the wedding planner. My maybe wedding planner!

We gabbed and giggled the whole way to the address Katrina had written down.

When we arrived at the planning firm, the receptionist told Carrie and me to take a seat in the modern-looking waiting area, and after just a moment a curvy, early-twenties woman with five different shades of blonde highlights in her hair emerged from upstairs.

She looked from me to Carrie. "Hello there," she said to Carrie. "You must be the bride. I can always tell."

"Um, no," Carrie said. "Actually . . ."

"I am." I held out my hand.

"Oh," the woman said, shaking my outstretched hand. "I'm sorry. I'm Jenna Finch. Welcome to Save the Date. Shall we?"

Jenna led us upstairs to her office and sat down behind a rather messy desk. She motioned for Carrie and me to take the two seats opposite her.

"So, Annabelle, congratulations on winning the Dream Wedding! This is our third year doing this. We are going to have so much fun! Is this your Maid of Honor?"

"Yes. This is Carrie Fields. Oh wait—it's Carrie Newton now. Does that make her my matron-of-honor, since she's married?"

Jenna shook her head. "Oh, no. Never say matron. It sounds too old."

"Okay. But traditionally . . ."

Jenna practically pounded a fist on the table. "You are the bride. You make the rules. This is your day. If you want to say maid, you say maid. If you want a hunk of a model to walk you down the aisle instead of your old dad, you do it."

Carrie's eyes got wide.

"Actually, I'm going to be having a small religious ceremony," I said. "So as far as the prize, um, funds, is it possible to use them for the reception only?"

"Of course," Jenna said. "More cash for the big bash! Now, first things first: the contract. I will need it signed by both you and your fiancé before I start booking the vendors." Jenna placed a multi-page form in front of me. "Take it home, go over it, and fax it to me as soon as possible. Preferably by Monday."

I breathed a long, internal sigh of relief. That gave me just enough time to accept Isaac's proposal, meet his family, and tell everyone all about the Dream Wedding!

"Okay," I said in regards to the contract.

"Great," Jenna said. "Now let's get to the fun part. I've put together a wedding personality quiz that really helps me get to know you as a bride. I'll give you a few minutes to fill it out."

Jenna handed me a questionnaire printed on pink paper and a fancy Waterman pen. "Would you two like something to drink?"

"Cranberry juice," I requested.

"Sparkling water, please," Carrie said.

Jenna disappeared for a moment and returned with crystal

glasses filled with our drinks and garnished with lemon slices. She also placed a tray filled with fancy fruits, nuts, and cheeses in front of us. "Here you are. I'll leave you two to work on the quiz."

Jenna excused herself, and I nibbled on a dried apricot as I read the first quiz question aloud.

1. If you could cut anyone out of the wedding who would it be?

A) Mother
B) Mother-in-Law
C) Sister-in-Law
D) Best Man

I looked at Carrie. "Is this for real?"

Carrie shrugged. "I don't know."

"What should I put?"

"Well . . . who's Isaac having for a best man?"

"Carrie!"

"I'm just wondering."

"I'm sure it will be Ethan. He is his brother."

"What if it's that guy he knows from high school . . . Dust Rag?"

"It's Dirk Bag," I said. "And I'm sure Isaac won't pick him. I'll just write in E) None of the above."

Carrie nodded as if to say, "Good idea."

I wrote in my answer and moved on to question 2.

2. Which of the following should your bridesmaids be willing to do?

A) Go on a liquid diet
B) Cut or dye hair
C) Take out a loan to buy a dress
D) All of the above

I stared at Carrie. "I would never ask you to do any of

these things." I added an option E) Have fun! and put a smiley face by it. Then I moved onto question 3.

3. If you found out another bride reserved the reception hall you wanted, would you . . .

A) Ask her to move locations
B) *Tell* her to move locations
C) Ask your parents to buy the hall

I wrote in "Find another reception hall," and resisted the urge to add "like most normal people" to the end.

4. If a member of your wedding party tripped while walking down the aisle would you . . .

A) Cry
B) Never speak to her again
C) Do something even more appalling during her own wedding

I left question 4 blank. The ceremony we'd be having wouldn't include long walks down an aisle. Thank goodness, since I'd be the one to trip for sure.

Carrie made an almost frightened face. "Annabelle . . . this quiz is crazy. Are you sure—"

"You are never going to believe this!" Jenna rushed into the office, carrying a red PDA.

Carrie and I both looked up.

"Monique's Bridal Couture has a 7:30 opening. They've been booked solid for four months, but they just had a cancellation. Should I tell them you'll take it?"

I had heard of Monique's Bridal Couture. When the girl from one of the seasons of the TV show *Bay Area Bachelorette* bought her wedding dress there, the place was instantly famous.

"I thought we needed to wait for my fiancé's signature before we started planning the wedding," I said, rather enjoying saying the words "my fiancé."

"This is Monique's!" Jenna shouted. "This appointment won't last another ten minutes. And if we wait, I just know Layla from A Formal Affair will snatch it up. I had a suit for a groom on an unofficial hold at Barrington's last month, and she stole it right out from under me! That woman has some gall bladder!"

Okay . . .

"Well," I said, glancing over at Carrie. "I guess we could go look."

"Great." Jenna typed frantically on her PDA "I'll have a car pick you up downstairs in ten minutes. And you'll probably want to call your Mom. She'll want to see you when you find your wedding gown."

"O-kay," I said, slowly.

I'd have Mom come along to look. It would be fun. But that's all we were doing: Looking. Because I wasn't going to do any official planning until after the weekend, after the proposal was made and the contract was read and signed. Today would just be a fun day looking at wedding gowns.

Because honestly, it's not like I'd find the perfect dress on the first day of looking, right?

Chapter 15

Wrong.

I knew the second I saw it.

I had just stepped into Monique's Bridal Couture and there in front of me was the most beautiful wedding gown I had ever seen, currently being worn by a lovely bride with dark wavy hair.

"It makes me look pregnant, doesn't it?" the bride asked the yawning redhead sitting on a leather chair beside the dress-fitting platform.

The redhead looked up from her gossip magazine. "It looks great."

And it did. The dress was right off a bridal show runway. Gorgeous, luxurious silk cut into an A-line silhouette with three-quarter length sleeves. A handmade lace overlay on the bodice, accented by a perfectly placed ribbon tied at the waist. It was an absolute dream.

I had always thought when it came time to shop for my wedding gown I would go to San Francisco to one of those discount bridal outlets and get in line at 5:00 am and then elbow my way through the crazy-bride crowd. But here I was looking at a couture beauty I could actually have.

I wanted that dress.

I stared at it longingly as the shop assistant greeted me, Mom, and Carrie at the door.

"Welcome to Monique's Bridal Couture. I'm Victoria. You must be Annabelle." The tall, elegant woman—who looked a bit like Naomi Campbell—spoke with a slight accent that sounded almost South African and wore a perfectly fitted suit and designer shoes.

I smiled a huge bride-to-be smile. "Yes. And this is my best friend and Maid of Honor, Carrie, and my mom, Marjorie."

Mom beamed at Victoria. "Can you believe how fast they grow up?"

I couldn't help shaking my head. When I called Mom from the wedding planner's office to tell her I had won a Dream Wedding and that I was going shopping for a wedding dress, I was worried about how she would react. But to my surprise, she whooped—yes, I heard my Mom whoop—with excitement and confessed that she booked her honeymoon two weeks before Dad proposed because the travel agency was running a special.

Victoria smiled at Mom's comment and led us down a line of mirror-doored dressing rooms, to the very last one. With a sweeping motion of her hand, she pointed us to a plush leather couch outside the room. "Would you like some champagne?"

"No thank you," I said. "We're more . . . sparkling cider kind of girls."

"We have that too," Victoria said with a wink.

"Great."

As we waited for our refreshment, our little dress-shopping group peered to the other end of the row of dressing rooms, where the wavy-haired bride was still standing on the platform, surveying herself in the mirror.

"I don't think this is the one," she said finally. She stepped into her changing room and soon emerged wearing another gown, this one a lovely creamy-color with a satin sash and a little jacket.

Yes.

Victoria swept by, clutched the rejected gown with one hand, and hung it on a rack behind the redhead. Then she sauntered over and handed flutes of sparkling cider to me, Mom, and Carrie. She did it all in one motion, like a dance.

I took a small sip of my cider and smiled giddily at Mom and Carrie as I got up and headed straight for the rack my dream dress was hanging on. I checked the tag and . . . it was my size! I felt my heart skip as I clutched the—

"What are you doing?" the wavy-haired bride scowled at me.

"I'm . . . going to try this on."

"I don't think so. That was on my 'I don't think this is the one, but I still need to think about it a while longer' rack."

I surveyed the rack the dress had been hanging on. It was completely full of dresses. Did she really think she could hoard all of them like that?

"But I . . ."

"Annabelle," Victoria said, quickly coming to my side. "Let's find you some dresses."

I moved to another rack. "Okay. What about these?"

The wavy-haired bride glared at me out of the corner of her eye. "I don't think so. Those are my 'Tried them on twice, but maybe the third time I'll like them better' dresses."

What? So which dresses weren't already claimed by the woman?

"Why don't we start over here?" Victoria led me toward the front of the store. "I apologize," she whispered. "Missy should only be here for a few minutes longer. I have a couple gowns similar to the one you like in the back. They're colored gowns, but you could try them on and see if the style suits you."

"That sounds great."

I returned to the leather couch, sat down next to Carrie, and took a sip of cider. "Victoria's looking for some dresses for me to try on," I explained to her and Mom. Then I lowered my voice to whisper, "I really want to try on that one that bride over there was wearing when we walked in, but she wouldn't let me."

I was interrupted by the loud sound of the song, "Diamonds are a Girl's Best Friend."

Missy's redheaded friend searched a cream patent leather handbag until she located a baby blue, crystal-studded cell phone.

"It's your man," she said after checking the display.

"Ugh," Missy grumbled loudly from inside her dressing room. "Why is he calling me? I told him not to call while I was looking at dresses."

The redhead shrugged and flipped the page in her magazine with one hand as she held the phone with her other. "Do you want me to decline the call?"

"No. I'll get it."

Missy emerged from the dressing room wearing a white slip and grabbed the phone.

"What," she said into the receiver.

She listened for a minute.

"No, no, no! They promised those to me a long time ago!" She listened again.

"What? No! If I can't have the off-white napkins, we might as well not even get married!" Missy hung up the phone. Her face was all red and she looked like she might cry.

The redhead put down her magazine. "Come on, honey. Let's go to the restroom."

"This is not happening!" Missy wailed.

"It'll be okay," her friend consoled.

The two disappeared in the direction of the ladies' room, and I suddenly had an idea.

"Um, I'll be right back," I said to Mom and Carrie.

Before either of them could respond, I dashed off and pretended to be looking at a pair of shoes until they lost interest in what I was doing.

Then, when Carrie was showing Mom her wedding ring set, I rushed over and took my dream dress right off of Missy's 'I don't think so, but maybe if . . .' whatever it was, rack and jumped into her dressing room to try it on.

My heart was pounding hard as I locked the door behind me and began to unzip the dress. It was even more gorgeous up close. I stepped into it and looked in the mirror.

I was transformed. Everything about the dress was amazing. The way the silk lining felt against my skin. The way the skirt was just full enough. The way the beading on the lace bodice looked like hundreds of tiny diamonds.

But still something was missing.

Maybe I needed . . . a veil. I looked behind me and saw three veils hanging on gold hooks.

Hmm. I wondered if the pieces belonged to Monique's or if they were Missy's own.

"Where did Annabelle go?" I heard Carrie ask.

And with no time to mentally debate the appropriateness of trying on a veil whose ownership I wasn't sure of, I quickly selected the longest one and put it on.

The veil helped but . . . Now I looked a little too short. I needed . . . shoes.

I peered at the five pairs of wedding heels lined up on the bench in the room. I quickly slipped into a pair of amazing peep-toes, listening for any sounds outside the room.

There. Perfect. I twirled around in front of the mirror, feeling like Cinderella.

If only I had a little bit more makeup on, then I would really know how I would look on my wedding day . . .

My eyes zoomed in on a MAC makeup bag.

No. I couldn't. This was not the makeup counter.

"Seriously," I heard Carrie say. "It's like she disappeared."

"I'll go check the bathroom," Mom said.

No. They were going to find me.

Panicking, I opened the makeup bag. And, as if some kind of explosion had just occurred, all the contents flew to the floor. Lipsticks. Eyeshadows. Mascara. Blush. Concealer.

"I think maybe I need to get a new wedding planner." Missy's voice pierced my ears. She couldn't have been more than a few yards away.

Oh no. Oh no. Oh no!

I frantically tried to simultaneously clean up the makeup; remove the shoes, veil, and dress; and figure out a plan of escape.

But before I achieved any of the above, the dressing room's gold door handle began to jiggle.

"Why is my dressing room locked?" Missy asked, sounding perturbed.

I gulped.

Would she believe temporary insanity?

"There's someone in there!" I heard Missy yell.

"Wearing your Jimmy Choos!" her friend added.

Uhh . . . .

Maybe I should fake a fainting spell.

Missy banged on the door. "Open this door right now!"

"What's going on?" I heard Mom ask.

"Someone is in my dressing room!" Missy hollered. "That's it! I'm going under the door!"

"No," I said quickly. I shoved the last of the makeup into the bag and put it back where I found it. "I'll come out."

"Annabelle?" Mom's voice sounded confused. "Is that you?"

I slowly opened the door and stepped outside, still wearing the dress, veil, and shoes.

"What in the world are you're doing!" Missy yelled, her face flaming red.

"I'm sorry . . . I . . ."

"Take that off!" Missy reached for the veil and yanked it off my head. "And my shoes!"

I quickly slipped the shoes off my feet.

Missy picked them up and sniffed them. "You better not have made them smell."

"Yeah," her friend added with a deadly glare.

Mom and Carrie watched the whole scene, completely bewildered and unaware of what to do.

"I'm sorry," I stammered. "I didn't realize . . ."

"Okay," Victoria's voice trilled through the air. "Here are those dress—" She stopped short and looked from me to Missy to the redhead to Mom and Carrie and back to me. "Is there a problem?"

"Yes," Missy said with bite. "She went into my dressing room and put on my veil and shoes while I was in the restroom trying to make sure my wedding doesn't fall apart!"

"I apologize," Victoria said quickly. "I told Annabelle I had something for her to try on. She must have misunderstood what I meant."

I looked at Victoria in amazement. She was totally covering for me.

"Well," Missy said, hand on her hip. "I suppose if it was a mistake I can look the other way. But if anything like this ever happens again, I'm taking my business elsewhere."

"I assure you nothing will," Victoria promised.

"Okay." Missy folded her arms and frowned at me. "Now I see why that dress didn't look good on me; it must be made for people with weird proportions. It looks pretty good on you."

"It really does look pretty amazing," Carrie said softly.

"Whatever," Missy said as her phone started to ring again. "What does he want now?!" she hollered as she moved to a more private phone-answering spot.

Her friend shot me a disgusted look and followed.

I bit my lip as I walked barefoot to the dress-fitting platform. Mom and Carrie followed, and I stood up there for a good five minutes, imagining Isaac's face when he first saw me in the dress.

"You look absolutely beautiful," Mom said, taking my hand. "Like a princess."

I smiled a ridiculously huge smile as I continued to stare at the dress.

Okay. I know I was planning on just looking at dresses, but was it so awful that I found my wedding dress *a few days* before my official engagement? I mean, I've heard of women who buy their dresses before they're even seriously dating anyone.

"What do you think?" Victoria asked, suddenly beside me.

"I think it's perfect," I said.

Carrie clapped with glee. "You're going to be the most beautiful bride!"

"You really are." Mom's eyes were suddenly filled with tears.

I stepped down from the platform, and quickly handed her a handkerchief I saw on a nearby table.

Victoria saw this and leaned over and whispered to me, "Did you know that was a $200 Jon Ling bridal handkerchief?"

We both watched as Mom blew her nose into it.

Victoria winked at me. "I'll put it on your tab. Your first official Dream Wedding purchase."

I beamed at Victoria, her words sinking in. I couldn't believe it! I'd found my wedding dress. My Dream Wedding dress! The moment was absolutely perfect.

So why did I have a not-so-perfect pit in the bottom of my stomach?

Chapter 16

"How do you think he's going to do it?" Carrie asked as she removed the organic cotton balls from between her toes.

I secured the lid on my new bottle of Candy Heart Red toenail paint. "I don't know. He wouldn't tell me anything he has planned for tonight other than it includes dinner."

Carrie and I were in the guest suite in the company house, eating fresh organic fruit, sipping Perrier, and wearing matching white robes as we celebrated our first post-Carrie's-wedding Paint and Popcorn Night and got ready for our Valentine's Day dates. Miles was taking Carrie to dinner at the Spyglass hotel, and Isaac was taking me to an undisclosed location so he could—let's say it together—propose!

Clothes from each of our closets were strewn on the fluffy white bed, our cutest shoes were lined up in front of the fireplace, and a ton of Sephora beauty products had been pulled from the cupboards in the bathroom and scattered on the marble countertop.

Carrie plopped onto the bed and nibbled on a pineapple chunk. "I bet he'll hide the ring in some kind of food."

"Really?"

Carrie nodded, a grin on her face.

"Oh my goodness! I'm getting engaged tonight!"

"And you better call me tomorrow and tell me everything."

"Of course I will." I hopped up from my chair, my insides bubbling with excitement. "Okay. My toenails are done. Which top do you think I should wear?"

I stood in front of the full length mirror and held up the two choices: A red cashmere v-neck and a light pink satin top—both bought for 35 percent off at Sass, this great boutique in Carmel.

I turned and looked at Carrie. "Which one is a better engagement night top?"

"The cashmere."

I slipped on the v-neck and my favorite pencil skirt and looked at the clock. I had fifteen minutes until Isaac arrived, and I still had to finish my hair and makeup. I was rushing into the bathroom when Carrie stopped me.

"Hey, you still have a tag on your top."

I twisted around to see.

"I'll go get you some scissors," Carrie offered. "Where do you think they would be?"

I leaned toward the bathroom mirror and applied some blush. "Probably in the office. Down the hall, third door on the right."

"Okay. Be right back."

I was all ready and putting emergency-touch-up makeup, Altoids, and my wallet into my handbag when Carrie came back into the suite with scissors in one hand and a brown box in the other. She set the box down on the bed and cut the tag from my top.

"What's that?" I asked, pointing to the mystery box.

"Pictures and stuff from high school. It was open on Alex's desk."

"Really?"

I watched as Carrie removed a photo from the box. It was a picture of Joe, Carrie, Alex, and me on the beach at Santa Cruz during the senior class trip. Ever since Alex had come back to town, the day had been coming to my mind, but here it was in full color.

I looked at my eighteen-year-old self and wished someone would have told her about eyebrow plucking.

"And look," Carrie said. "Here's one of us when we all went to Shrimpy's after we got our Cal Poly acceptance letters. Remember that?"

I nodded and looked at the photograph. Alex had his arm around me, and I was snuggled up against him. We were both holding up our Cal Poly letters with huge smiles on our faces.

Carrie flipped through a few more photos, and I began to notice a pattern. They all had one thing in common: Me.

"I don't think we should be going through Alex's stuff," I said in a tight, odd voice.

Carrie's frowned. "Um. Okay. I'll put them away."

Ding dong.

"That's Isaac." I shoved thoughts of Alex out of my mind as I zipped my bag shut and headed for the door. "Don't forget to lock up and set the alarm on your way out."

Carrie hugged me, careful not to mess up my hair. "Okay. You have a great time. And call me"

"I will!"

⁂

"Wow. You look amazing." Isaac kissed me on the cheek and offered me his arm as he led me toward his Firebird, which I noticed had been freshly washed.

"Thanks," I said with a flirty smile. "You look pretty spiffy yourself."

And he did. Dressed in charcoal pants and a striped dress shirt, he looked hot and cool at the same time—if you know what I mean.

As Isaac and I got closer to the car I noticed something that made my heart start pounding: There was a man in the back seat.

"Don't panic," I whispered to Isaac. "But someone is in your car. Let's just slowly back up and go inside and call the police."

Isaac's reaction was not what I expected: He laughed. "That's Dirk Bag," he said.

What?

Isaac opened the passenger side door for me and I got inside.

"Hey Annabelle," Dirk said from the backseat. "How's it going?"

"Fine," I said, completely confused.

Isaac got into the car. He looked back at Dirk and then at me. "Can you believe it? I was pulling into the parking lot of that flower shop down by the airport picking up a bouquet for you when I saw Dirk Bag standing at the bus stop."

Dirk continued the story. "I flew up here for a few days for work, but the rental car place lost my reservation. I didn't want to pay for a cab, so I just went out to the bus stop. That's when this guy showed up." Dirk punched Isaac in the arm. "It couldn't have worked out better."

"Except that I forgot to go into the flower shop and get your flowers," Isaac said, and Dirk laughed like it was the funniest thing he'd ever heard.

I, however, didn't really see the humor.

Isaac started the car and moved down the driveway. "He's in town for the rest of the week."

I looked over my shoulder slightly and saw Dirk nodding. "Yep. I was planning on staying at the Marriot, but Isaac's letting me crash on his couch."

"That's nice," I said, wondering if and how this new development was going to affect Isaac's and my evening plans.

Our *engagement* evening plans.

"You smell like perfume," Dirk said to me. He leaned forward in his seat. "And you look all fancy. What's the occasion?"

"February 14th," I said.

Dirk stared at me, a blank look on his face.

"Valentine's Day," I spelled out.

Dirk scratched his messy blond-haired head. "Is that today?"

If you haven't already guessed, Dirk is single.

"Yes." I changed my focus from Dirk to Isaac. "So where are we going tonight?"

"Yeah," Dirk said. "Where are we going?"

I looked over at Isaac, waiting for him to answer with a "*We* aren't going anywhere. Annabelle and I are going to—insert amazing place here—so I can propose," but he didn't. He seemed to be concentrating on the road or something.

Please. This is California. No one concentrates on the road.

"Well," I said. "*Isaac and I* are doing something special. He hasn't told me exactly what yet. But I know we're starting with dinner, somewhere nice I'm sure."

Dirk snorted. Usually I hate it when I'm reading a book and it says "so and so snorted" because I don't really know anyone who actually goes around snorting when talking. But apparently Dirk does.

"A nice restaurant?" Dirk asked. "No way. Those are going to be full of lovey-dovey couples if it's Valentine's Day."

Um, yeah. Me, Isaac: lovey-dovey couple. You: stop trying to ruin my Valentine's/Engagement Day!

"I know where we should go!" Dirk said, clapping his hand on his knee. "Hoagie Hal's! I wonder if they still have our pictures up in there?"

Isaac laughed.

"What's Hoagie Hal's?" I reluctantly asked.

Dirk was eager to explain. "It's this sandwich shop with these huge, two-foot long hoagies, and if you eat the whole thing in under thirty minutes you get a free T-shirt and they put your picture on the wall. Isaac and I went there the last time I visited and got on the wall. We should go!"

Yeah. Just what I wanted to do on Valentine's Day: watch Dirk inhale a two foot hoagie.

I could see it now: me squished in a booth with a group of beefy guys who were all watching Dirk eat a humungous sandwich, yelling, "Eat, eat, eat . . ."

"I would rather do what you had planned," I said to Isaac pointedly.

He glanced over at me and then at the watch he used as a clock in his car. "We probably have time for both. Our dinner reservation is actually at eight. I had a little something planned before dinner, so that's why I picked you up at seven. But if we skip it, we'll have time to hang out with Dirk and still make our reservation."

He had a little something planned before dinner? And now he wanted to *skip* it? So we could hang out with a guy whose *friends* basically refer to him as dirt. What if the something special was the proposal? I couldn't let Isaac's plan be ruined like this. No. Absolutely not. I was going to put my foot down on this one.

"Don't worry," Isaac said. "We'll still get to do everything I planned."

"All right," I heard my mouth agree. Apparently it wasn't in on what my foot wanted to do.

"Sweet!" Dirk celebrated.

I swallowed hard. I could handle an hour at Hoagie Hal's.

Or maybe not.

Hoagie Hal's was jam packed with college-age kids and it was really, really loud.

"I'm starving," Dirk announced as we stepped inside and walked toward the long line that snaked out from the ordering counter. "Are you guys gonna get anything? We could get a three-footer and split it or something."

"That's all right," Isaac said, looking at me. "We should

save room for dinner. We'll probably just get some drinks."

"Uh huh," I said, trying to hide my perturbedness. Is that a word?

"Suit yourselves."

For the next twenty minutes, we waited in the barely moving line, and Dirk and Isaac chatted about everything from their Hoagie Hal memories to the current college basketball season.

I laughed and smiled at all the right times, but inside I was fuming. It was Valentine's Day and instead of being somewhere quiet and romantic with my soon-to-be-fiancé, I was listening to a juke box play a bad Ace of Base song while my carefully styled hair took on the smell of onions.

After what seemed like forever, our orders were finally in our hands and we sat in a cramped booth near the bathroom.

"This brings back so many memories," Dirk said as he ripped into a mustard packet. "I can't believe—"

Dirk's words came to a halt as the mustard packet suddenly went haywire on him.

Or shall I say went haywire on me.

My throat felt hot as I turned my eyes down and saw a big splotch of mustard on the front of my cashmere top.

"Oh, man," Dirk said. "I'm so sorry. Here, let me get you something to . . ." Dirk looked around as if a dry cleaning shop would suddenly appear before his eyes.

Isaac quickly turned around and asked a girl in the booth behind us for some napkins. He dipped them into my soda water and handed them to me.

I spent a good minute wiping, until I was left with a wet mustard stain covered in shredded pieces of napkin on my brand-new top. "Oh well," I said as neutrally as I could muster. "I'll take care of it later."

"You sure?" Isaac asked.

"I'm sure."

"She was cute," Dirk said, nodding his head toward the napkin girl. "Not really my type. But definitely yours."

I looked over at Isaac, waiting for his "No one but Annabelle is my type, and you better fork over fifty bucks so she can buy a new top" reply, preferably with a loud, authoritative bang on the table, but all he did was laugh.

He laughed!

I'm telling you, I was this close—right now I'm holding up my hand with my forefinger and thumb very close together—to leaving. But I didn't. I stayed in that loud, smelly, awful hoagie place while Dirk polished off a two-foot long sandwich and washed it down with 32 ounces of Sprite.

When we were finally leaving the sandwich shop Isaac held the door open for me, but I gestured for him and Dirk to go ahead. They did, and Dirk was so busy talking about his new video game that he let the door slam right on me.

The perfect ending to a great Hoagie Hal's experience.

After dropping Dirk off at Isaac's place—where he clutched his stomach and collapsed on the couch to watch ESPN—Isaac and I were sitting alone in his car.

"Thanks for being so great tonight," he said, taking my hand in his. "It means a lot to me that you care about my friends."

I swallowed hard, feeling suddenly bad that I wasn't as great about the whole thing as Isaac may have thought. Isaac kissed me before starting the engine, and I immediately felt myself begin to relax and enjoy our evening. But, alas, the enjoyment was short-lived.

Parking outside the restaurant—which turned out to be La Bonne Violette—was awful, and since we didn't want to pay a valet, by the time we found a spot it was past eight.

"You don't think we'll miss our reservation do you?" I asked Isaac as we jogged to the restaurant.

He squeezed my hand. "We'll be fine. I'm sure they hold the table for at least fifteen minutes."

"Okay."

Isaac held the door open for me as we maneuvered our way through the people clogging the restaurant's entrance. "Matthews, party of two," he said to the tall, skinny *maître d'*. "We have a reservation for eight o'clock."

The *maître d'* consulted his book and then looked at his watch. "I'm sorry, monsieur. It is nine minutes past eight. We have given up your table."

"What?" I asked, my heart sinking into my empty stomach.

"We do not have a table for you."

"Can't you just put us on the list?" Isaac asked.

The *maître d'* laughed. "Sure. Your wait will be approximately 48 hours."

I shot Isaac a do-something look, and he spent the next twenty minutes trying to bribe the man to give us a table.

It didn't work.

"I'm so sorry, sweetie," Isaac said as we walked outside.

Dejected, I peered into the restaurant's window and saw a couple enjoying La Bonne Violette's critically acclaimed *crème brûlée*. *Crème brûlée* I was no longer going to find my engagement ring hidden in.

"It's fine," I said half-heartedly. Oh let's face it, quarter-heartedly.

"We'll find somewhere else to go," Isaac said.

We walked in silence to the car and then drove around for two and a half hours looking for a place to eat. Yes, that's right, two and a half hours.

Every few miles or so we'd stop at a restaurant, where Isaac would jump out of the car to see if they had any tables available, and then come back looking disappointed.

When he came back from Jimmy's Pancakes and Lobster—yep, that's a real place, as I now know—I had given up on dinner. In fact, I'd kind of given up on the evening completely.

"You know what," I said as Isaac buckled his seat belt. "I think we should just call it a night."

"We can't do that, it's Valentine's Day."

"You're right," I said. "Let's just grab a quick something to eat at a grocery store or something and continue with whatever surprise you had planned, which I'm pretty sure includes a proposal."

Actually, no, that's not what I said. That's what Mr. Hindsight tells me I should have said.

What I actually said was this: (And just so you know I was operating on a painfully empty stomach, and the onion smell in my hair had kind of gone to my brain.) "Yeah, well, it was also Valentine's Day when you let Dirk talk you into going to that ridiculous hoagie place."

Isaac looked taken aback. "That's not why we were late. We were late because the parking was so bad."

"Yes but we would have been there a whole lot earlier if it wasn't for Dirk Bag." I used Dirk's nickname—which I never used—with a little bite.

"I thought you liked Dirk," Isaac said, sounding defensive.

"He's fine. But Isaac, look at me. Other than the mustard stain, this outfit doesn't exactly scream 'Take me to a hoagie joint.' It just . . . it wasn't where I hoped we'd go tonight."

"You didn't seem bothered that we went."

"Well it's not like you would have even noticed if I was bothered. You were too busy talking about cute napkin girls."

"Is that what this is about?"

"No, Isaac. It's about our very first Valentine's Day being ruined." Not to mention the night I was supposed to get engaged.

"I was just trying to be a good friend to Dirk Bag."

"Well maybe I wanted you to be a good boyfriend more than a good friend."

"So now I'm a bad boyfriend?"

I shook my head and released a long sigh.

"Maybe you're right," Isaac said. "Maybe we should just call it a night."

I felt tears threatening. Angry, disappointed, frustrated tears. "Fine," I said, forcing the tears to retreat.

Isaac clenched his jaw and threw the car into gear.

Chapter 17

I heard a loud bang the second I walked into the kitchen. I jumped about a mile, and my heart felt like it was trying to leap out of my chest. I knew the maid and cook had already gone home for the night. What could the noise be?

I reached for the first thing I saw—which happened to be a huge bag of oranges—and tiptoed toward the sound. I don't quite know why my natural reaction was to head *toward* the possible danger, but it was.

As I walked, I yelled out: "Oh, hi there . . . Flesh Ripper, my huge . . . Doberman Pinscher. You look hungry. I guess I haven't fed you in a while. I'm sure you'll devour the next food you see. Oops. I just stepped on the silent alarm. But that's okay. The police will turn it off when they get here. Which should be in what? Thirty seconds now?"

I heard another bump and realized it was coming from the office. I gulped and readied my thumb to dial 911 on my cell, which I was clutching in my hand.

"Don't worry, Flesh Ripper," I hollered. "Daddy will be home soon from his job as . . . The World's Strongest Man. And hopefully he found those brass knuckles he was looking for."

Suddenly, I heard footsteps, and they were heading right

toward me. I threw myself behind a nearby armoire, shaking as the figure got closer and closer until it looked like it was coming right at me.

"Ahh," I screamed as I hurled the bag of oranges.

"What the—" a voice hollered as the oranges made a thud on the floor. The voice sounded oddly familiar.

I was practically hyperventilating as none other than Alex flipped on the light and removed a pair of headphones from his ears.

"I thought you were a robber!" I shouted.

Alex raised his eyebrows. "And you throw oranges at robbers?"

Was he laughing at me? "It was all that was available."

"Where's your car?" I asked, confused as to why I hadn't seen it in the garage.

"I parked down the road. Thought I'd get a little walking in. I miss that when I'm not in New York."

Okay.

"Sorry I scared you," Alex said. "I thought you'd be out late with what's-his-name. I needed to get some things out of the office."

"It's okay," I said, my breath returning to normal. "It's your house."

My mouth got dry after I said the words. Did this mean Alex was going to show up unannounced all the time? Was I going to have to lock the door when I took a bath and wear a robe over my pajamas? This could be bad.

"Don't worry," Alex said, reading my mind. "I won't come over again without calling first. My visit to the area today was last minute." Alex's eyes zoomed in on the mustard stain on my shirt. "What happened to you?"

"Nothing. Awful day."

"Really? So your Valentine's date with Icarus wasn't a hit?"

"Isaac," I said. "And I don't really want to talk about it."

"Well okay. But I bet I have something that will cheer you

up. Come on, it's in the kitchen."

"Actually, I think I'm just going to go to bed."

"You don't want to miss this," Alex said. "A little house-owner to house sitter Valentine's gift."

Don't do it, my brain warned.

But somehow I found myself nodding and following Alex to the kitchen.

"Sit," he said when we reached the breakfast bar.

I took a seat and watched as Alex retrieved a Cheesecake Factory New York cheesecake from the refrigerator.

I was taken back to the night he asked me to prom. The night we sat on the beach and ate nearly the entire New York cheesecake he had made.

I was starving. And the cake looked great.

Alex removed two forks from the silverware drawer and the two of us ate from opposite ends of the cake. It was the creamiest, butteriest, yummiest cheesecake I had ever tasted.

"You like it?" Alex asked.

"Mmm hmm," I mumbled through my full, satisfied mouth.

"Great. I hope you also like this." Alex handed me a lacquered robin's egg blue box.

I stared at it, stunned.

"Open it."

Feeling almost like someone else had taken charge of my hands, I opened the box and saw a delicate Tiffany diamond-pendant necklace. The kind so amazing you have to call for the price.

"Alex," I said, looking at him with a bewildered expression on my face. "I can't accept this."

"Yes you can," he said resolvedly. "No girl like you should have a bad Valentine's Day."

I set the box on the bar. "But . . ."

Before I could finish, Alex's cell rang from inside his pocket. He checked the caller ID and gestured toward the necklace. "I'm leaving it here. It's either yours or the maid's."

Alex disappeared in the direction of the garage. I heard him answer his phone and then his voice trailed off.

I stared at the jewelry box and bit my lip. The closest I've ever been to wearing anything Tiffany is ripping the ring ads out of magazines and taping them to my finger. But I only did that once.

Okay fine, four times.

In the past month.

I drummed my fingers on the bar. Maybe I could just put the necklace on for a second. Just to see what it looked like.

Without further deliberation, I creaked open the box and removed the necklace. It was gorgeous. I looked over my shoulder and then began to put it on. I stood in front of the microwave, using it as a mirror. I was fumbling with the clasp when Alex came back into the kitchen.

"Here let me," he said.

Before I could say no, Alex clasped the necklace closed. And then, just for a second, his hand brushed against my neck.

The touch shocked me so much that I jumped away from him and shouted, "Oww!"

Alex looked panicked. "What is it?"

"Um . . ." I improvised by grabbing onto my foot. "Foot cramp. Oww. Must be these shoes. I better take them off. And go to bed. Yeah. That's probably the best thing for me to do. Go to bed." I was talking a million miles a minute.

The sound of the doorbell interrupted me.

"You expecting someone?" I asked Alex.

"No. Are you?"

Maybe it was Isaac, coming back to apologize.

Suddenly a panicky feeling filled my chest as I had a moment of déjà vu.

You see, back when Isaac and I first started dating, there was this guy who . . . let's just say caused a misunderstanding that created a monster of a problem between me and Isaac.

I was not going to let that happen again.

"Hey Alex," I said.

"Yeah?"

"I think Isaac's at the door. Come with me."

Alex looked at me as if to say "Why?"

"Just come on." I grabbed Alex by the arm and felt my palms begin to sweat.

I threw open the front door. "Alex is here!" I shouted.

But it wasn't Isaac at the door. It was Jenna the wedding planner.

Jenna smiled broadly at Alex. "It's nice to finally meet you," she cooed in that taffy sweet voice women always seem to use around Alex.

I furrowed my brow in confusion. Why was my wedding planner excited to meet Alex?

No . . .

"Um, Jenna," I said quickly, "I—"

"Would you look at that necklace," Jenna said, her mouth dropping open. "Well isn't Annabelle lucky to have you as her fiancé?" She tilted her head and flashed a coquettish smile at Alex.

"Oh no," I said "Alex's isn't—"

"I definitely think Annabelle is lucky to have me," Alex said with a mischievous wink in my direction. "Won't you come in?"

Alex ushered Jenna inside and smiled at me over her head.

I shot him a very dirty look. *This is not funny!*

"Jenna," I said as soon as we were seated in the living room. "There's been a bit of a misunder—"

Jenna ignored me and reached into her handbag. "I'm so glad you two are here. I got into a little bit of trouble for taking you to Monique's without getting the Dream Wedding contract signed. I was hoping you two could sign it for me tonight."

Um.

"Well . . ." I stammered. "I thought you said you didn't

need it until Monday."

"That was before we found your dress. I'd really feel more comfortable if we took care of it right now."

Alex took the contract from Jenna's hand. "I don't see any reason why we can't sign it tonight."

I clenched my teeth. "Alex. Could I speak to you in the kitchen for a minute?"

"Sure, cupcake."

"We'll be right back," I said to Jenna as I pushed Alex into the kitchen.

He was grinning from ear to ear.

"What are you doing?" I said, hitting him on the arm.

"So you're marrying Ian," he said without responding to my question.

"It's *Isaac*! And yes."

Alex leaned lazily against the breakfast bar. "How did I not know this? When did he propose?"

I turned my head away from him and bit my lip.

"He didn't propose yet," Alex said in a Sherlock Holmesesque voice.

I whipped my head back to face him. "It's none of your business. You have no right lying to my wedding planner. Knock it off."

"How do you have a wedding planner? What wedding? You're not engaged!"

"Be quiet! It's a long story."

"I have time," Alex said, apparently riveted.

"Well I don't. Now. I'm going to go back out there and talk to Jenna. Can you please just stay in here?!"

Alex responded to my pleading tone. "All right. If that's what you want."

"It is." I moved to go back to the living room.

"I have to admit, it was kind of fun to think about," Alex said to my back. "You know, me, you, together. We used to talk about it all the time."

I spun around slowly. "That was a long time ago, Alex."

Alex's expression turned very serious. "Maybe. But when I'm around you it doesn't feel long at all."

"Don't do that," I said. "I'm with Isaac now. And I'm happy."

"Then why are you here with me on Valentine's Day?"

I stared at Alex and felt a sort of achy feeling in my stomach. "I—"

"Excuse me."

I jumped at the sound of Jenna's voice echoing in the kitchen.

"Yes," I said in a squeak.

"I have an emergency to take care of with a bride in Carmel. The wedding's this weekend, and her Maid of Honor refuses to wear any dress color except white. I'll need to hire a new one. Just sign the contract and fax it to me ASTAT okay."

I wasn't sure if she meant ASAP or Stat.

"Okay," I said.

"See you two later." Jenna dashed out of the room, typing into her PDA as she went.

"Bye," I said in a much-too-chipper voice.

The front door slammed and Alex looked at me. "I guess I should be going too." His eyes focused on my face and then on the necklace around my neck. "That really does look good on you. Happy Valentine's Day, Annabelle."

I didn't respond as Alex left, the front door banging slightly behind him. The kitchen was eerily quiet in his absence, and I quickly removed the necklace from my neck.

What the heck was Alex doing?

Chapter 18

"Still mad at me?" Isaac walked into my office just after 9:00 am the next day, bearing a dozen red tulips and a wrapped gift.

"I wasn't *mad*," I said.

Isaac set the flowers on my desk. "I'm so sorry, sweetheart. I've been thinking all night about how dumb I was. Here."

Isaac handed me the obviously-wrapped-by-a-guy box. I unfolded one of the badly taped ends and removed my gift: A box of SweeTarts, my favorite non-chocolate candy. A note attached said: "Sorry last night was so sour. I promise I'll make it up to you with a very sweet weekend."

I couldn't help but crack a smile. Isaac's apology gestures are always so deliciously corny. "Thanks," I said, smiling up at him.

"I'm sorry yesterday was a bust," Isaac said. "But I promise: this weekend will make up for it."

My stomach flip-flopped at Isaac's words. The proposal was coming over the weekend! So Valentine's Day didn't work out. Who cares? Getting engaged on V-day is cliché anyway.

I got up from my desk, and put my arms around Isaac. "I'm sorry too. I shouldn't have gotten so mad. It's just . . . I had all kinds of high hopes . . ."

Isaac squeezed me. "You deserved to have the perfect Valentine's Day. You shouldn't have had to watch Dirk Bag stuff his face instead of going to La Bonne Violette. I really will make it up to you."

I opened my box of candies and popped one into my mouth. "You're off to a good start."

Isaac kissed my forehead. "Good. So, I'll pick you up at your place at five and we'll head to the airport. I hope you're already packed."

If having my suitcase on the floor with one pair of jeans in it counts. "I'll be ready," I said, with a quick kiss to Isaac's cheek.

"Good," he said with a smile that said he knew I wouldn't be.

I pulled away from Isaac and moved toward my office chair, my face suddenly serious. The mention of "my place" had brought up something I really needed to tell him. "Hey, Isaac."

"Yeah?"

"I have something to tell you."

"Okay."

"Last night after you dropped me off . . ."

The sound of my cell ringing from within my handbag caused me to stop. I made an apologetic face at Isaac as I retrieved it. "Hello?"

"Annabelle. It's Jenna."

My body tensed from head to toe as I looked over at Isaac. "Oh, hi, Jenna. Can I call you back in a minute?"

"No," Jenna said in her wedding planner/drill sergeant way. "Listen. Love at First Bite has an opening for a tasting today at 11:30. I immediately thought of you. I have a handful of brides who would rip your eyes out if they knew you got this over them, but I thought you'd appreciate it more. What do you say?"

I jumped slightly when Jenna said the word, "Brides," and looked to see if Isaac had heard. He was flipping through a copy of *Fab* magazine I had on my desk—hey I'm a magazine writer, reading magazines is *research*—and didn't seem to notice.

"I don't know if it's such a good idea," I whispered.

"What?"

"I said I don't know if it's such a good idea."

"Look!" Jenna shouted, causing Isaac's head to shoot up. "I'm your wedding planner! I—"

"La, la, la, la, la!" I sang loudly, in an attempt to cover Jenna's voice. And, as if bursting into song wasn't enough, I added a weird little dance. Kind of an Irish Jig.

Isaac looked at me like I was a head trauma victim.

"Um, I'll be right back Isaac." I dashed out of my office and hid near the floor's fax machine.

"What on earth are you singing in my ear for?" Jenna was saying.

"I'm sorry," I said, feeling panicked. "Listen. I have to go. But I'll go to the tasting."

"Great. I'll meet you there. This is something most brides appreciate me being there for. "Probably because of my business cumin."

Or your business acumen. *You know, whichever.*

"And don't forget to tell your fiancé," Jenna added. "Grooms don't really care about a lot of the wedding details. But the food is something he will care about."

"He won't care," I said, my voice rushed.

"I've been doing this a long time," Jenna said. "You don't want to be sitting down at your reception and have him turn to you and say, 'Salmon? I hate salmon. What kind of idiot picked this out?' sending you to the bathroom where you cry so hard your false eyelashes fall off. Because that happened to a bride of mine: Mimi Carter."

"It'll be fine," I said. "See you at 11:30." And with this, I hung up the phone.

I headed back to my office and saw Isaac standing in the doorway. "There you are. What was that all about?"

"Just some work I have to do during lunch."

Isaac nodded. "You were going to tell me about something

that happened last night."

"Yes. I was." I cleared my throat. "Last night Alex gave me a house owner to house sitter gift. It was so nothing, but I just wanted to tell you."

I couldn't read Isaac's expression. "What was the gift?" he asked.

"Well . . . it was . . . a necklace."

"A necklace?"

"Yes."

Isaac made another face I couldn't quite decode. "Well, thanks for telling me."

I blinked. "Uh huh."

Isaac stared out the window for a second and then looked back at me. "I know you say the gift was nothing, but there's something I really have to get off my chest."

"Okay."

"That guy bugs me. There's just . . . something about him. Something that tells me he can't be trusted. There. I said it."

"Isaac—" I began.

But I was interrupted by the sound of Isaac's cell ringing from inside his pocket. He retrieved the phone and checked the caller ID. "Sorry, hon, but I should answer this."

I made a go-ahead gesture and sat down at my desk—trying to work, but honestly I could never get anything done with Isaac around—while he talked.

When he hung up he was frowning. "That was one of my clients. He wants to go over some prints in half an hour. So I'd better go." Isaac bent down to kiss my cheek lightly. "See you at 5:00. Just think, in a few hours, we'll be in L.A."

My stomach churned. Meeting the family. I was beyond nervous. "Okay. See you soon."

Isaac waved good-bye and as I watched him walk away—which I have to say, he looked so good doing—I couldn't help wondering if I should have mentioned the necklace at all.

Because, honestly, it was a stupid necklace from a wealthy publisher who apparently liked to throw his money around. It didn't even really warrant mentioning. Because it didn't mean anything.

Did it?

❦

"Welcome to Love at First Bite," a woman with a brunette bob, who looked like she never ate more than air, greeted me inside the gourmet, invitation-only eatery nestled in the Carmel Highlands. "You must be Annabelle Pleasanton?"

"Yes. I'm meeting Jenna Finch."

"Of course. Right this way."

The woman led me to the back of the restaurant. Jenna was waiting for me at a cherry table with a single calla lily in a vase in the center. I took a seat across from her and opened up the tasting menu that had obviously been left for me.

Jenna looked up from her own menu. "Hi, Annabelle. Where's your fiancé?"

"I told you, he's not coming."

Jenna shook her head. "I called him after I talked to you. He's here. He said he was going to wait for you out front."

The blood drained from my face. *What?*

"Oh, don't look so shocked. I didn't want you two to miss this experience."

My mind raced. How had Jenna gotten a hold of Isaac?! What had she told him?! Oh my goodness! This was bad.

I mean, that's bad, right? Having your almost-fiancé find out you've already started planning your wedding. He'd think I was a complete nut. Like the women in those movies who are so obsessed with babies they wear pregnancy bellies and throw themselves baby showers. Only in this case it was weddings, not babies.

I tried to fake composure in front of Jenna. "So you called him," I said, the words squeaking out like those of a twelve-year-old boy whose voice is changing.

"Yes. I saw his business card on the kitchen counter last

night and grabbed one. And good thing too, because I know you would have regretted not having him here today."

My whole body froze.

No.

Just then, Alex approached the table, looking all spiffed up in a designer suit. "There you are," he said with an amused grin.

It took a lot of effort not to lunge at him. "Yes. Here I am," I said in the most monotone voice I could muster.

Jenna looked at me as if she could sense something was wrong.

"Jerkface," I said to Alex. Then I turned to Jenna and smiled a sweet smile. "That's my pet name for him. It's a long story."

Jenna nodded, looking confused.

I whipped my head back toward Alex. "Jerkface, could I talk to you for a second?"

"Sure, sugar pop. What do you want to talk about?"

"I mean in private," I said through gritted teeth.

"Oh brother," Jenna said melodramatically. "It's started already. You take a good solid couple and toss in a wedding and suddenly it's *Days of Our Lives*. Look. You only get one chance at this. Don't waste time fighting. You're about to have the best crab cakes of you life. Don't spoil it."

"You're right, Jenna," Alex said with a charming smile. "No fighting."

Alex sat down. And I was so mad I kicked him under the table.

Or at least I thought I kicked him.

But Jenna's loud, "Ouch!" told me otherwise.

"Sorry," I stammered. "I, um, have this tick, and I sometimes, you know, kick stuff, it's a kick tick . . ."

Jenna reached under the table and massaged her shin. "That's going to leave a bruise. I'd better find some ice to put on it." She glared at me as she walked away.

"What is wrong with you?!" I shouted at Alex the second

Jenna was gone. "Why on earth did you come down here?"

Alex leaned into the back of his chair in that cool, smooth way he did everything. "My assistant called me about an hour ago and said someone left a message about a tasting at Love at First Bite. She didn't remember who called or why. She's not really on her game today because she broke up with her boyfriend last night. Poor thing. Broke up on Valentine's Day."

I scowled at Alex. "Does this story have a point?"

"Just that I didn't know who called. But since I've never been here before, I thought it would be a nice place to have lunch. Then when I got here, I saw Jenna waving at me—"

"Because she thinks you're . . ." I let my voice trail off. I wasn't going to say the words. "The point is, once you knew what was going on, you should have told her you couldn't stay. You should have told her—"

"I should have told her what?"

I stared at Alex. He had me with that one.

"Come on," Alex said. "Now that we're both here and it doesn't look like Izod is coming, let's just have lunch."

I didn't even bother to correct Isaac's name. That's just what Alex wanted. "Let's not," I said, arms crossed over my chest.

"Is there a reason we shouldn't have lunch together?" Alex asked, his voice all kinds of insinuating.

"No," I said. "Of course not."

Alex opened the tasting menu on the table. "Good."

Before I could argue more, Jenna returned with some ice wrapped in a chef's hat, and we began a round of tasting.

I have to say, the company was awful, but the food was amazing. Spicy tuna tartare. Dungeness crab cakes. Pizza with white truffles. Mushroom caps. Creamy risotto. The kind of food they serve at celebrity after-parties.

Alex seemed to know a lot about the food and told me to stop worrying about price and just choose what I wanted while Jenna nodded and shot me wow-don't-you-have-an-amazing-fiancé looks.

After about an hour of tasting I had my favorites picked

out. Jenna went to find an ordering-packet, and Alex and I were again alone at the table.

"So, I heard you're planning on applying for the editor-in-chief position," he said, setting down his water glass.

I choked on the crab cake in my mouth. "What!? How do you know that?"

"This morning I found out about an article idea you ran by George."

"What?!" I said. Apparently, it was my word of the day. "How?"

"I hear things."

"Oh." I leaned back in my seat, a feeling of discomfort forming in my full stomach. I wasn't sure I liked Alex knowing so much about me and my plans.

"I'm glad I know," Alex said. "It made me snap into the realization that you're not just housesitting for me for a little while. We're going to be working together for a long time; for as long as you stay at *CCL*.

"And I realized that maybe I need to switch gears where you are concerned. It's only natural to go back to the age you were when you last saw someone, but I can't do that anymore. I apologize if I've been living in the past a little bit lately."

"I appreciate that," I said.

"I'm glad." Alex smiled and then stood up from his seat. "I had a very nice lunch with you today. I'll see you later, Annabelle."

"See you," I said in a weird, far away voice as he walked away.

I stared at the lily on the table as I thought about Alex's words. He realized he needed to switch gears and not live in the past. He wasn't going to do it anymore.

Good. Things would finally get back to normal.

What? I can kind of see a concerned look on you face. Do you not think I should trust him?

Chapter 19

"Miss, could you please make sure your seat is in the upright and locked position? We're preparing for takeoff."

I snapped my head to the left and looked at the red-lipped flight attendant.

"Um. Okay." I slowly pushed the button and moved the chair up until it felt like I was going to fall forward. Apparently "upright" in plane-speak, means "falling out of your seat."

"Are you all right, sweetie?" Isaac asked, looking over at me.

I nodded.

A lie of a nod.

You see, here's the thing: I'm kind of, maybe a little bit, afraid of flying.

Okay, fine, a lot afraid of flying.

Up until the moment I packed my bags for the trip—thirty minutes before leaving for the airport—I was excited to be going to L.A. with Isaac. Excited to take Friday off work. Excited to get away from Monterey and everyone that was there. Okay, just one person that was there. And especially excited to finally become a real bride instead of the imposter I was beginning to feel like.

But as I packed for the trip after work, the terror of flying hit me like a ton of bricks.

I've only done it once before, when I went with my family to drop my sister Sarah off at college in Washington, DC, and I was so terrified I threw up in my dad's San Francisco Giants hat. The one signed by Barry Bonds.

I think Dad's okay with it now that Barry has been in the news so much, but that's beside the point. I really, really didn't want to throw up in anything of Isaac's.

I tried to relax as I watched the flight attendant demonstrate how to secure the oxygen mask.

I took a quick scan of the plane and saw that I was pretty much the only person paying any attention. How could they not be paying attention?!

I listened to every word like my life depended on it, because I was completely convinced it did. And when she said the last bit way too fast, I tapped Isaac on the shoulder in a panic.

"What did she say? Secure it on the child first then myself? Or secure it on myself first and then on the child? What am I supposed to do?!"

Isaac took my hand and squeezed it. "Relax. You're not traveling with any children. I'll take care of my mask and you take care of yours."

"Oh," I said, my breath shallow.

I leaned back into my chair—well as much as you can lean back in an upright airplane seat—and tried to calm myself.

After the plane remained in the same spot for what seemed like an hour but was actually around seven minutes, the silver-haired woman next to me started to look worried.

"Do you hear that odd grinding noise?" she asked me.

I squeezed Isaac's hand with a death grip. "What . . . there's a grinding noise?" I whipped my head toward Isaac. "The lady next to me hears a grinding noise? What could that be?"

Isaac patted my hand. "That's you grinding your teeth, honey."

Oh. Oops.

"Are you sure you're okay?" Isaac looked more concerned

than he had the last time he asked.

"Yes. I'm fine."

"Why don't you listen to that relaxation CD Carrie lent you?"

The relaxation CD! Of course! I nodded as I pried my non-Isaac's-holding hand from the armrest and shakily reached into my carry-on bag to retrieve the disk Carrie had lent me when I stopped by her place to borrow some comfortable sandals for the trip.

I loaded the CD and pushed play.

The woman on the disk had a very soothing voice.

"Gently close your eyes," she instructed me. "Pay attention to your breath. No need to change it, just become aware of the breath moving in and out of your body. Now imagine yourself softly releasing the stress and anxiety through your mouth . . ."

I let out a deep breath. Hmm. It actually made me feel better. The CD was working, it seemed.

"Now to further your relaxation, imagine you are in a cloud of white."

An image of me in the airplane traveling through a cloud came into my mind.

"Suddenly you feel yourself beginning to fall into the cloud."

What?

"You fall deeper and farther . . ."

I watched as my mental-image airplane began to fall. I was pummeling to my death!

I threw off the headphones. "What kind of crazy relaxation tape is this?!"

A few heads turned to look at me, and a male flight attendant instructed me to "Discontinue the use of my portable electronic device."

The plane finally began to move and I chanted, "I'm relaxed, I'm relaxed," with my eyes tightly closed and Isaac's hand in mine as we sped down the runway and took off.

The rest of the flight went pretty much like this:

I freaked out when we hit a bit of turbulence and made a "dying confession" to Isaac that I hated the scarf he gave me for Christmas.

I freaked out when the lights on the plane went out and exclaimed, "Is there an electrician on board?!" until Isaac calmly reached over and turned on my reading light.

And I freaked out when I could have sworn I heard a bird fly into one of the wing engines. Isaac kept asking me to describe exactly what I heard and I kept telling him "a bird noise and then a clunk."

He and the woman beside me pointed over to the boy across the aisle playing a duck-hunting video game.

One hour, twenty minutes, and ten years off my life later, we finally landed.

I've never been so happy to see the ground.

"You did great," Isaac said, kissing me on the nose. "I had no idea you were so afraid of flying. I'm sorry to put you through that."

"No problem," I said. "I'm just glad it's over."

"Okay," Isaac said, pointing to the left. "Baggage claim is this way."

Suddenly my fear of flying transferred to my fear of meeting my soon-to-be in-laws.

"Is there a ladies' room near there?" I asked, mentally planning the freshening-up I needed to do.

"Yes. When we get down there I'll point you toward it, and I'll get the bags. Well, my bag and your Mack truck."

"Very funny."

My suitcase wasn't *that* big.

LAX was bustling. As I moved across the marble tile floors, I looked around for celebrities.

We had just passed a store selling books, magazines, and newspapers when I saw Bob Barker coming out of a little restaurant. I was so excited. I totally missed seeing him on The Price is Right.

"Bob! I neutered my dog!" I hollered at him, thinking I was very clever.

Bob looked right at me and . . . It wasn't Bob. Just some random man who was looking at me as if he were trying to figure out what kind of nutcase yells "I neutered my dog" in the middle of an airport.

Isaac also looked at me like I was crazy, and I hid behind him, remaining quiet the rest of the way to baggage claim.

When we arrived, my black suitcase with the polka-dot ribbon on the handle was already circling the baggage carousel. Isaac lunged for it and struggled to get it off the moving conveyor belt. His muscles were in full flex and his face was a little red, and for a second I thought he might not be able to grab it. But when he finally did and set it next to him, he played it off like no big deal. Like fifty pounds was a feather to him.

Men.

I dug through the suitcase and found my silk top, my makeup bag, and my favorite heels—these gorgeous Italian leather stilettos I found hidden behind a huge bottle of bubble bath at Nordstrom Rack. I think someone was doing the ole' "I'll hide them here until I can come back for them" trick, and I felt a little bad for snagging them. But not quite bad enough to leave them there. What can I say, once you enter the doors of Nordstrom Rack, it's every woman for herself.

I put on the heels, tossed my flip flops into my suitcase, and headed toward the ladies' room. "I'll be right back," I said to Isaac.

Inside the bathroom I stood in front of the mirror as I removed my travel T-shirt and slipped the silk top on over my camisole. The silk was a bit wrinkled, so I decided to splash it with water and hold it under the electric hand dryer. I thought it was a good idea.

I thought wrong. Not only did the water not dry all the way, but the water spots got rings around them. The top looked ten times worse than it had when it was just wrinkled. I slipped it on and inspected the damage: I looked like I had been rained on by dirty rain. Not exactly the I-am-a-classy-girl-who-will-make-a-great-daughter-in-law look I was hoping for. I made a mental list of every top in my suitcase to see if I could come up with a way to save the outfit.

I finally decided to wear my black cardigan over the top. I'd just have to rifle through my suitcase again to find it.

Okay. Next thing: Makeup.

I touched up my cheeks and eyes in the bathroom mirror, and got ready to fix my lips. By fix I mean fill them in with lip liner because I was currently suffering from the makeup crime of visible lip lines. You know, when the liner or lipstick on your lips has faded away, but the outline on the lips is still there. Not too pretty.

Of course, as luck would have it, when I moved to apply my "3 Carat Girl," lip pencil—which I saw on sale at the Clinique counter in Macy's and thought would be perfect for the occasion—I realized I tossed it into my suitcase because it had a built-in sharpener that I didn't think they'd let me take on the plane. I added to my mental checklist: get the lip pencil when I grab the cardigan out of my suitcase.

I felt the beginning of beads of sweat forming under my arms as I walked back to meet Isaac. I fanned my underarms with the airplane-reading magazine that was luckily in my handbag.

"There you are," Isaac said when I came to his side. He looked at my blotched shirt. "What happened?"

"Nothing. I just need to get in my suitcase." I reached for the bag, but Isaac started walking away with it.

"Sorry," he said over his shoulder. "But my parents just called. They're only a couple minutes away, and if we're not out there waiting, they'll have to go all the way around again."

"But my shirt. My lips. My—"

Isaac didn't respond and headed out the automatic doors. I followed him, trying not to lose my shoes as I jogged.

Outside was utter mayhem. Busses, taxis, rental car

shuttles, and tons of other vehicles were zooming by as if there weren't crowds of people on the sidewalks. I saw one lady try to catch her rental car shuttle and almost get creamed by a hotel shuttle. I won't tell you which hotel, because you might like it and I wouldn't want to sully your opinion, but I'm telling you, I'm certainly going to think twice before letting them "leave the light on" for me.

"We need to get to the second curb," Isaac hollered at me over the sound of people and traffic and airplanes.

I followed as he approached a crosswalk and waited for a break in traffic. As I watched the cars rushing by, I suddenly felt like I was in that old video game, Frogger. You know the one where the frog has to get across the street without getting squished by the passing cars and trucks. That was me: Frogger.

"We're never going to get across!" I called to Isaac.

"Yes we will! Wait for it. Wait for it. Go!" Isaac said the word "Go," with such intensity I half-expected it to be accompanied by an action movie theme song.

I clutched my handbag to my side as I jogged behind Isaac.

We were almost out of the danger zone when my right shoe caught on a crack in the ground. As I continued forward the shoe flew behind me.

"My shoe!" I yelled, looking back to where it had landed. A Hummer limo was headed right for my beloved stiletto.

"No!" I cried.

Isaac looked back at me. "Leave it! There's no time!"

"I can't!" I shouted.

I lunged toward the shoe, but before I could get close enough to grab it, the limo laid on its horn and seemed to pick up speed. I jumped back and quickly crossed the crosswalk. Only to see my shoe get smashed to smitherines by a billion pound limo.

It's just a shoe. It's just a shoe. It's just a 70 percent off retail Italian leather perfectly gorgeous shoe.

"There they are!" Isaac dashed toward a blue Pontiac, and I followed, alternating between five foot seven and five foot ten.

"I can't meet your parents like this," I shouted to Isaac. "I need to get in my suitcase. Just really quick!"

"You'll have to do it when we get to the house," Isaac said as he knocked on the trunk of the car. "Hurry and get in!" he looked over his shoulder at an approaching Alamo shuttle and tossed our suitcases into the now-open trunk.

I got in the car and slammed the door shut. I could immediately smell the strawberry Yankee Candle air freshener hanging from the rear view mirror.

Isaac jumped in the car seconds later and closed his door. "Let's go!" he said, out of breath.

Isaac's mom looked over her shoulder and surveyed my shell-shocked face. "Hello, Annabelle. It's so nice to finally meet you."

"It's nice to meet you too," I said, my voice a bit shaky.

"All righty then," Isaac's dad, Dennis—who had the same ears and hair color as Isaac, only with a touch of gray—hit the gas and weaved in and out of cars expertly as he headed for Airport Road.

As we drove, Isaac's mom, Doreen, turned around in her seat and looked at me. She was pretty with dark hair and blue eyes. She looked a bit like Jaclyn Smith only less office-womany. Her eyes took in my VLL (visible lip lines) and then lingered for a moment on my disaster of a shirt, but she politely looked away. "Welcome to L.A., Annabelle," she said with a smile.

"Thanks. It's very . . ." I almost said crazy, but this was her hometown, so I didn't want to insult it. "Populated," I said finally.

Populated?

Dennis slammed on the brakes, and Doreen braced herself on the car door and faced forward to see what was going on in the road. "Don't get so close to the busses!" she said to her husband.

"I wasn't close until he decided to slam on his brakes for no reason," Dennis said, sounding stressed. Who wouldn't be in this mess?

Doreen turned back around. "How was the flight?"

"It was . . ." Awful. Horrible. "You know . . . flighty."

It was flighty? What is wrong with me?!

"Annabelle's a bit afraid of flying," Isaac explained.

"Oh," Doreen said.

For the remainder of the drive to the Matthews' Santa Monica home, I tried to remain quiet as Isaac and his dad talked about the weekend's upcoming UCLA basketball game. It worked pretty well. But when we got to the house and I got out of the car with my one shoe on, I saw Doreen and Dennis exchange looks.

I took off my single shoe and followed Isaac into the house barefoot. All I wanted to do was get into my suitcase, get myself together, and fix this disastrous first impression I was leaving.

Once inside, Isaac showed me to the guest room. As he propped my suitcase against a wall, Doreen stuck her head in the door. "What do you two think about going out for some Mexican food?"

"That sounds great," Isaac said.

"I'd really like that too," I said. "If it's all right though, I'd really like to, um, change first."

"Sure," Doreen said. "See you in . . . twenty minutes?"

"That's perfect."

Once Doreen was gone Isaac took me into his arms and kissed me. "I love having you here."

"I'm glad to hear that."

"See you in a few minutes, beautiful girl."

I smiled flirtatiously, completely forgetting about my lip problem. I'm sure I looked ridiculous. "See you," I said to Isaac.

About fifteen minutes later I was changed, made up, and ready to go. I was on my way to find Isaac when I heard him and his parents talking from a room at the end of the hall.

I moved toward the voices.

"Are you sure she's okay?" Doreen was asking. "She doesn't have some sort of . . . condition?"

"Mom. No!" Isaac said. "She's just nervous about meeting you guys."

"Well, she was definitely acting funny," Doreen continued. "And what was with the one shoe?"

"She was a little overwhelmed by LAX," Isaac said, defending me.

"Well," Dennis said lazily. "She does have some pretty nice feet."

Great. Way to leave an impression.

Chapter 20

"Good morning, sweetie."

I jumped about a mile and flung my arms in the air when I heard the words, sending the porcelain bunny rabbit knickknack on the nightstand flying to the floor.

"It's okay," Isaac said in a gorgeously soothing voice. "It's just me."

I sat up in the homemade-quilt-covered bed in the Matthews' guest room. "You scared me half to death," I said, my mouth beneath the powder blue sheet. "I hope the bunny didn't break."

Isaac looked to the floor. "It's fine. As are you."

Ooh, I liked that transition.

"How do you look so gorgeous when you first wake up?" Isaac asked.

I batted my eyelashes as if to say, "I don't know, I'm just naturally lovely I guess." Which was a total lie since I had slept in my waterproof mascara and added some long-wearing lip gloss when I woke up to use the bathroom at 6:00 am.

Isaac came in for a kiss, but I turned my head coquettishly. No way was he getting near my pre-Colgate mouth. Not until at least six months after the wedding. If then.

"So what are we doing today?" I asked, mouth still hidden.

"I'm not telling you. Meet me in the breakfast nook in half an hour."

"How about forty-five minutes," I said. I had already looked like I had "a condition" when I met his parents. I wanted to start today out on a much better foot.

"Okay. Forty-five minutes. I'll see you then."

After showering, doing my hair and makeup, and dressing in what I thought was a good redemption outfit, I made my way into the breakfast nook. What I saw made my mouth turn up at the corners so much it almost hurt.

The dining room table was covered in bouquets made out of candy. There was a gumdrop bouquet, a caramel-covered marshmallow bouquet, and a saltwater taffy bouquet.

I looked at the treats in shock. Since when did Isaac know how to make candy bouquets?

But it was what my eyes focused on next that really floored me. Hanging from the sheer curtains that framed the window beside the breakfast table, were photos Isaac had taken of me. The interesting thing about the photos, though, was that they weren't all of me. Each one was a part of me, just one part.

I walked closer and inspected my personal photo gallery: A picture of my flip-flop-clad feet. A picture of my eyes, crinkled at the corners, so I knew I had been smiling. A picture of my hands holding an open Bible. A picture of my mouth, smiling so big, I knew I must have been looking right at Isaac when he had snapped it. There were no words attached to the photos. No captions or notes. But there didn't need to be. The photos said everything Isaac had meant them to.

It felt a little strange to see pieces of me in such large, full color, but something about seeing myself the way Isaac saw me made me feel so lovely, so real, so cherished.

"It's . . . amazing. I love it." I kissed Isaac softly on the lips and then rested my head in the crook of his neck. "What's all of this for?"

"It's for you," he said. "I love you, Annabelle. You are the best thing in my life by far. Plus, I want today to be perfect."

My legs suddenly felt like they wanted to dance. "Why," I asked, pulling away to look at Isaac. "What's today?"

Say our engagement day! Just say it!

"Not yet," he said. "First, breakfast. I made a waffle bar."

Isaac headed toward the kitchen, and I walked in back of him, my arms wrapped around his shoulders. Sure enough, an entire waffle bar was waiting for us. Isaac poured a premeasured cup of batter onto the hot waffle iron, and I stood back (yes, I was afraid, so what?), looking at the topping spread: Maple and strawberry syrup, fresh strawberries, chopped bananas, chopped nuts, whipped cream, even some chocolate chips. There's nothing like having candy for breakfast!

"Well if you want today to be perfect," I said as I put a few chocolate chips into my mouth, "you're doing a good job."

Isaac grinned. "This is just the beginning."

⚜

"Come on. Tell me where we're going."

Isaac merged onto the freeway and shook his head. When we came to a dead stop in traffic after going about .1 miles, he reached over and squeezed my hand.

"Is it a garden?" I asked.

Isaac smiled a tight-lipped smile and shook his head again.

"A theater? Ooh . . . is it that beach with all the hippie guys doing weird stuff?"

"I'm not going to tell you. But you're going to love it."

Isaac's words made me feel warm and tingly all over, like I was in a bathtub filled with soda pop.

We drove for quite a while, chatting as we wove through traffic.

Finally we exited the freeway, and when I saw the signs, I knew.

"Oh my goodness!" I shouted. "We're going to Disneyland!"

Isaac smiled as I bounced in my seat excitedly. "When you

wish upon a star . . . makes no difference who you are," I sang loudly. And probably off-key.

I kept singing as Isaac pulled into a packed parking lot and placed a ticket inside my hand. "Your ticket, m'lady," he said in a terrible accent. I think he was trying to sound English or something, but it came off more Japanese.

I giggled as I unbuckled my seat belt and kissed Isaac hard on his sweet, delicious mouth.

Disneyland!

I have loved Disneyland since the first time I visited when I was six years old. Isaac discovered my love for Disney fairytales when he found my collection of Disney Princess Barbies. I tried to explain the dolls were a hot commodity and I had them for *investment* reasons, but he didn't really buy it.

I hadn't been to the park since my high school senior trip, but it was just as amazing as I remembered. As we passed through the front entrance, I held onto Isaac's hand and took it all in. Everything was bright and clean and magical, like living inside a fairytale.

"All right," Isaac said, excitement in his eyes. "Follow me."

He guided me further into the park, and we had only been walking for a minute when I saw a shop selling those cool vintage-y Mickey Mouse T-shirts. Again, probably a very good investment.

"Mickey shirts!" I shouted, pointing to the shop.

Isaac reached into his pocket. "Go get one," he said, handing me a fifty.

I was really beginning to like this whole Isaac-wanting-to-make-the-day-perfect-for-me thing.

I kissed him on the cheek and grinned all the way to the shop.

After I bought the shirt, I found Isaac's dark hair and blue surf-style shirt in the crowd. I snuck up behind him, grabbing onto his hand.

When he turned around, I was expecting to see his smiling

face but instead I saw ... A complete stranger! A complete stranger whose hand I was holding.

Quickly I dropped the hand, which if I'm being honest, was pretty sweaty.

"What are you doing?" The man, who looked nothing like Isaac from the front, glared at me.

"Vas er wrongenhand," I said quickly. I guess I thought pretending not to speak English made everything better. Of course, what language I was supposedly speaking, I have no idea.

"What?" the man asked, still shooting me that glare.

"Uh . . . Auf Wiedersehen," I said before dashing away.

And yes, I did learn that on *Project Runway*.

After a moment of searching, I found the real Isaac sitting on a bench. He was wearing a grey shirt. Whoops.

"Hey," I said, trying to suppress the tiny shudder I felt coming on as I remembered my encounter with Sweaty Hands.

Isaac stood up and took me into his arms, hugging me tightly. "You ready?" he asked.

"Yes."

"Okay. Let's go."

I took in the sights, sounds, and smells of Disneyland as we walked hand in hand through the park.

After a bit of walking we reached the park's center.

"Sleeping Beauty's castle!" I said with glee when I saw the pastel-painted edifice.

Isaac's eyes brightened as he gently pulled me in the direction of the castle.

My heart started pounding as if it knew something I didn't.

Could this be it?

Isaac led me to an area at the left of the castle. Waiting there was a bench that had been covered in glitter and flowers, and a little girl with brown ringlets dressed in a blue fairy costume.

Isaac looked at the little girl and said, "Hello, good fairy," in the most adorable voice I think I have ever heard.

I felt the corners of my mouth turn upward.

"Hello," the little girl said, looking at me. "I'm Merryweather, the good fairy. Please sit down."

I did as I was told and looked over at Isaac. "Did you actually watch Sleeping Beauty?"

Isaac raised his eyebrows and didn't answer.

"Thank you, Merryweather," I said to the little fairy—whose Mom, an attractive woman in designer jeans—was apparently watching us from a few feet away.

"You're welcome, Princess Annabelle. This is for you." The girl placed a gold-toned Sleeping Beauty crown on my head.

I love how in a place like Disneyland a grown woman can get away with wearing a crown.

"Thank you," I said to the sweet girl.

"You're welcome, Princess Annabelle."

Is it bad that at that moment I decided I could get used to being called "Princess Annabelle?"

"Since you already have beautiful hair and lips," the little girl said as if she were reciting lines for a play—in case you don't know, that's what the good fairies give Sleeping Beauty in the movie—"I'm dusting you with happiness, laughter, and love." The girl waved a little wand around me as she said the words.

"Did he tell you to say that?" I asked, pointing to Isaac.

The little girl giggled and nodded her head.

I couldn't help but smile as my insides danced like, well, fairies.

"Thank you, Merryweather," Isaac said.

"You're welcome, cousin Isaac. See you later." The little girl scurried off in the direction of her mom and the woman smiled at Isaac before escorting her little fairy away.

Isaac waved good-bye and then sat down beside me. "I had the hardest time figuring out the perfect way to do this," he began. "A way that would be worthy of you. Everything

I thought of seemed like it wasn't good enough. I wanted everything to be magical, perfect. I thought this was as close as I could get."

Isaac took a deep breath and then began to lower one knee to the ground, kneeling in front of me.

I covered my mouth with one hand, and felt tears begin to form in my eyes. My chest felt like it was on fire, and my heart was going crazy.

I felt like the world was in slow motion as Isaac removed a John Wilfred ring box from his pocket and opened the box so the ring was facing me.

"Annabelle," Isaac said, his voice deep and full of emotion, "I am so madly, deeply, crazily in love with you. You are the single most incredible person I have ever known. And you deserve to be the happiest girl in the world. I promise you, I will do everything in my power to make that happen. Will you marry me?"

"Yes!" I exclaimed. "Yes! Yes! Yes!"

Isaac took me into his arms and the two of us stood up almost as if we were one person. He held me close, kissing me as if he were trying to memorize everything about my lips.

The members of the small crowd that had formed around us started clapping.

Isaac slid the ring on my finger, and I glanced at it through my teary eyes. It was the exact one I had wanted. A single princess-cut diamond in the center of a white-gold band with small diamonds on the sides. Isaac picked me up off the ground and twirled me around, my feet high in the air.

This was it! My fairytale proposal!

It couldn't have been more perfect.

Chapter 21

"I'm engaged!" I shouted into Isaac's cell phone.

Isaac pulled my left hand up toward his lips and kissed the finger that now bore my engagement ring as he pulled out of the Disneyland parking lot.

"She's engaged!" Mom yelled so loudly I had to move the phone away from my ear.

"Isaac finally got smart, huh?" I heard Dad say.

Then I heard Cammie ask, "Did she like the Sleeping Beauty thing?"

I answered all of their questions and told them I'd call back later. They were all so happy for Isaac and me.

Next I called Carrie. She cried, which made me cry, which made Isaac reach for a Kleenex in the glove compartment and almost crash into the lit brake lights of a Chevy Impala in front of us.

Thirty minutes later we pulled into the parking lot of a fancy Italian restaurant called Severino's.

"What are we doing here?" I asked.

"We're having an engagement party." Isaac put the car in park and unbuckled his seatbelt.

I looked at him with narrowed eyes. "You must have been pretty confident I'd say yes."

Isaac shrugged. "If you hadn't, I would have changed the party to a console Isaac party."

I grinned as Isaac swung open his door and the two of us walked into the restaurant.

"Congratulations!"

The ten-seat table in the back of Severino's was halfway filled with people. I recognized Doreen and Dennis, and after Isaac and I sat down and were handed our menus, Isaac introduced me to the others.

To our right were Isaac's Aunt Margaret and Uncle Wayne, who, he said were the resident genealogists in the family,

"It's nice to finally meet you, Annabelle," Margaret said, touching the bun in her hair that was secured with an antique clip. "Isaac says your last name is Pleasanton?"

"Yes."

"We actually have some Pleasantons in our bloodline. Wouldn't that be funny if you and Isaac were distantly related?"

Um. No. "Well—"

"That's Grandma Malette," Isaac interrupted, pointing to the spunky-looking gray haired woman who was seated next to Margaret and Wayne. "You're going to love her."

"I'll take a half-diet, half-regular," Malette was saying to the waiter in a commanding, gravelly voice. Then without missing a beat she said to Isaac, "Get over here and hug your grandmother."

Isaac motioned for me to follow him as he went to Malette's seat. He gave her a hug and then introduced me.

"She's pretty," Malette said to Isaac. "How'd you get a girl this pretty?"

"I was looking for someone just like you, grandma."

"Save it," Malette said. "I know I look like an old raisin. Luckily, my eye sight's so bad; I look in the mirror and see Marilyn Monroe."

"I think you look great," I said.

Malette frowned at me. "You don't have to kiss up to me, sweetheart."

I felt my cheeks burn.

"We're here," I heard a voice say from behind us.

I looked toward the voice and saw the woman I had seen with the little fairy at Disneyland approaching with a thin man in rimless eyeglasses. I now noticed the woman looked like a younger, blonder version of Doreen.

"Hi, Aunt Ginny," Isaac said. He went to hug her and got caught on her trendy, dangly necklace.

"Isaac," she said, frowning at him as she inspected her jewelry for damage. "And Annabelle. Let me see." She reached for my hand and examined my ring so closely I almost expected her to whip out a jewelry loupe.

"What is it? A full carat?" she asked.

I don't know, I thought. I hadn't exactly said, "Yes, Isaac, I'll marry you, how many carats are in this thing?"

"Probably somewhere around there . . ." I said vaguely.

Isaac put an arm around the man in glasses. "This is my uncle Cal and aunt Virginia, we call her Ginny."

"It's good to meet you," Cal said, pushing his glasses up on his nose.

"Nice to meet you too," I said, flashing what I hoped was a charming smile.

Ginny narrowed her eyes. "You don't color your hair, do you?"

I fingered my brown locks. "No."

"Well. You might want to think about doing it for the wedding. It looks a little flat. I have this great guy." Ginny lowered her voice to a whisper. "He does pretty much all the celebrity Jessicas. His work is *beyond!*"

I scrunched up my lips. "Okay. I'll think about it."

Isaac and I sat back down and Doreen touched my arm.

"Look at you two," she said. "My little boy is getting married. I still remember when he and his brother made a fort in the backyard with a sign that said 'No girls allowed, especially our stinky sisters.' One night I let the girls go in and paint the whole thing pink." Doreen winked at me.

"Where are Ethan and the girls?" I asked.

"Well. Ethan actually went to Monterey with Rona for the weekend to visit her folks."

Okay, reader. Just to fill you in, yes, Doreen was talking about *that* Rona. The one who I nearly pelted with the pantyhose when I threw them at lying, cheating Alex. She's actually dating Isaac's brother Ethan now and is a realtor in L.A.

And, even crazier, she and I are almost what you would call friends.

"And the girls are in the middle of midterms," she continued. "They're at Pepperdine, you know."

I nodded.

"They're doing great there," Dennis said in a proud dad tone. "Not a grade below a B between them."

"They said they might stop by later if they can," Doreen added.

"Oh, so is the extra seat for one of them?" I asked, pointing to the seat a few down from mine.

"Oh no," Isaac said. "That's actually for—"

"Sorry I'm late!"

"Chloe's here," Ginny cooed as if the queen of England had just appeared. I looked up and saw the beautiful blonde approaching, dressed in a great black dress and a pair of designer heels that something told me she hadn't found hidden behind a bottle of bubble bath in Nordstrom Rack.

"Hey, kid," Cal said. "We were starting to think you weren't going to make it."

"Well," Chloe said a bit dramatically, "I'm lucky I did. I had a bit of a disaster at the hair salon."

"Oh please," Ginny said. "Your hair is always perfect."

Chloe brushed off the comment with an I-know-but-I-have-to-pretend-I-don't wave.

"This must be Annabelle," Chloe said to Isaac.

Isaac put an arm around me. "This is her."

Chloe bent down and air kissed me. "It's so nice to meet you. Isaac's told me so much about you."

"Nice to meet you too," I said.

I watched Chloe walk to her seat and talk to Isaac's family as if they were her own.

Wow, I thought, *she's stunning. And I am completely and utterly comfortable with her being here at my engagement party because, as Dr. Harmony says it should be, my focus is only on my love for Isaac and his love for me.*

What? You don't believe me? You don't believe that this is all I thought when I saw a woman come into my engagement party looking like she was a contestant on one of those "Bag a Man" reality shows? Well, then you just don't know me.

All right. I guess after more than 150 pages you do know me pretty well. So, I'll be honest. There may have been a little bit of "Who does she think she is and what does she think she's doing?" running through my mind.

But that's only because I accidentally left my Dr. Harmony book at home and hadn't been able to do the Harmony Exercises.

The waiter took our orders and set four loaves of bread on the table. I watched as Chloe refused the bread and Ginny praised her for her "discipline."

I couldn't stand it anymore, so I leaned over and whispered in Isaac's ear. "Why's Chloe here?"

"She's my agent," Isaac said, as if he had said, "She's my cousin." "Plus, she's a friend of the family."

"Oh," I said, biting into a slice of warm buttered bread.

"So, Annabelle," Chloe said, watching as I struggled to chew the slightly-too-big piece of bread. "Are you enjoying L.A.?" She elegantly cut a piece of lettuce and put it into her mouth.

I swallowed. "I am. It is a little . . . fast paced for me though."

Chloe nodded. "I know what you mean."

"Oh, Chloe," Doreen said. "You've always fit in here. Ever since you were a little girl in all those dancing classes and pageants. You were destined for fame."

"I'd have to agree with that," Dennis added.

Chloe smiled, soaking up the compliment.

My fists clenched. *Breathe out the envy. Breathe in the sisterly harmony.*

"I still remember you in Swan Lake," Doreen said. "You moved me to tears. And then when you were first runner-up for Miss California. I still say you should have won."

"I won a bubble gum bubble blowing contest when I was in sixth grade" I said, thinking it was pretty cool.

Doreen frowned at me. "That's . . . nice."

Apparently bubble blowing didn't come close to Miss California.

When our entrees arrived, the conversation turned from Chloe's dance performances and pageants to the fact that I was a food writer.

"What would you write about this place," Chloe asked as she cut her fish fillet the way all the etiquette books say to do.

I squared my shoulders, glad to have a moment to demonstrate that I was not a total loser.

But as everyone at the table looked at me, my mind suddenly went blank.

Completely and absolutely blank.

I stared at the plate of ravioli in front of me. "Um, well . . ." I cleared my throat and Isaac's ears perked up with interest. "Severino's is a great place for . . . people who like to eat Italian food. The bread is very warm and . . . white. And the pasta is . . . white too." I gulped when I saw the looks on everyone's faces. "For those who enjoy seafood," I added with a weird squeak in my voice, "Severino's . . . has it."

I shifted in my seat. "Usually I have a little time to think about what I write, plus I usually write more about the—"

"I didn't mean to put you on the spot," Chloe interrupted.

"I was just thinking that my fish is an absolute dream. All the elements dance on the tastebuds; the tender, flaky meat, the savory herb rub, the perfectly proportioned dash of lemon. And the red roasted potatoes on the side are both bold and beautiful."

"Maybe you should be a food writer, Chloe!" Margaret said.

Everyone at the table laughed and I gritted my teeth.

Stinking little show off!

I mean . . . Breathe out the envy, breathe in the sisterly harmony.

After dessert, Doreen clinked her spoon against her glass, eliciting everyone's attention. "It's so nice to have us all together like this. And I just want to say how happy we are to have Annabelle joining our family. We hope you feel right at home. Cheers!"

After the toast, wrapped gifts started to magically appear on the table.

"Score," Isaac whispered into my ear.

I smiled at him and couldn't help but notice that Chloe was watching us.

Isaac and I spent the next while opening our gifts: A geneology notebook from Margaret and Wayne. A crystal vase from Ginny and Cal. A Wholesale Wonders gift card from Doreen and Dennis. A set of Ginsu knives from Malette.

"Thanks so much!" Isaac and I said in unison.

"Don't forget mine," Chloe said. She passed a Macy's bag down the table.

Isaac nodded for me to open the gift. I don't know why, but my hand felt a little clammy as I looked into the bag. I clutched the gift inside and removed . . .

"Matching cashmere sweaters," Chloe said, with the clap of her hands.

Isaac took the two sweaters out of the bag. They weren't matching at all. His was a nice dark blue and mine was a pukey lime green color.

Reader, please refer back to page fourteen to see what I think of lime green.

"This is nice," Isaac said, holding his sweater up. "Thanks Chlo."

Chlo. Was he kidding me?

"Why don't you put them on?" Chloe suggested.

Isaac didn't hesitate before pulling the sweater over his head. He looked handsome in it, of course.

"Yours too, Annabelle," Chloe said.

I looked at the tag on the sweater and my mouth got dry: Size Xtra small. I am not an Xtra small kind of girl. I'm a medium kind of girl. I work out regularly because it makes me feel good, but I eat bread and dessert when I'm out to dinner.

"I'd better not. I don't want to get it dirty," I said.

Chloe looked at me. "You just said you were cold."

Why oh why had I said that after eating my gelato? "Okay," I relented.

I closed my eyes and willed the shirt to be a very big Xtra small. Or maybe even to grow.

But it wasn't. And it didn't.

I tugged and pulled as much as I could without looking like I was actually tugging and pulling as I put the sweater on. But once it was on, it didn't even cover my stomach. You know those football players who wear stomach-bearing shirts? Well, I looked just like one. Who had just been puked on.

Doreen and Ginny looked at me with mortified expressions on their faces.

"Oh no," Chloe said, her voice all innocent. "I thought for sure it would be okay. I tried it on and it fit me just fine. Oh well. You can return it. The receipt's in the bag."

"Thank you anyway," I said through clenched teeth.

"I think you look cute," Isaac said, kissing me.

I tore off the sweater and endured the rest of the "party" feeling absolutely miserable. This was not how engagement dinners were supposed to go.

After the festivities were through, Isaac and I said good-bye to everyone and he walked me out to the car, my leftovers in a little tin-foil swan.

"I think that was a really good dinner," Isaac said, sounding satisfied.

I stared at him, my face covered with bewilderment. *What dinner was he at?!*

Chapter 22

"My family does not hate you."

I sat down on the floor next to Isaac's childhood bed and pulled my pink-pajama-clad legs into my chest, resting my chin on my knees. "Yes they do. Your mom thinks I'm suffering from some sort of 'condition;' your dad thinks I have nothing more going for me than good feet; Ginny thinks I have bad hair; Malette thinks I'm a kiss up; and Margaret thinks I'm an inbreeder. Plus, the whole family thinks I'm a terrible food writer who can't fit into a sweater."

Isaac sat on the floor beside me. "I promise they don't think that. When you were changing into your pajamas Mom and Dad told me they're really looking forward to getting to know you better." He kissed my cheek as if what he just said was the sweetest thing in the world.

"They're looking forward to getting to know me better? As in, if they were going on what they know now, they *would* hate me? Is that what you're saying?"

Isaac furrowed his brow, as if he were figuring out what to say next.

"Oh my goodness, that is what you're saying! They think I'm awful. They think I wear bad lip liner and one shoe and can't even come up with a way to describe pasta. But they sure seem to think Chloe's perfect," I added under my breath.

"What about Chloe?"

"Never mind," I said, channeling every ounce of sisterly harmony I had in me. "I just . . . I wanted to make a good impression."

"Sweetie," Isaac said, putting his arm around me. "I love you. You could be dressed in a potato sack speaking Pig Latin and everyone would still be able to see how funny and kind and amazing you are."

My lips curved slightly.

"Come on." Isaac squeezed me gently. "I've missed you so much lately. Let's just enjoy our engagement night."

I released a breath. "Okay."

I leaned into Isaac's shoulder, and looked around the room. My eyes took in the basketball trophies, the Boy Scout awards, the photos of Firebirds. It felt strangely exhilarating to be near something so Isaac, like I was being invited into his private world.

I was looking at an L.A. Lakers sticker stuck to the desk in the room when my eyes focused on a storage container beneath the chair. "What's in there?" I asked, pointing to the box.

"Pictures and stuff."

"Can I see?"

"You're going to be my wife; you might as well know what you're getting into."

The word "wife" made my neck tingle, and I beamed at Isaac as I reached for the box and began to look through pieces of his past.

I saw his high school diploma and photos of him at graduation. I saw photos of his basketball teams, and my eyes immediately went to his face.

It was a weird kind of cool to see him in those old photos.

"What in the world?" Near the bottom of the box I found a photo of a bunch of guys with completely bald heads. And there, right in the middle, was my future husband with a completely bald, completely white, completely weird looking head. "You're bald!" I said, looking at Isaac with an open mouth.

"At least my head doesn't look like Ethan's."

Isaac pointed out his brother, who looked, I must say, a bit like an alien. Poor guy.

At the very bottom of the box, I found Isaac's high school yearbooks. I flipped through the one from his senior year, reading the signatures and messages.

"Hey Isaac!" I read aloud in my best teenage-girl voice. "Science was totally boring this year. Maybe I'll see you around this summer. Stay cool and don't change. Shelly."

"Pretty compelling stuff," Isaac joked.

"Dude," this time I read in my teenage-boy voice. "You still owe me five bucks. See you around. Harmon."

"What were you like in high school?" I asked, looking up from the book.

"You would have loved me," Isaac said with an adorable smile.

"I'm sure I would have. What did you do? I mean, were you in clubs or anything?"

"Not really. I did basketball. I didn't think much about being well-rounded. I was in the French club though. Only because they ate bread and cheese at all their meetings."

"I was in the French Club too! I still have the T-shirt and everything."

Isaac winked at me. "I knew we were a good match."

"Was Dirk your best friend?" I asked. "Like me and Carrie?"

"Not really. I hung out with a group of guys: Dirk Bag, Jesse, Robert, Trevor. We'd go to lunch every day in my Firebird and hit the taco stands. And we had a pickup game of basketball that never ended. I think in the end the score was 9,000 to something."

I smiled. I loved how being in Isaac's old room naturally led to my discovery of new things about him.

"Did you get good grades?"

"Yeah, I guess. I graduated tenth in my class."

"Pretty impressive. Any hobbies besides basketball?"

"I was into photography even back then. I took photos for the Santa Monica High School newspaper."

Now that was cute. "Seriously?"

"Yeah. In fact, I took a lot of these yearbook photos."

I flipped through the yearbook some more, and sure enough many of the photos were accompanied by a "Photo by: Isaac Matthews" tag.

I was about to close the yearbook, when a picture caught my eye. At first I almost missed it. But I would recognize that face anywhere. That one that was just perfect for a model. I stared at it, my heart speeding up a little. I silently read the blue glitter pen words next to the picture.

"Hi Cutie. I had such a blast with you at State this year. I'm so glad the cheerleaders got to go with you guys. Let's hang out this summer before you leave for San Jose State." Then a big heart and the name Chloe.

I'm not going to lie; my insides clenched. In my mind I knew the words were written years ago, but the truth was, everything that was going on back in Monterey had made me feel that sometimes the past has a way of not being all that past.

"You okay?" Isaac asked.

"Yes," I said a little too quickly.

"You sure? It looks like something's wrong."

I closed the book and looked at Isaac dead-on. "What's the story with Chloe?"

"What do you mean?"

"Did you date her?"

"No." Isaac paused for a minute. "Everyone thought I should, though."

Okay reader, can you do me a favor, can you just reach in here and smack Isaac right upside the head. "Everyone thought I should date her?" Who says that to his new fiancée who just had to sit through an entire dinner with his family going on an on about how great another woman was? Who?!

"Well that's great," I said, my words sharp. "I'm glad everyone thought she was so perfect for you."

Isaac flinched. "That's not what I said."

"Well how am I supposed to take it?"

"My family just liked her and thought that since she was into photography and a lot of other things I was into that we'd make a good match."

Okay. I think I deserve a cake or something for staying in the room after that. Something chocolate.

"Yeah, well some of them apparently still think she's a good match for you," I said before I could stop myself.

"What are you talking about?"

"Isaac. Didn't you see what happened at dinner? Your family couldn't stop talking about how great Chloe is. And your mom kept giving me looks that said, 'Well you're certainly not who I pictured for my son.'"

Isaac had the nerve to roll his eyes. "She did not."

"Yes she did. They all did. And it stinks, Isaac. It really stinks. I've been waiting for this moment for a very long time. And I finally get it, and everything is a mess. This isn't how things were supposed to go."

How *was* it supposed to go?

Well, we were supposed to get engaged and Isaac's family was supposed to run to me with open arms and put flowers around my neck while they told me I was the daughter-in-law they always dreamed of. And then I was supposed to tell Isaac about the wedding I'd won, and we were all supposed to stand in a circle holding hands. And there was supposed to be dancing, a light breeze, and maybe even a guitarist playing Kumbaya.

Isaac touched my hand. "I think most of the stuff you're talking about is just in your head. But I'm sorry today wasn't everything you wanted it to be. I tried. I really wanted it to be the perfect day."

I suddenly felt supremely awful. He really had tried.

"I know you did," I said, looking into Isaac's sweet face.

"I'm sorry I'm stressing about this so much. Today really was amazing. I loved breakfast. I loved the photos. I loved Disneyland. I love you." I touched his cheek with my hand and kissed him.

Isaac brushed my hair behind my ear and spent a minute just looking at me. "I love you too, Annabelle. You are so incredibly beautiful in every way. I can't believe I get to marry you."

I melted into a pile of mush. "I can't believe I get to marry *you*. And tomorrow, I have a surprise for you that I think might make up for my little freak out tonight."

I was going to tell him about the Dream Wedding, fill him in on the things that were already in motion, and get that contract signed.

"That's interesting," Isaac said. "I think my mom has some sort of surprise planned for tomorrow too. She won't tell me what it is, but she told me it was something very cool."

Doreen had something "very cool" planned huh? Well, that sounded good to me.

Of course, I was soon to learn that Doreen and I have very different definitions of "very cool."

Chapter 23

"Annabelle . . ." I heard a woman's voice whisper.

"I'm not fat, you just bought me a tiny sweater," I muttered sleepily.

"I'm sorry?"

My sleepy mind began to wake, and I soon realized Chloe wasn't talking to me, but Doreen.

I sat up and saw that I was hugging the yellow-raincoat-clad bunny that had been on the bed as a decoration. I shoved it aside. "Sorry," I said to Doreen. "I was dreaming."

"That's all right. I was just coming in to see if you were ready?"

"Ready for?"

Doreen smiled. "We're having brunch at Ginny's. Didn't Isaac tell you?"

"No . . ." But suddenly a memory of Bigfoot coming into my room and talking to me came to mind.

"We're leaving in an hour," Doreen said.

"Okay. I'll be ready."

I hopped out of bed and spent five minutes in the bathroom brushing my teeth, applying Foxy Glossy lip gloss, and perfecting an I-just-rolled-out-of-bed-looking-like-this ponytail before going to find Isaac to say good morning.

His bedroom door was half open, and I knocked softly.

"Come in," Isaac said in that gorgeous deep voice of his.

I went inside and he was sitting on the floor building something with Legos. It was quite possibly the cutest thing I have ever seen.

"Good morning my beautiful wife-to-be." Isaac stood up from the floor and kissed me.

See, the teeth-brushing and lip-glossing was a good idea.

"Did you come in my room this morning and try to wake me?" I asked.

Isaac nodded. "Yeah. You said something like, 'Go away, I know you don't exist.' I didn't know what you were talking about."

I laughed as I looked at Isaac's track pants and T-shirt. "Is that what you're wearing to brunch?"

"I'm not going to brunch."

"What?"

"Mom says it's girls only."

I gulped. "But . . ."

"Dad and I are going to the UCLA basketball game with some of his buddies from work."

"But . . ." I repeated.

You can't leave me alone with those women!

"You'll have fun," Isaac said, hugging me.

"Why don't I go to the basketball game with you," I suggested, eyes bright and hopeful.

Isaac looked confused. "You'd really rather go to a basketball game than to a classy, girls-only brunch? I thought there was no way you'd want to go. But if you really want to, I can always tell my mom and my aunts and grandma . . ."

Oh brother. He might as well have said, "If you really want to stab my poor mother in her kind thoughtful heart, and possibly send my sweet little grandmother to the hospital with disappointment and shock, I'll see what I can do."

"I guess it will be fun," I relented. Because, let's face it, I *would* much rather eat yummy fruit and muffins than wave around a foam finger and pretend I actually cared that #12 had the best rebound record in the league.

"It will be," Isaac said.

"But I have dibs on tonight," I said. "I have something really important to talk to you about. Something amazing."

"A surprise?"

"Maybe."

Isaac playfully tickled my side, and I left the room to get ready.

I showered—hopefully no one heard the loud yelp I let out when I squished my toes with the Wholesale Wonders gigantic-sized shampoo I dropped on them—and dressed in a pair of nice tweed trousers and a designer silk-chiffon top that Katrina gave to me because it reminded her of her ex-boyfriend. I added a pair of hoop earrings and a great pair of heels. Then I styled my hair into a pretty mini-bouffant style and applied my makeup.

I surveyed myself in the mirror. I would definitely want me as a daughter-in-law.

"Have a good time," Isaac said as he followed Doreen and me into the garage when it was time to leave.

"You too. Go Brewers!" I added, raising a fist in the air.

"It's Bruins," Isaac said in that reverent tone guys use when talking about "their team."

I shrugged. "I was close."

Isaac opened the car door for me, and I reluctantly got inside, resisting the urge to grab onto him and not let go. But I could do this. I was a big girl.

Isaac smiled. "See you soon, sweetie."

"So tell me, Annabelle," Doreen said as we drove to Ginny's house. "What makes you think you're good enough for my son?"

No, she didn't really say that. But I'm telling you, it's what she was thinking as she asked me about my job, my family, and my aspirations for the future. I tried my best to give intelligent answers and even managed to use the word "obsequious" in a sentence.

And I'm even 99 percent sure I used it right.

We arrived at Ginny's house—a modest dark brown two-story—in Brentwood Flats after a short drive. I got out of the Pontiac and followed Doreen to the front door where she knocked for only a second before entering. "We're here!"

I walked in behind her and immediately smelled a mixture of warm cinnamon rolls and new furniture.

"Wow," I said aloud as we passed through the marble-tiled entryway.

The house was nothing like I expected. From the looks of the outside, I thought the interior would be simple, but it was far from it. With marble floors, luxurious furnishings, thick draperies, and gold accents, the look was somewhere between posh Fifth Avenue townhouse and Las Vegas casino.

I suddenly remembered something Isaac had told me. Apparently Ginny's house had been appraised for over a million dollars before the real estate bubble burst. And after that, Ginny had the whole place revamped to fit her "millionaire" lifestyle.

Soon Doreen, Ginny, Margaret, Malette, and I were all sitting at a beautifully set table with a rose centerpiece, helping ourselves to the delicious-looking spread of cinnamon rolls, fresh fruit, fresh-squeezed juices, buttermilk biscuits and assorted jams, perfectly cooked eggs, and mini sausages.

"Well," Ginny said when we were all comfortably nibbling. "Welcome to my home for this little get-together. I hope you all have a lovely time. That jam came from this place where Gwyneth buys all her spreads and jams. It's *beyond*. Love it."

I caught a glimpse of Malette rolling her eyes.

"And since I just can't wait anymore . . ." Ginny reached beneath the table and retrieved something from a Coach handbag. "I think it's time for Annabelle's surprise."

I felt my insides flutter. A surprise?! For me?!

I watched excitedly as Ginny set a white book on the table. I squinted and made out the words on the front of the book, which were written in pink and silver writing: *Annabelle and Isaac: To Have and to Hold.*

What?

Ginny smiled and fiddled with the pearl necklace she was wearing. "I've recently picked up a new hobby: event planning. Just last week, I successfully planned my next door neighbor's 'Just Ten More Years Until I Can Start Thinking About Semi-Retirement' party, so it's only natural that a wedding would be my next step!"

My stomach dropped. *What?*

"It works out perfectly," Doreen said. "This way we can all be involved."

I cleared my throat. "I, um, really appreciate the offer but . . ."

How was I going to finish that sentence? "I really appreciate the offer, but I actually won an all expenses paid wedding at a bridal fair and in fact have already started planning that wedding, and I don't need any help, but thanks?"

No way. I didn't want to give them anything more to add to their list of "Reasons why Annabelle is a crazy nut who we should not only persuade Isaac not to marry but to dump completely."

I cleared my throat. "I really appreciate that, but I think I have things covered. Do these have spinach?" I held up a mini-quiche.

Ginny laughed. "No bride has things covered! And that's why we all stayed up late last night looking over the bridal checklist on page two of your planner and started to come up with some plans!"

I opened my mouth to respond, to say something, but nothing came out. Except for a tiny piece of mini-quiche—but I don't think they saw.

"The first thing we found is a really exciting honeymoon

idea!" Ginny smiled as she reached back into her bag and handed me a brochure with a photo of frozen tundra on the front. "A cruise to Antarctica! All the celebs are going high adventure these days. It's *the* thing to do. Beach honeymoons are so out. You do have to sign a waiver that says if you die while on the cruise you won't sue. But honestly what are the chances of that?"

She couldn't be serious.

"And I was thinking," Doreen said, eager to interject her big idea, "Wholesale Wonders has these blenders that are always on demonstration. They can blend anything! Who says you have to have food at a wedding reception? Why not have a buffet of shakes and smoothies?!"

Okay. This was . . . not good.

"Look," I said, clearing my throat. "I really appreciate your help. But—"

Doreen looked at me like I was standing next to a pile of her hopes and dreams with a match and some gasoline. "Yes?"

"Never mind," I said with a sigh.

"I guess it's my turn then," Margaret said.

"I thought you didn't have anything," Ginny said, confused.

Margaret smiled as she got up from her chair and returned with a white garment bag.

"I was doing some genealogical research online when I came across a website that rents special occasion and wedding dresses that are in the style of pioneer times."

My mouth turned dry. *Oh no. Tell me she didn't.*

Margaret unzipped the garment bag to reveal a dress that bore a striking resemblance to the one I wore the year I was a pioneer girl for Halloween.

I mean, I'm as big a fan of the pioneers as the next girl, but that doesn't mean I wanted to look like I was about to go play a game of "kick the cow pie" on my wedding day.

"What do you think?" Margaret asked, looking at me.

I blinked. "It's . . ."

Ginny tapped the side of her mouth with a well-manicured finger. "You know . . . the antique look actually is very in this season. You should try it on Annabelle."

But I didn't ask for Margaret to rent a dress for me. I already had a dress. I . . . "What's the matter?" Doreen asked, surveying my face. "Are you afraid it won't fit? Like Chloe's sweater."

Ten seconds later, I was in Ginny's bedroom, trying on the pioneer dress while the three women sat in the living room, discussing whether or not my "oddly shaped head" could pull off an updo.

After a minute, I emerged from the room looking like I had somehow wandered off the set of *Little House on the Prairie*.

"You look adorable!" Margaret said, beaming.

"She looks like she hates it," Malette said with a deep frown.

"You don't like it?" The way Margaret asked the question, I felt like if I said no, it would be akin to saying I hated little puppies.

"Well. I'm just not sure it's me."

Malette rolled her eyes. "Oh don't be such a politician. Just say you don't like it."

"I . . . well . . . I . . ."

"Oh, for crying out loud," Malette said. "Just spit it out. I'm having flashbacks to Ginny's fifth grade play."

"Hey," Ginny protested. "I was a good Martha Washington!"

"Thanks for the thought," I said to Margaret as I looked down at the dress. "I really appreciate it. I—"

"Save it for the campaign trail." Malette frowned and pushed me back into the bedroom, and I noticed she was pretty strong for such a small woman.

I had the dress unzipped and was about to remove it when something on Ginny's bed caught my attention: The midnight blue satin sheets.

"No. Timmy Chester played George," I heard Ginny say from the living room. Apparently the women were now on the subject of the fifth grade play. Better that than my weird head. I stared at the sheets, an idea brewing in my head.

No. I couldn't.

I shouldn't.

You see, the thing was, Isaac and I planned to register for gifts when we got back to Monterey—I'll admit it, I couldn't wait to get my hands on that little scanner gun. And, well, I'd always kind of wanted to see what satin sheets were like, but never had the chance. All I really knew about them was that Cliff and Clair Huxtable seemed to like them on *The Cosby Show*.

I felt myself inch toward the bed, my hand outstretched.

A quick little touch wouldn't hurt.

I ran my hand across the satin sheet peeking out from beneath the duvet and felt it's coolness against my skin. Nice. Very nice.

Of course . . . feeling the sheet with my hand hadn't really given me the full effect. They might feel entirely different against other parts of my body.

I heard the sound of the women laughing in the living room and, before I could stop myself, hopped on the bed, throwing the sheet and covers over myself. I hiked up the pioneer dress to bare my legs.

Ahh.

Yes. We were definitely registering for satin.

"Annabelle, are you decent?" Ginny's voice at the door made me jump about a mile. "I need to grab something."

"Just a second!" I frantically tried to get out of the bed, but somehow the fabric of the dress had gotten twisted up in the bedding and I was trapped like a swaddled baby.

"Annabelle," Ginny repeated.

"Yeah . . . I'm almost . . ." I twisted, turned, wriggled, and tried to free myself.

I was just about there when Ginny came in the door.

And there I was, just sitting in her bed in an unzipped, hiked-up pioneer dress.

Ginny's mouth was wide open. "What in the world?!"

If she weren't in on the whole "Does Annabelle have some sort of 'condition'?" thing with Doreen already—she would be now.

"Ginny . . . um . . . hi," I stammered. "Nice sheets."

Oh boy. I knew I should have gone to the basketball game.

Chapter 24

"So she comes in and you're sitting on her bed. *Under* the covers." Isaac was laughing so hard I wasn't sure he should be driving.

I made my best mad face and crossed my arms. "It's not that funny."

Isaac reached over and touched my cheek. "I'm sorry. It's just such a cute mental image."

I shook my head, trying to wipe the whole fiasco from my memory. "How was the game?"

"It was fun. We won. But I missed you like crazy."

I smiled, the warmth of Isaac's words partially erasing the mortification of The Satin Sheets Incident.

"So where are we taking those flowers." I looked into the backseat, my eyes focusing on the floral arrangements Ginny had purchased for the brunch.

"It's a place called Caring Blooms. My mom was going to drop them off, but I thought you might like to. It seems right up your alley."

Caring Blooms. Why did that sound so familiar?

About twenty minutes later, Isaac pulled into the parking lot of a flower shop. We grabbed the floral arrangements from the backseat and went inside.

The woman behind the counter, who was dressed in overalls and had a red bandana over her blonde hair, put her hand on one hip. "If it isn't Isaac Matthews."

"Hey Linda."

The woman I now knew as Linda regarded me. "And who is this lovely girl?"

"My fiancée," Isaac said, a smile in his voice.

Linda's eyebrows shot up. "Well what do you know," she said.

Isaac and I set the flowers on the counter. "Mom wanted me to bring these over," Isaac explained.

"Perfect timing," Linda said. "I just got a call from Nina at the Crestview Care Center. They had a couple residents who didn't get a thing for Valentine's Day. I told them we'd take care of it. These will go right over there."

"Caring Blooms!" I shouted.

Isaac and Linda looked at me, confused—and a bit startled.

"Sorry," I said. "It's just . . . I've been working on this article, and I've been looking for wedding vendors who give to the community in interesting ways. I'm almost positive I remember reading about you."

"Oh, you're a journalist," Linda said the words like they were an answer, not a question.

"Yes. This is so crazy. I was so inspired by what I read about you online, but I couldn't really find much."

"We're a pretty small operation," Linda said. "But we're growing."

"Do you mind . . . ?" I took a quick glance at Isaac before continuing. "Do you think I could ask you a couple questions about what you do and what gave you the idea? I mean, if you have time. If not, I can give you a call . . ."

Linda was already on the other side of the counter, taking a seat at a whicker table in the shop's quaint waiting area. "I'm always up for a chat," she said.

"Great." I smiled excitedly at Isaac as the two of us joined

Linda. "Thank you so much."

Once seated I reached into my handbag and retrieved the professional-looking writing notebook I carry with me at all times, just in case a writing opportunity like this ever arises.

Actually, if I'm being 100 percent honest, it was actually a stack of Delta Airlines drink napkins from the flight to L.A.

I really should start carrying around a professional-looking writing notebook at all times in case a writing opportunity like this arises.

"So," I began. "Tell me a little bit about how Caring Blooms came to be."

"I've always been a gardener," Linda explained. "Always loved how working in my garden can change a bad day into a good one. Then five years ago, around the middle of May, a young mother in my neighborhood lost her husband in a terrible car accident.

"I cried for her and the five little ones she now had to care for alone, but honestly I hadn't the first clue what to do to help. I didn't have any money or anything to give, so to be completely honest, I kind of hoped someone else was doing something. Then one afternoon I was in my garden and something just kind of hit me: This is what I could do.

"So the next day I went over to the house and left a bouquet, a card, and a cherry pie that wasn't really any good, on the doorstep. The weeks passed and I didn't hear anything about it. Which was fine; I didn't need to.

"But then about four months later the two oldest kids in the family knocked on my door. 'Our Mommy's Birthday is tomorrow,' they said. 'We want to buy her a present. But we don't have any money, and we don't think she does either because last night we heard her crying in her room after Jeffrey told her that his t-ball stuff would cost a hundred dollars. But she loved those flowers you gave us when our Daddy went to heaven. So we were wondering if maybe you could make us some flowers to give her. We could pay for it by doing chores for you."

I felt tears welling up in my eyes.

"I know!" Linda said, grabbing hold of my wrist like she had known me for ages. "That's exactly what I did! How could I resist a request like that?! So what did I do? I made the biggest, best arrangement I had ever made and those little angels were so excited to give it to their mother. And that's when the power of it all hit me. And I decided to 'make flowers' for the people who need them, whether or not they can pay for them. With money or with chores," Linda added with a laugh.

I couldn't help staring at Linda in admiration. "Wow. How do you finance that?"

"We sell flowers to the people who can afford them, and then we recycle them. We do the flowers for weddings, Hollywood parties—all sorts of events. And the people we sell the arrangements to usually don't need them for more than a few hours. So our little army of delivery people, who are basically volunteers because what we can afford to pay them is barely enough to cover gas, deliver the flowers to hospitals, care centers, homes—wherever they're needed."

I looked up from my napkins, which were quickly running out of blank space. "And it works?"

Linda winked at me. "It more than works."

❦

Pink Note #133
Name: Caring Blooms

Why They're Noteworthy: I have moments sometimes where I stop myself from helping someone who maybe needs it because I feel like I have nothing to offer. Caring Blooms is in existence because of a woman who decided not to do that. I think I have a lot to learn from her.

"Writing down some more stuff for your article?" Isaac asked, looking over at me from the driver's seat as we made our way to his parents' house.

I held up my notebook. "Pink Note."

"You carry that notebook with you everywhere, yet you had to take notes for work on airplane napkins. I guess we know where your priorities are." Isaac winked at me. "So . . . now that we're done with the delivery, is it time for the surprise I've been told about?"

I pressed my lips together as if to say, "Not yet."

But, in just a little while, I was going to tell Isaac all about the Dream Wedding.

I could not wait to see his reaction!

Chapter 25

"You did what?"

"I won a wedding!" I held out my arms, ready for Isaac to hug me and tell me how happy he was, but he just frowned.

Wait a minute. Why was he frowning? Where was the hug, the praise, the "Oh, Annabelle, you are the cleverest most wonderful fiancée in the world and since you've saved us gobs of money on our wedding you can spend as much as you want on shoes for the rest of our marriage!"?

I raised my eyebrows and gestured with my hands. "Isaac, did you hear what I just said? I won a wedding! Everything on our wedding day, paid for by someone else!"

Isaac shifted in his seat on his parents' living room couch. "I heard you. I'm just . . . How in the world did you manage to win a wedding between last night and today?"

I bit my lip. "Well . . ."

Isaac looked at me the same way Mom did when I was four and told her my goldfish Fishy was the one who ate the last two cookies in the jar. "What did you do?"

"It's nothing bad," I said, upset at his insinuating tone. "I entered a drawing I thought was for a cake and ended up winning a wedding!"

"When did this happen?"

"Justafewdaysago," I mumbled, my hand over my mouth.

Isaac furrowed his brow. "Are you speaking Russian?"

"No," I said. "I just . . . don't really feel that when I won the wedding matters. What matters is that now we can start planning with no worries. So, for colors I'm thinking chocolate brown and—"

"But we just got engaged yesterday," Isaac said. "You couldn't have won the prize before yesterday." He looked at me for confirmation.

"What is yesterday, really?" I asked, channeling the overly pensive tone of my college philosophy professor.

"Annabelle . . ." Isaac tilted his head slightly to the right and employed this tactic he loves to use on me where he just stares at me until I crack.

"Fine!" I blabbed after one measly minute—no where close to my personal best. "I won it on Tuesday! This lady called me at work and said my name was randomly selected and that I won a wedding."

"And you didn't say, 'This is a great surprise, but I'm not currently engaged.'"

"I was going to . . . But then Katrina got on the phone and . . . The point is: I didn't have to officially accept the prize or sign the paperwork right away; so I knew I had a little wiggle room."

Isaac looked at me like I just told him I have evaded my taxes for twenty years, and I have all of my money in Swiss accounts. "So you were just planning on 'unofficially' holding onto the prize until we got engaged?"

I didn't answer. It sounded bad when he put it like that. But what he didn't know was that I knew our engagement was right around the corner at the time.

Isaac's head was just beginning to tilt when I shouted, "I knew! Okay?! I knew you were going to propose!"

Isaac's mouth dropped open. "What?"

I gulped and nodded my head. "I knew."

"How in the world could you have?"

"Well. You'd been dropping all kinds of hints. And it was almost like I could feel it or something. Plus . . . someone might have let it slip."

"Someone who?" Isaac asked, his tone sounding very NYPD.

"Carrie," I said quickly. "But she didn't mean to. You told her you were going to propose on our anniversary. So when she got back from her honeymoon she thought we were engaged."

"So you've known since Carrie got back from her honeymoon?"

"Yes."

Isaac looked like a boy who's just been told his favorite baseball player uses steroids.

"But it was good," I said. "Because then I won the drawing, and it all worked out for the best." I put my two thumbs up in the air.

"I can't believe you knew," Isaac said, slumping into the back of the couch. "All this time. Why didn't you say anything?"

I shrugged one shoulder. "I knew you wanted it to be a surprise."

"But it wasn't a surprise!"

"Everything about the proposal was," I said. "Just not the fact that it was coming. Which, like I said, was obviously for the best because we won a free Dream Wedding!"

Isaac shook his head and smiled slightly. "You really won a free wedding?"

"Yes!" I shouted. "Can you believe it?"

Isaac's lips broke into a wide grin. "Only you would enter a drawing and accidentally win a free wedding. This is really cool, sweetie." He wrapped his arms around me and kissed the top of my head. "I can't believe it. A free wedding!"

"I know!" I said. "Fifty thousand dollars all ours!"

Isaac's face whipped toward me so quickly I was surprised it wasn't accompanied by a snapping sound. "Did you just say fifty thousand dollars?"

I nodded. Now this was more like it. He was practically

speechless. Soon would come the tears of joy at how good I did and an announcement to his family that no matter what any of them think I am a wonderful woman and am so much prettier, cooler, and smarter than Chloe.

I mean . . . not that I need to be prettier, cooler, and smarter than Chloe. *I . . . respect my earth sisters' qualities and the positive energy such qualities channel into the universe, and thus I don't feel the need to have the "upper hand," but to "join hands" with my sisters . . .*

"Fifty thousand dollars," Isaac repeated. "That's a lot of money. Who did you win this wedding from, the Gates Family?"

I laughed. "No. The prize is sponsored by John Wilfred, the jewelry company."

"So what is it, some kind of promotional thing?"

"What do you mean?"

"I mean, are we going to have to do endorsements for the store? I bought your engagement ring there, so I guess we're off to a good start. But will they want more? Like . . . are we going to have to sign releases for all our wedding photos and do weird shots where we're looking down at our wedding rings smiling."

The mental image of Isaac looking down at his hand smiling was a pretty good one. "I don't know. I'm sure all that's in the contract. It's in my desk at work. I seem to remember reading something about using 'affiliated wedding vendors,' but it didn't seem like a big deal. And honestly, I'd be willing to dress up like a diamond ring and stand in front of the store singing songs for fifty grand."

"That would be cute to see," Isaac said. "But that doesn't sound like John Wilfred's style. We'll look over the contract when we get home. At least we're not locked in yet and can still get out of the deal."

Whoa. Whoa. Whoa. Did he just say "Get out of the deal?"

"Why in this crazy world would we want to get out of it?"

Isaac shrugged. "I'm just saying, if there's something in the contract we're completely opposed to, we still have options."

Options? I don't want options. I want my couture silk gown and crab cakes and tuna tartare from Love at First Bite. I closed my eyes and opened them again. "I really want this, Isaac. I can have the wedding of my dreams and not worry about putting us and our families in the poorhouse. It's perfect."

Isaac traced my engagement ring with his finger. "I promise you'll have the wedding of your dreams whether we have fifty thousand or five hundred dollars. My mom said she and my aunts and grandma are ready to help in any way they can. We'll make it happen."

"I'm sure the contract is just fine," I said quickly. "I'm sure everything with the Dream Wedding will be just fine."

And the funny thing is: I actually believed it.

Chapter 26

Oh no. Oh no. Oh no.

I was running in my beloved pair of Christian L's—a steal I found on Craigslist just five seconds after the ad had been posted—down the hill to Barrington's Custom Formalwear in Carmel.

Why was I abusing my favorite shoes? Well, because on the drive to Carmel, I'd realized something horrible: Jenna thought Alex was my fiancé. And she was meeting me and *Isaac* at Barrington's for some groom/groomsmen-attire shopping.

Hence the running.

"Sorry," I said as I bumped into two tourists carrying shopping bags from various Carmel boutiques.

"Hey!" one of them shouted. "You could have broken my bottle of Monterey Bay sand! I paid twenty-five dollars for that!"

"Sorry!" I said again.

Twenty-five bucks for a bottle of sand? I could have gotten a bottle and filled it with sand for about twenty-five *cents*. Well, if the writing career didn't pan out . . .

I reached the shop's famous green awning and rushed past the doorman. It was only a second before I spotted Jenna standing in the tie section, talking to a man in a pinstripe suit. Isaac was nowhere in sight, thank goodness, so I jogged up to Jenna and pulled her into the bathroom.

Out of breath, I explained the whole crazy Alex-posing-as-my . . . well, you know the situation.

"So, Mr. Abercrombie isn't your fiancé?" she asked, brow wrinkled.

I sighed. "His name is Alex and he and I used to . . . Anyway, he's just been acting crazy lately, and he thought it would be hilarious to pose as my . . . Well, the point is, I'm sorry you were misled. I just never really had a chance to—"

Jenna waved a hand dismissingly. "I once planned a wedding where the groom's sister was so against him marrying this girl that she started making telephone calls and sending messages to her brother, pretending to be his ex-girlfriend saying she wanted him back. In the end the groom actually changed his mind and wanted to get back together with the ex and, well, you can imagine the disaster. So . . . A guy pretending to be your fiancé because he still has feelings for you. That's nothing."

"Wait a minute," I said. "Has feelings for me? No. Alex doesn't have feelings for me. He just thought it would be funny to mess with me. That's just how he is."

"Whatever you say," Jenna said with one eyebrow raised.

I've always wished I could do that. It looks so cool.

"No. Really. He's just like that. He—"

"All right," Jenna said, looking at her watch. "Enough of this drama. We need to get back to our appointment. I'm glad I decided to come because Antoine's working, and he has the taste of a Vegas costumer. Let's go."

When we returned to the shop floor, Isaac was there, looking delicious in jeans and a T-shirt.

"Hey there," I said, planting a kiss on his slightly stubly cheek. "Ready to do this?"

He nodded. "Yes. Let's find something for me to wear the day I solidify my position as the luckiest guy in the world."

Wow. How was it that words could do such funny things to my spine?

For the next forty-five minutes I bounced around the store with Jenna, Antoine, and Isaac, excitedly finding suits—designer suits—I thought would look great on Isaac.

But every time he emerged from the dressing room he was frowning. The coats were too shiny. The pants were too skinny. The details were too fancy.

"Come on, Isaac," I said as he was unbuttoning a grey suit that, I'll admit, did have a bit of a prom-dress-like sheen. "These are designer suits! They're going to be a little bit fashion forward. But that's what's so cool about them. It's something you would have never been able to wear before."

Isaac, who looked completely exhausted, forced a smile as he removed a Roberto Cavalli suit from the hook outside the dressing room. "I'll try one more," he said.

"Yay!" I flashed my I-can't-believe-I'm-shopping-for-a-wedding-suit-with-you grin at him for the hundredth time. "I bet this is the one!"

I sat with my fingers crossed in the chair outside the dressing room. But when Isaac finally emerged, he looked absolutely miserable.

And, just between you and me, I was kind of with him on this one. The suit was pretty avant-garde, and, to be completely honest, looked a little bit like something a guy would wear on a rink of ice while doing a bunch of triple lutzes to a song by Tchaikovsky.

If you get my drift.

"Are you kidding me," Isaac asked, lifting his hands—which were covered by the slightly ruffled dress shirt under the suit coat.

"It's not that bad," I said. "It's Roberto Cavalli. Jenna said a lot of grooms ask for him. Orlando wears him all the time."

Isaac looked at me like I was speaking Cantonese. "This shirt has flowers on it," he said as if the fact spoke for itself.

I inspected the shirt. "Maybe they're not flowers.

Maybe they're little . . . windmills. Windmills are cool. Very Holland-y."

Isaac frowned. "They're little flowers. And I'm pretty sure there's pink in them." He moved his face really close to the sleeve to check for pink.

"So what," I said. "A lot of guys are wearing pink these days. They say 'real men wear pink.' "

"Yeah. Real girly men." Isaac looked at the suit in the mirror and tugged at the lapels.

"Well you're going to have to pick something," I said. unbuttoning the suit coat to see if it made any difference. It didn't.

"I know," Isaac said. "But I really don't think I'm going to find anything here. How about we try a department store?"

Jenna, who was sitting nearby, gasped slightly at Isaac's words.

"This is the nicest store on the Dream Wedding list," I said. "In fact, it's the best men's formalwear shop in the Monterey Bay area—maybe all of Northern California. It's as good as it gets around here in terms of designers."

"I don't care about that," Isaac said. "I just want a nice suit for me and something my groomsmen won't feel like idiots wearing."

"Nice," I said, not able to hide my disappointment. "So we're catering to Dirk Bag then. Great."

"Who are you?" Isaac asked, staring at me. "This isn't you—obsessed with expensive clothes and looking down on my friends. Where did Annabelle go?"

I felt myself physically move back, like I had just been kicked in the shins. It hurt that Isaac would say that to me. He didn't know what it was to be a girl who dreams of her perfect wedding all her life. He didn't know what it meant to finally have those dreams coming true.

"Fine," I said, slinging my handbag over my shoulder. "If you think I'm a *different* Annabelle, and you don't want my help, I guess there's no reason to continue this wonderful day of wedding planning!"

"I guess not!" Isaac said, his obvious frustration at the day revealing itself.

"Fine!" I said again, because when you're acting twelve, it's kind of your favorite word.

I turned on my heels to leave, but stopped short when I remembered something. Tonight my family was throwing Isaac and me a little engagement party. Mom had spent all weekend cooking and baking and planning; I couldn't let her down. So I turned back around and looked at Isaac.

"I almost forgot. Tonight is that party my family planned. Don't forget."

"Well I guess I'll see you at your parents' house then," Isaac said, removing the Roberto Cavalli jacket like it had done something wrong. "Can't wait."

"You and me both."

Chapter 27

When I arrived at my parents' house, Isaac was already there, sitting in his Firebird. I could hear the car stereo playing a loud rock song from a yard away.

I knocked on the car window. "We should probably get in there," I said, my voice agitated as I nodded toward the house.

"Yep." Isaac opened his door, and we walked side by side to the house. I could feel the tension in the air between us.

"Hello!" I called as we stepped inside.

A few seconds later, Camden raced through the entryway, a pudding cup in his hand, and pudding all over his face.

"Camden!" I heard Cammie holler. "You're supposed to stay at the table with that! Mom, I told you he shouldn't have that pudding."

I followed the sound of my sister's voice and found her, Mom, and Carrie in the kitchen.

"You're here!" Mom gave me a huge hug and I breathed in the scent of brown sugar mixed with freesia perfume. "My daughter and her future husband!" Mom embraced Isaac like she would a son.

Isaac and I may have just had a bit of a spat, but seeing him and Mom like that made me all warm and fuzzy inside.

"Finally I get to see you!" Carrie threw her arms around me. "Congratulations!"

I smiled at her, my dearest friend in the whole world. "Thanks, Carrie."

"I want to see the ring!" My sister grabbed my hand. "It's really pretty, Annabelle. Just your taste. You didn't do too bad a job," she added with a nod in Isaac's direction.

"I'm glad," Isaac said with a polite smile.

I knew that smile. It was the one he used when he was a little miffed inside but didn't want to show it.

The kitchen grew very chaotic as Cammie asked me when we wanted to start our premarital counseling, Carrie told me I should really think about using eco-friendly linens at the reception, and Camden finger-painted the refrigerator with pudding before being told it was time for bed.

Amid the commotion, Dad, Cameron, and Miles came inside through the sliding glass door, the smell of Dad's famous barbequed tri-tip wafting in with them.

Dad, tongs still in hand, came up and gave me a big hug. "Bellie!" he said, beaming.

Bellie is Dad's nickname for me. It comes from my name, Annabelle, and in no way refers to my abdominal area. I only explain this to you because once in college I brought home a boyfriend—a very short-lived boyfriend—and Dad called me Bellie in front of him. Then when we were alone, the guy looked at me and said, "Why does your dad call you that? Your stomach's not *that* big."

Like I said, he was a short-lived boyfriend.

"And Isaac," Dad patted him on the back, "I see you finally got some sense knocked into you."

Usually Isaac would have responded to that by saying, "Yes I did," and putting his arm around me or something. But tonight he just nodded and smiled that same polite smile.

I'm not going to lie; I was starting to really dislike that smile.

Dinner was a medley of tri-tip, an organic cucumber salad

Carrie made, and Mom's amazing twice-baked potatoes. The table had been decorated with little scrapbook-style collages of photos of me and Isaac and confetti words that said "love," "joy," and "smile."

But Isaac and I were pretty much silent during the lively "remember when we got engaged" dinner discussion, and I stared enviously at the other couples at the table, who seemed to be enjoying this, our second engagement celebration, much more than I was.

After dinner, everyone migrated to the living room where Cammie announced: "All right, everyone, it's time for the entertainment portion of the evening!"

I looked at Carrie to see if she knew what was going on, but she just shrugged.

Hmm . . . Last time we had an "entertainment portion of the evening," Dad showed us some "magic tricks" he'd learned on the internet. Cammie and I ended up in the ER, handcuffed together. The doctor had to free us with some heavy-duty metal cutters, and all the while Dad was insisting he could free us if we'd just give him a minute.

"Everyone needs to sit in couples," my sister instructed.

We all obliged, and Cammie grinned, looking excited. "In honor of Annabelle and Isaac's engagement," she said, "we are going to play . . . The Nearlywed Game!"

She pushed play on a CD player behind her, and the theme song from *I Dream of Genie* boomed from the speakers.

Chuckles sounded through the room.

"Now here's how we play." Cammie doled out whiteboards and markers, two per couple. "I'll ask a question about one person on the team and both team members should write their answers on their boards. If you both have the same answer you get a point. And whoever gets the most points wins a prize Mom made especially for this game!"

"Homemade chocolate truffles with assorted fillings," Mom said.

The couples in the room mmm'd excitedly, and I snuck a

glance at Isaac, wondering what he was thinking.

"Look," I whispered to him. "My family wanted to make this night special for us. Can we just put everything aside for their sake?"

"Sure," Isaac said in a tone I couldn't quite decipher.

"The first question is for me and Cam." Cammie turned to her husband of five years. "What was I almost named?"

Cameron twisted his mouth up in thought. "Um . . ."

I felt my eyebrows shoot upward. I so knew this one!

"It's something from The Bible," Cameron stalled.

That was true. Mom apparently gets a little loopy under the influence of the labor-pain-killing drugs and gets it into her head that we should have biblical names and not the ones she and Dad have spent months picking out.

Cameron was squirming in his seat, watching Cammie give him an intense if-you-don't-know-this-about-me-you're-dead-meat look. Finally Cameron scribbled on his white board and flipped it around.

"Thessalonia!" he shouted.

"Very good!" Cammie flipped over her board, which said the same thing in much better handwriting. She kissed her husband on the cheek.

"Oh, boy," Dad said with a shake of his head. "I do remember that."

"It's a pretty name!" Mom insisted.

Cammie smiled triumphantly. "We get a point. Now on to Mom and Dad. Dad, who was Mom's first boyfriend?"

"Brett Markson," Dad said as he flipped over his board. "But his name should have been Brett Throwslikeagirl."

Mom revealed her answer. "The only boyfriend I remember is Dad."

"No point!" Cammie said loudly.

I suddenly had all sorts of flashbacks to playing Candyland with my sister.

"It was worth it," Mom said as she winked at Dad.

Cammie flipped to her next question card. "Okay. That

brings us to the Nearlywed couple. Isaac, what was Annabelle's first word?"

I quickly jotted my answer on my board, and Isaac looked toward the ceiling in thought. "I don't know . . . Mama," he said with a shrug.

"Use your board," Cammie instructed.

Isaac scribbled the word on his board and then turned it over.

I smiled as I revealed my answer: *Mama.*

"We get a point!" I shouted. It was nice to know that even when something was going on, we could still show everyone that we knew each other well.

"Except that wasn't your first word," Cammie said.

"Yes it was."

"No, sweetie," Mom said apologetically. "It wasn't."

I furrowed my brow. "Well then what was my first word?"

"It was actually two words." Mom bit her lip, like she didn't want to continue. "I stink."

"No you don't," I said, confused.

"No," Mom said. "Those were your first words: 'I stink.'"

Cammie giggled. "Zero points for you!"

Everyone in the room laughed as they pictured little baby Annabelle choosing, "I stink," as her first words.

"Hey," I said defensively. "Maybe you're wrong. Maybe I said. 'I think.' Maybe I was just really smart for my age and wanted you to know there was a lot going on up there."

I heard Isaac chuckle at my words and looked over at him. Maybe it was a signal that he wanted to quit squabbling and enjoy the night. I know I did.

I wanted to reach for his hand, but stopped myself for some reason.

Soon it was time for the ladies' round. Cammie made her way around the room, asking the women their questions, and I don't know why, but I felt myself getting more sad and upset with every question.

This was not the way today was supposed to turn out. Isaac and I were supposed to find him the perfect wedding suit and then come to the dinner all smiles and giddiness, like the annoying engaged couple we deserved to be! We weren't supposed to be fighting our way through the Nearlywed Game!

"Okay," Cammie said when it was my turn. "Annabelle. Who was Isaac's first girlfriend?"

"I don't know," I said, my voice way more snippy than I intended it to be. "But Ashley Dawes was his first fiancée, and apparently he used up all his wedding-planning niceness on her!"

The room grew dead silent as all eyes turned to me, the crazy outburst girl.

"Well maybe if you weren't trying to dress me up like some sort of ballet dancer," Isaac said through gritted teeth.

Cammie held up the question cards in her hand. "You guys aren't sticking to the rules!"

"She dressed him up like a belly dancer?" I heard Miles whisper to Carrie. She shook her head as if to say, "Not now."

"What do you care what your suit looks like?!" I said to Isaac. "Don't you want our wedding to be perfect?!"

"Oh so you agree it is *our* wedding," Isaac said

I shot out of my seat. The nerve! "I can't believe you would even say that to me!"

"How about we have dessert now," Mom suggested in a soft tone as she stood up.

"But we're not finished with the game!" Cammie protested.

"Thanks, Mom," I said. "But I'm not very hungry." I turned to leave the living room and all I could think about was getting outside, getting some air, and getting rid of the awful feeling in my chest.

Chapter 28

The wedding day was here.

I was standing in front of a fountain in my beautiful white dress, exotic lilies in my hand, doves flying above my head. Isaac was walking toward me, looking like he couldn't believe his eyes.

But before he reached me, a bright lime green Cadillac pulled up in front of him, and out stepped Chloe dressed in a white bridesmaid dress that was basically a shorter version of my gown. She looked me up and down as the Cadillac's driver emerged, and I saw it was . . . Doreen?

Doreen sidled up to me. "I told Chloe I didn't think you'd mind if she was a bridesmaid," she said, beaming at Chloe. "Since I can't have her as a daughter-in-law, at least she can be in the wedding pictures."

"And, Annabelle," Chloe said, "I've already promised when *I* have *my* wedding, I'll let Doreen, Ginny, and Margaret plan it all. I'll wear a pioneer wedding dress, and let my fiancé pick out whatever suit he wants, and we'll honeymoon in Antarctica."

"Oh," Doreen gushed. "You're such a sweet girl, Chloe. You'll make some guy's mother very happy someday!"

"No she won't!" I shouted. "She'll make some guy's mother very—"

I was about to come up with a great zinger, hopefully one that rhymed with happy, when the sound of a clearing throat made me shoot up in my office chair.

Wait a minute? My office chair? I thought I was in front of a fountain holding lilies.

I blinked my eyes and oriented myself, realizing I had fallen asleep with my face on my computer keyboard.

"Bad dream?" I heard a male voice ask from the doorway of my office.

I turned my head and saw Alex looking at me, an amused expression on his face.

"No," I said quickly.

"What are you doing here?" he asked.

I rubbed my eyes and looked at the clock on my computer: 8:48 pm. "Working," I said, trying to sound nonchalant.

"At nine o'clock at night?"

"Yes. Studies have shown that working at night is good for the . . . you know for . . . the hypothalamus."

"All right," Alex said, eyes narrowing. "You okay?"

"Perfect," I said.

Total lie. I had left my parents' house fuming after the Nearlywed Game Blowup and had come straight to work. I just really needed to be alone. I had typed like a madwoman for about an hour, and then put my head down, tears threatening. I must have fallen asleep while trying to fight them by saying the alphabet backwards.

"Well," Alex said, taking a seat. (Without being invited, I might add.) "I'm glad I caught you. I wanted to congratulate you on your engagement."

What? How did Alex know? He'd been in New York the past couple weeks, and it had been kind of nice not to deal with him or his . . . antics.

"Thank you." I brushed my hair out of my face with my left hand, and Alex's eyes zoomed in on my ring.

"He's a lucky guy," Alex said. He straightened his shoulders. "I have something for you. Consider it an engagement gift."

"What?"

Alex reached forward and handed me some sort of document bound in a clear-covered folder.

I furrowed my brow as I examined it. "This is a copy of the sample article for my editor-in-chief portfolio."

Alex nodded.

"How did you get this? I haven't even finished it."

"I have friends on the IT staff."

My brow even more furrowed, I flipped through the pages and noticed the article had been marked up with a red pencil. "What in the world?"

"I thought you might like a little feedback," Alex said. "I know how hard you've been working on the article. And I figured you'd appreciate this more than say . . . a toaster oven."

"Feedback? You mean you read this?"

"I did."

I stared at Alex. I mean, he was the publisher. If I was going to get anyone's feedback, he was the one. "Is that allowed?"

"What?"

"I mean, are you allowed to give me help like that?"

"I don't know," Alex said. "Let me ask the company VP." Alex made an exaggerated face. "He says it's fine."

"I'm just saying . . . I don't want to have an unfair advantage. I don't want to get help the others aren't getting just because they didn't happen to get engaged this month."

"How very *Full House* of you," Alex said. "If others want my help, I'm here. I just thought I'd offer it to you since I thought you might feel awkward to ask because . . ."

"Because of our history," I said softly.

The corners of Alex's mouth turned up. "Well that's not what I was going to say, but if our history is on your mind—"

"Not *our history*," I said quickly. "I just meant . . . the history of . . . the country . . . of America."

"The history of America?"

"Yeah," I said, my voice rushed and squeaky. "You know,

how we're 'All for one and one for all.' "

"Actually I think that's The Three Musketeers."

"I just mean . . . the fact that everyone has the right to life, liberty, and the pursuit of . . . you know . . . that we hold these truths to be self-evident . . . that everyone should be able to . . . do something . . ."

"What in the world are you talking about?"

"Nothing. I appreciate your help. Thank you, Alex."

"It was my pleasure," Alex got up from his seat and saluted me as he headed for the door. "See you later, Annabelle."

He was almost gone, when I heard myself blurt, "So did you hate it?"

Alex stopped short and turned around. "Not at all."

"Are you just saying that because you read it and thought it was completely ridiculous and not up to snuff and now you think all I have left is my pride so you might as well let me have that and—"

Alex cut me off. "It's true you don't have the same experience as some of the others. There are a lot of talented people going out for this position; people who've been at *CCL* and other local publications for five, ten, even fifteen years—including your own editor."

I felt a big, fat lump forming in my throat. I didn't stand a chance at this thing. I mean, this was an editor-in-chief position. It was way out of my league. Way out.

Looks like I'd be selling bottles of Monterey Bay sand sooner than I thought. My slogan could be . . . "Here's some sand."

Oh my goodness, that's the best I could come up with? No wonder this writing thing isn't going to work out.

"But what you lack by way of resume lines," Alex continued, "you make up for in creativity and heart. Your piece has a good angle, and your point of view is strong. We want *Central Coast Weddings* to have a powerful presence right out of the gate, and while I'm only one member of the hiring committee, I have to say you are pretty much exactly what we're looking for."

What?!

I felt the panic-filled throat lump begin to subside and be replaced by a swell of hope. "Are you serious?! I . . . Wow. I can't say how much I appreciate you having that kind of confidence in me! And I promise you, if I do get this job, I will give it 110 percent!" I sounded a bit like a hyper cheerleader. "Thank you so much for critiquing this for me. I really do appreciate it. You've really given me the boost I needed to keep pushing forward."

"Of course." Alex's face turned suddenly serious. "I really had no idea you could write like that. I guess there are a lot of things I never knew about you."

There was something in his tone that made me feel suddenly uncomfortable. "That's okay," I said with a weird laugh. "I don't want people to know everything about me."

Alex blinked a few times before speaking again. "Do you ever wonder what might have happened if we hadn't—"

I cut him off quickly, "Do you ever wonder who invented tape?!" I picked up the Scotch tape dispenser sitting on my desk and held it up awkwardly.

"I want you to know I'm sorry, Annabelle," Alex said, ignoring my crazy attempt at changing the subject. "About everything."

I put down the tape and shrugged one shoulder. "It's forgotten. It was a long time ago."

"I'm glad to hear that," Alex said. "Because if you get this job, we're going to be seeing a lot of each other. And I really don't want you to hate me. I've experienced that, and I didn't care for it at all."

"I never hated you, Alex."

He shook his head. "Well then you were a really good actress."

"I didn't. I was just . . . eighteen. I was eighteen and I thought you were . . ."

Alex's eyes fixed on me. "You thought I was what?"

I didn't answer, just fiddled with the stapler on my desk

until I almost stapled my fingers together.

"I thought you were too," Alex said.

I swallowed hard, staring at my desk.

Okay. Wait a minute. Wait just one minute!

Can you do me a favor, reader, and look over that little exchange one more time and tell me what you think Alex thought I was saying, and, therefore, what you think he was saying?

Maybe he thought I was saying, "I was eighteen and I thought you were a good tennis player." And then he said, "I thought you were too." In which case, no big deal, right?

What are the chances of that?

"Well I guess I'd better let you get back to work," Alex said with a knock on the office wall. "See you later, Annabelle."

"See you."

"And good luck with your editor-in-chief portfolio. I'm rooting for you." Alex left the office, and his words seemed to linger in the air.

No more than ten seconds later, my cell buzzed from atop my desk, causing me to jump slightly.

I picked up the phone. It was a text from Isaac.

Sweetie, I'm so sorry about tonight. Something really cool just happened. I'm going back to L.A. Please come with me.

Chapter 29

Less than a week later, I was back in Southern California with Isaac. I'll spare you the flight details, but let's just say I'm pretty sure a letter asking me never to fly Delta again was coming my way.

"Come on, give me a little hint," I pleaded.

Isaac shook his head. "Nope. It's a surprise." He took hold of my hand as he pulled his parents' Pontiac onto a beautiful palm-tree lined street I was pretty sure was in Santa Monica.

I stared out the window, chest gripped with anxiety. I'd spent all week wondering what the "something cool" was that Isaac texted me about. But every time I asked, he insisted it should be a surprise.

I must say, though, Isaac has a very good "surprise track record." To date, his credits include:

1) A book of black-and-white photos he took of Monterey Bay's most amazing sights especially for me.

2) A designer cashmere coat with pockets he filled with Starburst he had unwrapped and re-wrapped with love quotes.

3) A beautiful silver charm bracelet with a Chinese

character on it that Isaac said meant, "The Year of The Two of Us." Of course, now that I think about it, for all I know, the character could actually mean pork fried rice. But oh well, it's a really nice bracelet.

4) A dozen cupcakes Isaac had shipped to me all the way from Sprinkles in New York that I of course froze so they would last longer. Okay, which I meant to freeze, but ended up eating in a week. Fine, two days, but it was just after we switched to Daylight Savings time, so they seemed like really long days.

But, honestly, I'd never seen Isaac so excited about a surprise.

"Close your eyes," he instructed as he pulled the car over to the curb and began to slow down.

"What?"

"Close 'em!"

"Fine." I closed my eyes and felt Isaac wave his hand in front of my face.

"Are they closed?"

"Yes," I said.

I felt the car creep forward a while longer before it stopped completely and Isaac put it into park.

"We're here," he said. "Don't move."

We're here? Where?

I was tempted to sneak a peek as I heard Isaac get out of the car and jog around the back, but I didn't.

Okay, fine. I did for one tiny little second. But all I saw was that we were parked on the street in a nice, clean neighborhood before I felt bad and snapped my eyes shut again.

Isaac opened my door and took hold of my hands. Without a word, he helped me onto the sidewalk, down a walkway, and then up four stairs. At the top of the stairs, I heard the sound of a key turning in a lock and then a door opening.

I could feel my heart beat fast with excitement as I wondered where we were.

"Okay." Isaac helped me maneuver through what seemed to be a doorway and dropped my hands. "Open your eyes!"

I opened my eyes, and was completely thrown by what I saw.

And not in a good way.

No, my friend, not in a good way at all.

What I saw was an old, vacant, rather filthy house that had obviously been vandalized.

I scanned the graffiti that had been sprayed on the banged-up wall to my right. I'm not the best graffiti-translator, but I was pretty sure I could make out the words "Enter and die."

"What are we doing here?" I asked, huddling next to Isaac. "Are you doing some kind of before and after photos of this place or something?"

Isaac raised his eyebrows at me, his mouth tight-lipped.

"Come on, Isaac. What's up?"

"Come inside and see." Isaac extended his hand to me as he moved inside the house.

"Um . . . Okay." I followed behind Isaac, my arms close to my body.

Isaac watched me with an amused look on his face that said, "Silly female, why can't you deal with a little bit of dirt and grime?"

Of course, two seconds later, Isaac walked right into a spider web, and he must have felt the web's occupant crawl onto him because he let out quite possibly the weirdest sound I've ever heard come from him and started flailing around.

"Get it off!" he hollered as he brushed his head and body with his hands.

"No way!" I said, jumping away from him.

It took Isaac a good thirty seconds to get rid of the imposter, and once he did, he looked at me. "I was just afraid it was going to get on you, you know."

Uh huh.

After brushing his hair with his hand one more time, Isaac continued to walk further into the house, toward the kitchen.

I tried to stay close to the exit, you know, just in case, but Isaac pulled me in the direction he was going. I clung tightly to him as I walked.

Once inside the kitchen, Isaac pointed to a cabinet at our right. "Why don't you take a look in there?"

Let me tell you, I really, really didn't want to take a look in there. But, since Isaac looked so excited, and I trusted that this must be going somewhere good, I reached for the cabinet.

"Okay . . ." I bit my lip as I opened the door slowly, using only my thumb and index finger. The cabinet couldn't have been more than an inch open when I saw the creepiest, biggest, furriest, I-don't-know-what, sitting on the shelf just staring at me.

"Ahhh!" I screamed so hard I didn't even realize the cabinet door had come off in my hand and I was hurtling it across the room.

What happened next was all kind of a blur, but I can just barely remember seeing Isaac duck as the cabinet door whizzed past his head and hit the wall behind him and then run to my side, taking hold of me.

"Annabelle!" he cried. "It's okay. It's okay!"

"But there's something in there!" I hollered, feeling goose bumps of fear forming on my skin. "It's big and brown. And kind of mangy looking. And I saw these big beady eyes. And fangs!"

"Annabelle!" Isaac said, holding me tight in an attempt to stop the shaking. "It's just a teddy bear!"

"Huh?"

Isaac let go of me and retrieved the furry creature from the cabinet. It was a cute little brown teddy bear. All furry and sweet with little button eyes and no mouth to speak of.

"I could have sworn it had fangs," I said.

Isaac chuckled as he took me into a hug. "I can't believe you ripped off the cabinet door."

"I can't believe you put something furry in an abandoned house's cabinet and told me to open it!"

"I guess I didn't think that part through," Isaac said with an apologetic smile. "I just thought you'd think it was cool if I tied the key to the bear."

"What?" I grabbed the bear and noticed a silver key was tied to its neck with a pink ribbon. "I don't get it. My surprise is a key?"

Isaac smiled, looking into my eyes as my brain started to turn. "It's a key to this house," he said.

"Okay . . ."

"It was a foreclosure. Rona bought it and was planning on fixing it up and flipping it for a profit, but she's willing to sell it to me at a good price. Sell it to *us*."

I set the bear back in the cabinet. "What? Why? We don't want to get into the house flipping business, trust me. Haven't you seen those shows on the Home and Garden Channel? I'm telling you, the tagline should be, 'Couples who flip together, fight together.' I mean, they really go at it. I saw this one couple and the guy said he could re-tile the shower and when he messed it up his wife was calling him all kinds of names and telling him she could see why her father never liked him and—"

"We wouldn't buy the house to flip," Isaac said. "We'd buy it to fix it up for us. To live in."

My mind halted, just did a dead stop. "But we don't live in L.A."

Isaac came to my side and put his arms around my waist. "About an hour and a half after our engagement dinner at your parents' place, I was offered a job working for Pilar Sanchez— the press has dubbed her the Latina Martha. Anyway, she's producing a new show and wants me to be the primary stills photographer." Isaac shook his head as if in disbelief. "It's a huge, amazing opportunity."

"Wow, Isaac, that's fantastic." I put my arms around my fiancé.

"It is. The money's good. There's a complete benefits package. 401K. The whole deal. Working freelance was fine when it was just me, and I can still do some stuff on the side, but now that it will be us, and eventually . . . a family, I really wanted to find something more stable. And this just sort of fell in my lap.

"The craziest part is after I got the offer, I called Ethan because I knew Rona had just bought this house and honestly, real estate in Southern California is a nightmare, but this is something we could actually afford that's in a good neighborhood, with great schools, great shopping." Isaac winked at me after saying shopping. "Everything just kind of fell in to place. It's a lot like when you won the wedding, isn't it? How it all just felt so right."

"Yes," I said, feeling like my legs were about to give out right under me. "It is . . ."

Isaac searched my face, sensing how overwhelmed I was by this news. "Tell me what you're thinking."

"I'm thinking. I'm . . . thinking . . ." *Enter and die, for starters.*

I stared at the graffiti on the wall, trying to take in everything. This was so out of nowhere. Isaac got a job offer in L.A.? Isaac wanted to move to L.A.? Isaac already found us a house in L.A.? An old, vandalized house so run-down it has cabinet doors that a wimp like me can rip off?

"What about Monterey?" I asked. "This is the kind of thing people who meet at school or on the internet have to deal with, you know, where to live after they get married. But we both live in Monterey. Monterey is home. I mean, my family is there, my whole life. And I spent the past month working like crazy on an application for a job up there. What about that?"

Isaac scratched his chin. "I thought you said you didn't have a chance at getting that job."

I felt my face muscles tighten.

Note to any guy who may be reading this: If your girlfriend, wife, mom, sister, or friend says she doesn't think she has a chance at something—be it a job, a grand prize at

the quilting fair, even a starring role in a Matt Damon film—
don't agree with her!

I frowned. "Yeah, I did say that . . ." But that was before I
thought I *had* a chance. Before I talked to Alex. Before I looked
over his notes and saw that he had a whole bunch of nice things
to say about my ideas, about my abilities. " . . . But even so.
Moving to L.A.? This is just so . . ."

I had no adjectives.

Isaac scratched his head. "Wow. This isn't going how I
thought it would go at all."

"How did you think it would go?"

"I thought you'd be happy."

"It's not that I'm unhappy. It's just that . . . I'm a bit . . .
thrown off. Ten minutes ago I thought we were going to build
our home in the area where my mom, best friend, and sister all
live. The area where I've built a life I actually really love. But
now—"

"Yoo-hoo! Anyone home?!" I looked to the front door
where Doreen and Ginny were entering, arms filled with
Home Depot and Wholesale Wonder bags.

"My boy!" Doreen said, taking Isaac into a hug. "We just
couldn't wait to get in here and start redoing the place. We
went shopping with Chloe, and she said that lime green is very
in right now."

Of course she did. After the engagement dinner with
Isaac's family last weekend, I told Isaac I was going to return
the sweater from Chloe. He said he was sorry it didn't fit and
that it was odd Chloe had picked a lime green one since she'd
asked him what my favorite color was, and he'd told her I liked
pretty much anything but lime green.

Uh huh.

Doreen opened a bag with a set of rugs in it. "One for every
room in the house—and all for one low price at Wholesale
Wonders! And don't you just love that color."

Lime green. All of the rugs were lime green.

"And look at these sconces," Ginny said, revealing a set of

overly gaudy sconces. "Don't they remind you of something Trump would use?"

"Also," Doreen said with a smile as she reached into a bag, "we know you're considering having chocolate brown, sage, and cream for your wedding colors—a very *unusual* choice for a summer wedding—but we found this jumbo box of rose, lavender, and blue ribbons, just in case."

Doreen set the box on the counter and started talking to Ginny about her experience making tie-bouquets and saying how great she thought the lavender ribbon would look on one.

I stared at the women as they discussed what time of day the flower guy delivered to Wholesale Wonders.

Please tell me I hit my head with the cabinet door when I flung it open and this is all a dream and in a few minutes I'm going to wake up in my Monterey bed, ready to live my Monterey life.

Please.

Chapter 30

"Derek in subscriptions."

"Justine in advertising."

"Ted the copy editor."

"Yeah, but he was worse than Becca. And he'd been here for two years." Katrina took a casual sip of her Foamie—whipped hot cocoa with vanilla bean—and sighed.

We were sitting in my office, drinking cocoa as we went over the list of people who had been "let go" from the magazine this week. It was a pretty long list. And it was only Wednesday.

"At least you know you're safe," Katrina said.

"What? How?"

"Oh, please. You're so getting the editor-in-chief gig."

I held my cocoa in my right hand, swirled the raspberry flavored Party Wave around with a tilt of the cup. "I highly doubt it. But you know, maybe it's for the best. Maybe I'll just move to L.A. with Isaac and start my sand bottle company."

The mention of L.A. made my head hurt. Isaac and I had successfully avoided the subject for the past three days, and I kind of liked it that way.

Katrina tossed her cocoa cup into the trash and looked at her reflection in her black MAC compact. "Please. I bet you thirty bucks you don't get a call toda—"

The ringing office phone cut her off.

I put my hand on the receiver. "Still want to make that bet?"

Katrina looked up from the compact and bit her lip.

"This is Annabelle Pleasanton," I said after picking up the phone.

"Pleasanton, it's George. I need to see you in my office."

"Okay. Sure. I'll be right there."

I hung up the phone and gulped. I said a morose good-bye to Katrina and walked quickly to George's office, straightening my suit—a great tweed one I found on chickdowntown.com—as I walked.

George's door was ajar, and I breezed right past his assistant Gidget, who was at her desk reading a copy of *Soap Opera Scoop*.

"Pleasanton," George said once I was inside. "I've been asked to send you to the conference room."

My stomach dropped. Or maybe the sixteen ounces of cocoa in it dropped. Nevertheless, there was an unpleasant dropping in there. "Do you know why?"

"I guess we'll see." George lifted his eyebrows and shot me a look that seemed almost . . . bitter.

My insides tightened. He knew. He knew they were letting me go. And he actually seemed upset about it. Maybe after all this time I had begun to grow on him.

"All right," I said, putting on my best brave face. "I guess I'll . . . go to the conference room."

"Close the door on your way out," George said.

The walk to the conference room seemed longer than ever. And for some reason, the theme song to Jaws was in my head. When I reached the room, I swung the door open, and saw . . .

"Alex? What are you doing here?"

He smiled. "Waiting for you."

"But . . ." And that's when it hit me. Alex was the big boss.

He was the one who was going to give me the old heave-ho. Is that how you say it? The old heave-ho?

"Why don't you have a seat?" Alex said.

I slowly sat down, thinking of all the articles I'd never get to write, all the ideas I wouldn't get to think at my new job as I stood dressed in gloves and a hairnet next to a conveyer belt filling bottles with sand.

"So," Alex said with a smile. "The hiring committee has carefully reviewed each and every submitted portfolio. We spent all day yesterday and all morning today factoring the portfolios in with the interviews we conducted on Monday. We put a great deal of time into deciding who will best fill the editor-in-chief position. And we've decided . . ."

I didn't really listen to the words. My brain pretty much shut off after the word *so*. Kind of the way a girl in a bad relationship always shuts off her brain when a guy starts a sentence with the words, "I've been doing some thinking."

"Okay," I said with a sigh. "I guess I'll pack my desk and start toning my sand-pouring muscles."

"What are you talking about? Didn't you hear what I just said?" Alex's voice was slightly high, like he was excited.

"I . . . um . . . well . . ." I sighed. "Actually no, I didn't hear what you said. I don't really want to. Just tell me when I need to be out of here."

"Out of here? You're not going anywhere except to an executive office I'm having a decorator look at right now. You got the job, Annabelle!" Alex reached across the table between us, and touched my hand. "You're the new editor-in-chief of *Central Coast Weddings!*"

The whole world stopped. Like everything except me and Alex had been put on pause. "What?"

Alex smiled, his blue eyes seemingly bluer than usual. "You did it! You got the job. The committee has a lot of faith in you. We can't wait to see what you do."

I couldn't speak. I just stared at Alex, without blinking for longer than I thought it was possible for a human not to blink.

Alex laughed. "You're too adorable. Now, let's go over a few of the details: You will get a company car and a company house, which will actually be the home you're staying in now. You'll get a signing bonus, full benefits, and as for your starting salary . . ." Alex scribbled something onto a piece of paper and slid it across the table to me.

I stared at the paper. *What? I mean, seriously . . . What?*

I would tell you what the paper said except I think it's kind of, you know, bad form, to divulge information like how much I make.

Oh who am I kidding, I don't care! I want you to know what the paper said! Are you ready? Okay. Brace yourself. It said: $250,000. Yes, that's right. $250,000! Which is about a gazillion times what I'm making now.

I looked up from the paper and just sat there in that conference room chair, completely and utterly floored.

"We're going to be combining three of the executive offices into one for you," Alex said. "The view is spectacular; you should check it out. Let's see, what else . . ." Alex tapped his platinum pen on the table. "We want you to start three weeks from Monday. I know that's soon, but things are moving along pretty quickly. We're hoping to put out a fall issue. It's pretty optimistic, but I think we can pull it off."

At the mention of the fall issue, I turned from stunned to supremely excited and found myself jumping up from my chair and squealing with joy. I almost hopped onto the table, but figured that wasn't the kind of thing an editor-in-chief would do.

Editor-in-chief! I was editor-in-chief of *Central Coast Weddings.* "Oh my goodness!" I threw my arms around Alex in a moment of sheer elation.

"Wow," Alex said, his arms tightening around me. "This is a much better reaction than I was expecting."

The realization that I was hugging Alex was like a dart hitting my forehead, and I jumped back from him instantly.

Alex surveyed me as I shot away. "Everything okay?"

"Sure," I said, staring at the ground. "I just . . ."

The left side of Alex's mouth turned up ever-so-slightly. "Foot cramp?"

"What?"

"Nothing." Alex stood up from his seat and leaned against the table. "So can I assume by your reaction that you'd like to accept the position?"

Um. Yes! Of course! I—

My joyful thoughts were interrupted by a big, fat reality: I couldn't accept this position.

"What's wrong?" I heard Alex ask.

I rubbed my forehead. "Isaac got a job offer too. In L.A."

Alex frowned. "L.A.?"

"Yes. And he found us a house down there."

"So you're saying you might be moving to L.A.?" Alex sounded completely thrown.

The words burned my ears. Moving to L.A.? No! I didn't want to move. I didn't want to trade an in-the-bag editor-in-chief position for pounding the pavement, looking for writing work again. I didn't want to trade my beautiful, 17 Mile Drive house in Monterey for a place with graffiti on the walls and lime green rugs on the floors. I didn't want to spend the rest of my life having family dinners with "Chlo," the girl everyone wished Isaac had married.

But still, I heard myself say: "Maybe."

Alex crossed his arms. "I thought you hated L.A."

I didn't reply.

"Wow," he said. "You're honestly considering turning down this position."

I rubbed my hands together. "There are wedding magazines in L.A."

Alex looked at me. "Your resume would get thrown in the trash bin at those places, Annabelle. We at *CCL* know you, know your potential, but to those places you'll just be a girl with no experience."

I knew Alex's words were true, but they still agitated me.

"You have to make sacrifices sometimes! That's what people who are in love do. Just because *you* always do what you want when you want doesn't mean everyone else can live like that."

"You don't want to go," Alex said, his blue eyes burning into me.

"I . . ." The lie I was about to tell got caught in my throat.

"Well," Alex said, abruptly moving toward the door. "The offer's on the table. I'll need to know three weeks from today."

I nodded weakly as Alex left the conference room, the door slamming closed behind him.

Chapter 31

"So you still haven't told him?" Carrie looked over at me
as the seamstress at Monique's pinned the hem of her Maid of
Honor dress.

I frowned. Not at the dress—Carrie looked amazing in the
chocolate-brown silk—but at the question. It had been a week
and a half since I'd been offered the editor-in-chief position,
and, no, I still hadn't told Isaac. He was working in L.A., and it
just wasn't a conversation I wanted to have over the phone.

"He gets home tonight," I said, taking a sip of my sparkling
lemonade. "He's coming over and I'm just . . . going to do it."

"Don't worry," Carrie said in that reassuring way of hers
as she spun around at the seamstress's direction. "Everything
will be fine."

"I hope you're right. It's like the longer I've gone without
telling him the more scared I am." I set my glass down. "But, I
did get some pretty good advice on how to go about the whole
thing. It was weird . . . There I was just sitting in the living
room after work, listening to a little Dr. Leslie on the radio,
when a girl with a very similar problem to mine called in."

Carrie looked at me over her shoulder, her eyes narrowing
a bit. "Oh really?"

"Yeah. This local girl named . . . I think it was . . . Jennifer

Laniston, called in and told her story, which really was a lot like mine. Dr. Leslie told Jennifer she needs to explore why she felt she couldn't tell her fiancé her feelings. Her guess was that the girl probably waited a long time to find love, maybe had a difficult relationship where she was rejected and she never really recovered, and felt that if she rocked the boat, her love might be lost. She said the most important thing to do was to conquer that fear and be completely open and honest with the guy."

"What was the guy's name?" Carrie asked, sounding suspicious.

"Oh . . ." I said. "I'm not quite sure . . . Brad Spit, I think."

"Brad Spit and Jennifer Laniston?" Carrie interrupted, eyebrows raised.

"They sound like very nice people," I said.

"I knew that was you on the radio!" Carrie shouted, pointing an accusatory finger at me.

"What?" I asked innocently. "Why would you think—"

"I know your voice, Annabelle. Plus, you'd just spent the morning talking about Brad and Jen."

"Well they never should have broken up," I said into my lemonade. "And since when do you listen to Dr. Leslie?"

"Since the station has a Deepak Chopra segment right after her."

The seamstress told Carrie she was finished, and Carrie slipped out of the dress and joined me in the sitting area.

"I'm sad you feel like you have to call Dr. Leslie to get advice," she said. "I'm here for you whenever you need me."

"I know," I said. "I just . . . feel bad bothering you. The last time I called your house Miles answered and told me you'd 'just be a moment' because you were washing a load of his 'jumpers,' and I asked him what in the world he was wearing dresses for."

"'Jumper' means sweater in England," Carrie said.

"Well, in California it means those thin-strap denim dresses people wear over T-shirts."

"I know things are different," Carrie said. "But please call me. I still need you."

"I need you too. Carrie?"

"Yeah."

"Why did I have to get this amazing job offer in a town I love while Isaac got an equally amazing offer in a town I hate? Could it be a sign? I mean, Isaac's always been this . . . perfect guy. I honestly can't believe my luck that I found him. But what if it was all some kind of fluke? What if the way things are going now, with all these problems between us about the wedding and jobs and houses and families, is the fluke finally coming to an end?" The words burned my throat, like a hot drink. "What if Isaac and I aren't—"

"Annabelle," Carrie said, stopping me. "You are. Okay. Tonight, when Isaac gets home and you finally tell him everything it's going to be so fine you're going to wonder what you were so worried about."

I smiled hopefully at my friend. "You think?"

"I do."

"Sorry I'm late!" Jenna burst into the shop and approached us, bending down to kiss my cheek as she pushed her sunglasses up on her head. "Hey, Carrie," she said as she took a seat. "So what did you think about the dress?"

"It's beautiful," Carrie said.

I nodded."It really is. Margarita says it will be finished once she redoes the hem."

"You can never go wrong with French silk," Jenna said. "So what else did I miss?"

"She's telling him tonight," Carrie said, nodding her head in my direction.

Jenna raised her eyebrows. "About the job?"

"Uh huh," I answered.

"Finally," Jenna said. "You've been so tense this past week and a half. It's like you're a completely different bride. When you were deciding on the favors yesterday and Isaac called and told you his mom thought the idea of having a 'Matthews

Mini Sweet Shop' at the reception where guests could fill bags with assorted candies was 'something more suited for a tween birthday party than a wedding reception,' I thought you were going to have a culinary!"

I'm pretty sure she meant *coronary.*

And she was right. Lately, I *had* been a completely different bride.

"Well good luck," Jenna said. "And remember, I had a bride once whose fiancé got a job in New York City and the couple postponed the wedding so he could move over there and they could see how the long distance thing worked out. It's not your situation exactly, but I'm just saying, you have options. That's what the Cold Feet Clause is for."

"Cold Feet Clause?" Carrie asked.

Jenna nodded. "It's a clause in the wedding contract. The first part says the couple has twenty months from the date of signing the contract to hold the actual event. It's set up for couples who find they have to postpone the wedding, or just need more time to plan. And the second part of the clause is the cash-out option for couples who don't go through with the wedding at all. That has only happened once and I have to admit, I was kind of heartbroken. It was just so sad to—"

"Don't worry, Jenna," I said, cutting her off. "Isaac and I won't need to use either part of the clause."

"Good."

Friday, 4:54 pm: Operation Conversation.

Isaac looked almost painfully handsome in jeans and a trendy blue polo shirt when I answered the door. He stepped into the house and kissed me so good my knees nearly buckled.

"I missed you so much, sweetheart," he said, his voice all low and gorgeous.

"I missed you too."

Isaac touched the headband in my hair as we walked toward the living room. "Your hair looks really pretty like that."

"Thanks," I said, wishing the moment wasn't tainted by my anxiety over the impending conversation.

Isaac stretched as he approached the couch. "So you said you have something important to tell me."

I sat down beside him. "Yes."

Isaac watched my lips move. "Let's hear it," he said, following the words with a kiss.

I rubbed my hands together nervously. "Okay. Here goes. I guess I'll just . . . say it . . . I . . . I've been offered the position of editor-in-chief at *Central Coast Weddings.*"

Isaac's jaw dropped, and he took me into a tight hug. "Sweetie, that's amazing!"

"It is," I said. "But there's one pretty big problem: It doesn't really fit in with your plan to move to L.A. and work for Peeler Sanchez."

"It's *Pilar*," Isaac said with a chuckle. "Not *Peeler*. She's not a kitchen utensil."

Hmm. Was Jenna starting to rub off on me?

"Okay, whatever her name is. I have to admit, it's pretty hard for me to be happy about my news when I know you want to take a job in a completely different part of the state."

Isaac scratched his head. "Sure I want to take the job. But it's not like I'm just going to without discussion."

"Six days ago you were ready to make a down payment on a house in L.A. That doesn't sound like a job that's up for discussion."

"Well things were different six days ago. You didn't know you'd been selected as editor-in-chief of *Central Coast Weddings.* Wow. I just love saying that."

"Don't get my hopes up, Isaac," I said, my voice rigid.

Isaac looked a bit thrown. "What do you mean don't get your hopes up?"

"I mean . . . you want to move to L.A. You have a job and a house all lined up. And I've got to admit, I feel a little blindsided by that. I didn't even know you wanted to move back there."

Isaac drummed his fingers on his denim-clad leg. "I guess I didn't really know until it all happened."

"Okay. Well, I have to admit, I don't think I'm in the same place as you are about it all. Haven't you noticed how weird things have been since our last trip down there?"

Isaac shrugged. "I noticed things were a little . . . off. But I thought you were probably just stressed about work and the wedding and us being apart."

"It's more than just stress, Isaac. I hate L.A."

There, I said it.

"What?"

I closed my eyes tight. "I don't like the idea of living in a nightmarish fixer-upper. I don't like the idea of having to start my writing from scratch because my resume is going straight into the trash bin everywhere I apply. I don't like the idea of not seeing Carrie or Mom or my sister. I don't like the idea of constantly feeling like an idiot around your family. I think I would rather live in a cardboard box on Cannery Row with seagulls pecking at my feet while I sleep, than live in L.A."

Isaac's expression was a mixture of shock and concern. "Is that really how you feel?"

"How can you not already know the answer to that question?!" I threw my hands in the air. "Can't you tell how uncomfortable I am in L.A.? I mean, for the past couple weeks I've been running around feeling like I have to pretend for you. Pretend I like Southern California. Pretend it's not completely obvious to me that your family thinks I'm a total loser. Pretend I'd be just fine leaving Monterey."

"I don't want you to pretend," Isaac said. "I have never wanted that. You could have told me any time how you really feel. That's what I want."

"Is it really? Because lately it kind of feels like you just want me to fit in with your plans."

Isaac's face turned from tender to tense in 2.7 seconds. "That's not fair. You know I love you. You know I want you to be happy. And, honestly, you really don't have any room to talk. If you don't recall, you started planning a wedding worthy of a Hilton sister before I even proposed!"

"We were saving fifty thousand dollars!" I exclaimed.

"Do I look like someone who wants a fifty thousand dollar wedding?!" Isaac asked, eyebrows raised.

My mouth dropped open. "What are you saying? That you're unhappy with our wedding?"

"No," Isaac said, "I'm saying, as much as you hate L.A., I hate fancy raw tuna and frilly wedding suits."

I pushed my finger into my chest. "Well, I hate gold sconces and lime green rugs and sitting around all day talking about how perfect Chloe is!"

Isaac wrinkled his forehead. "What?"

"Never mind," I said, clenching my fists. "Listen to us! We're fine when we just don't talk about this stuff, but the second we do . . . it's craziness! The bottom line is . . . something isn't right. And it hasn't been right for a while. And now it's like everything that's wrong has come to a head with this new development; the one where I have every reason to stay in Monterey and you have every reason to move to L.A. And I really don't know what we're going to do about that."

Isaac took hold of my hand. "We'll figure it out."

"But what if we never do?"

"Annabelle . . ."

I pulled my hand away. "No, seriously. What if I always want to stay in Monterey and you always want to move to L.A. What then?"

"We'll arm wrestle," Isaac said with a grin.

"Why don't you care about what I'm saying?" I asked, my voice rising.

Because, I'm not going to lie, I was mad. At Isaac, for deciding he loved Southern California all of a sudden. At the universe, for not creating some sort of cosmic phenomena that caused L.A. to collapse into the sea. And at Chloe, though I'm not exactly sure why.

"I do care," Isaac said. "I just . . . don't really see what the big deal is."

"You don't see what the big deal is? The big deal is: We're planning our wedding Isaac. And our life. And now all of those plans could potentially change. Completely."

Isaac looked at me. "I guess I didn't really think of it like that."

"Well, I can't help thinking of it like that. Because I'm the one up here going over bridal shower and honeymoon dates that will change depending on where both of us are working in a few months, a gift registry that will change according to where we're living, and a million other little things that will be affected by these new decisions.

"And all I know is, I want us to be happy planning our wedding, and thinking of making a home out of your place or this place—because apparently the editor-in-chief position comes with this house—or whatever place it may be. But for the past couple of weeks, it's all felt sad and uncertain. I don't think that's how an engagement is supposed to be."

"It's not," Isaac said, putting an arm around me and kissing the top of my head. "So what do we do?"

Isaac looked at me intently, and it was like at that moment we both knew the only right answer to the question.

"Maybe the best thing to do is the one thing we don't want to do," I said softly. "Put the wedding plans on hold until we work all these things out; until we make all the decisions we need to make." I swallowed hard as if to rid myself of the awful taste of the words in my mouth.

Isaac touched my hand, his fingers grazing my engagement ring. "That can't be what you really want."

I felt tears begin to form in my eyes—the kind that make your throat sting. "Of course it's not what I want. I want for you to get the perfect job in Monterey. Or for my whole family to suddenly love the idea of Southern California. But that's not happening. And for now . . . this is the best we can do."

Isaac shook his head, looking toward the ceiling. "I hate this."

"I do too."

Isaac wiped the tears from my eyes. "We'll figure this out, Annabelle," he said. "We'll find solutions to everything that are so simple we'll wonder why we didn't think of them sooner. And then we'll get right back to planning everything."

I blinked, a fresh tear making its way down my cheek.

I never wanted him to be more right about anything.

Chapter 32

Ding. Dong.

I sat up on the couch and wiped my face with a dirty tissue from the pile on the coffee table.

Isaac had left with a strained, "I'll call you," and I'd closed the door behind him and sat down to watch TV, holding myself together like the mature adult I am.

Actually, that's a total lie.

I collapsed on the couch, a complete sobbing disaster, and attempted to soothe myself by watching the news. And after an hour of watching SUV owners complain about spending hundreds of dollars to fill up their gas tanks and listening to how bad the S&P 500 was doing, I did feel a tiny bit better.

I quickly shoved the pile of tissues into a drawer beneath the coffee table and rubbed my eyes to get rid of mascara residue.

My heart pounded as I headed to the door. Isaac must have been as messed up over this whole thing as I was and came back to the house so we could get through these miserable moments together.

I ran my fingers through my hair and threw open the door, and there stood . . .

"Alex?"

Alex studied my face. "You've been crying."

Awkward laugh. "I have not."

He stepped over the threshold. "Then why is your makeup all smeared like that?"

I touched my face, and Alex pointed to the foyer mirror where I took a quick look at my reflection. Sure enough, I was a puffy-eyed, mascara-run mess. I looked like a raccoon that just lost a boxing match.

"I did this on purpose," I said quickly. "I was going for a couture, fashion show kind of look."

"I don't believe you," Alex said, closing the door behind him. "Do you want to tell me what's going on?"

"What are you doing here?" I asked, dodging the question.

Alex walked to the living room—without being invited, what was up with him and doing that?—and I followed behind. He took off his jacket and removed a binder from his satchel. Then he sat down on the couch, and his attention went to the throw pillow I had been laying on. The pretty, expensive fabric was tear-stained and covered in nasty-looking smudges of makeup.

I immediately picked up the pillow and flung it across the room.

Alex lifted his eyebrows as if to ask, "What the heck was that?"

"I think I saw a bug or something," I said as I sat down on the opposite end of the couch. "So what did you say you came over for?"

"I wanted to bring you these swatches from the decorator who will redo this place for you if you take the job." Alex opened the binder and set it on the coffee table. "And . . . I have chocolate-covered gummy bears. I remember how much you like those."

Alex held out a baby-blue striped bag of gourmet chocolate-covered gummy bears. I, of course, remembered how Isaac had bought me chocolate-covered gummy bears on our first date, and immediately felt my eyes well up.

"Annabelle?" Alex said, sounding nervous in the way most guys do when a girl starts crying in front of them. "You've gotta tell me what's going on."

I shook my head and reached for a tissue on the coffee table. I wiped my face with it and noticed the tissue felt really coarse. I wadded it up and held it in my hand.

"That was a drapery sample," Alex said.

I opened my hand and looked down at the sheer fabric. "Sorry," I said to Alex. "You caught me at a bad time."

"It's okay. You're sure you don't want to talk about it?"

No, I didn't. Now was not the time. And Alex was definitely not the person. But somehow I just . . .

"Isaac and I . . . The wedding's on hold."

Alex shook his head. "He's an idiot."

"No he's not. He's perfect." And there were those darn tears again.

"Don't cry," Alex said, scooting to my end of the couch. "Remember when you pepper sprayed my uncle Fred?" Clearly he was trying to get my mind off things.

The memory was horrifying. "It was after midnight in the back of the movie theater parking lot!" I said. "And he came up to your car and knocked on the window. I thought we were being carjacked!"

"It *was* a nice car," Alex said with a grin.

And I couldn't help it, a quarter-smile formed on my lips.

"We had some good times, didn't we?" Alex said.

"If you can call that good."

"I do," Alex said his voice suddenly husky as he scooted closer to me.

I felt my stomach drop and swiftly felt very uncomfortable. Like I was wearing clothes that were two sizes too small. Desperately needing something—anything—to do, I reached for the candy dish filled with gumballs on the end table next to me and started shoving the things into my mouth, one after the other.

"You know," Alex said, his tone serious. "I've lived in New York, London, Milan—all over the world. And I've met and dated a lot of women. A lot. But I've never found anyone like you, Annabelle. Ever."

Umm . . . .

"And now your wedding is on hold," Alex continued. "Which makes me think maybe this is my window of opportunity."

I must have had six gumballs in my mouth when Alex leaned toward me and got a really weird look on his face. And before I knew what was happening, he was moving his mouth toward mine. Like he was going to kiss me.

His lips were mere inches away from my own when I did the only thing I could think of: I spit out my gum with a good amount of force. Yes, that's right, my friend.

A turn of the head would have worked, maybe even a little push. But no, I spit my gum at the guy.

Alex moved away, looking completely disgusted at the huge six-gum-ball blob that was now in his lap. "Geez . . . what are you doing?"

"What are *you* doing?!" I jumped up from the couch.

"I'm sorry." Alex wrapped the gum in a tissue with a grossed-out look on his face. "But I just couldn't help it. I've been wanting to do that since I saw you at Carrie's wedding."

This was not happening! This was not happening!

Actually, what in the world *was* happening?

"Um . . . well . . . Carrie's wedding . . . but . . . it didn't," I muttered, mastering my skills in jibberish. "The bathroom . . . I have . . . to go to."

Okay, Yoda.

I dashed into the kitchen and grabbed my cell from the counter top. Then I shut myself in the bathroom and pushed speed dial #5.

"Hello?"

"Carrie. What are you doing?"

"Miles and I were just about to watch a movie. Why?"

"I've got a code yellow!"

"You . . . need me to bring you a new pair of pants?"

"No!" I shouted. "And gross."

"Sorry. That's what I thought code yellow meant."

"No. Code yellow means I have an uncomfortable guy situation that I need you to rescue me from!"

"Oh," Carrie said with a sigh. "This is as confusing as the terror alert color scale."

I rolled my eyes. "Well I need you to get over here. Alex just . . ." I whisper-mumbled the words.

"He fried the fish meat?" Carrie repeated whe she thought I'd said.

"He tried to kiss me!" The sentence came out a little too loudly, and I turned on the bathroom fan to drown out my words.

"What?" Carrie said the word like it had five syllables.

I filled Carrie in on the dets. Oh, who am I kidding I can't get away with saying that. I filled Carrie in on the *details* all the way up to the kiss-attempt.

"I'm so sorry," Carrie said, sounding heartbroken about what had happened between Isaac and me. "You two will work it out. You are completely meant to be. And don't worry, I'll come over there and show that slimy little slime-faced scum Alex what I think about him! He's stupid. And dumb!"

It was so hilarious to hear Carrie trash talk. She's so horrible at it.

"Oh and maybe you should bring something with you," I said before we hung up. "So it looks like a coincidence that you came over while Alex was here."

"Okay. I'll be right there."

I hung up the phone, and waited in the bathroom until I heard Carrie's car outside. I wondered if Alex was curious about what was taking me so long in there—it had to have been a good twenty minutes—but I could hear that he had turned the TV to some sort of sports game so I figured he had lost all sense of time, like guys tend to do when watching sports. I mean, four hours for a football game? How do they do it?

I gave Carrie time to make it to the front door and exited the bathroom. Then I sauntered into the living room, ready to answer Carrie's ring any second, and thus avoid being alone in the room with Alex for any amount of time.

But I was just feet away from Alex and still no doorbell.

Gee whiz Carrie, what's taking you so long? I wondered as I tried to make my tiny steps seem as casual as possible—which had the exact opposite effect.

"What in the world are you doing?" Alex asked, looking over at me.

"You know . . . slowing down," I said. "You always hear about how no one slows down anymore. So I'm just—"

Finally I heard that beautiful bell.

"Gee. I wonder who that could be?" I said as I dashed toward the front door and flung it open. "Carrie!"

"Hello Annabelle. You left this at my house. And I thought you might need it." Carrie said the words in a loud, stilted, robotic voice.

She handed me a bag, and I began opening it. "Thanks Carrie. For bringing me my . . . garlic press?"

What? A garlic press? I'm not even entirely sure what the thing does.

"I just thought you might need it," Carrie repeated in the robot voice.

"Thank you," I said, reaching for her arm. "Now that you're here, why don't you come in?"

Carrie entered the house, and I saw her giving Alex a dirty look. Well, a Carrie version of a dirty look, which is just as hilarious as her trash talk.

"Hello Alex," she said.

Alex flipped off the TV. "Hey, Carrie. How's married life treating you?"

"Fine. Just fine." Carrie approached the DVD cabinet and retrieved my copy of *Pride and Prejudice*. "We should watch this!" she said to me with a gleam in her eye.

She knew exactly what she was doing.

"That sounds great." I took the DVD from Carrie, inserted it into the player, and aimed the all-in-one remote at the entertainment system.

And sure enough, the second the opening credits started rolling, Alex stood up from his seat on the couch and said, "I guess I'd better be going."

"Aww. That's too bad," Carrie said, making herself comfortable on the floor, a pillow under her elbows.

"Yeah," Alex said. "I have a pretty early meeting tomorrow."

"Well, have fun," Carrie said, eyes glued to the TV.

Alex put on his jacket and came up beside me. "I'm sorry if you think what happened just now was too forward of me," he whispered, his breath on my neck. "But I'd be lying if I said I won't be spending the rest of the night thinking about it. Good night, Annabelle."

Chapter 33

Ring, you stupid thing! Ring!

I shifted on my beach towel, flipped my cell open, and scrolled down the list of missed calls—again. But Isaac's number was no where on the list.

I slammed the phone shut and glanced miserably at my coworkers, who were all having a great time at the other end of Santa Cruz Beach.

When George had announced this little "work party" at our weekly editorial meeting, I'd decided I would come down with a convenient cold rendering me unable to make it, until Kat begged me to come and promised me two pairs of designer jeans and a black quilted Chanel bag if I did.

She knew just how to get to me.

But, honestly, I shouldn't have let myself be bribed. Because I was definitely not in the partying mood.

It had been one week. A week. And I hadn't heard a thing from Isaac. No calls. No emails. I would have settled for some words spelled out in shaving cream on my car. But I got nothing.

I knew he had a big project he was working on in Malibu, but did that mean he couldn't pick up the phone? Didn't he know how much I needed to hear from him?

Sure I had considered calling him tons of times, but he had said *he* would call. And I'd decided to let him make that first move.

But, as I sat on the beach, watching my coworkers laughing and chatting happily, I decided I couldn't take it anymore.

I speed-dialed Isaac's number, holding my breath as it rang.

"You've reached Isaac Matthews . . ."

Voicemail.

"Sorry I can't take your call right now . . ."

Wait a minute, I thought as I listened, *this is a new outgoing message. Why does Isaac have a new outgoing message?*

Suddenly my mouth went dry. Maybe he changed it because he wanted to add something like, "And guess what ladies; the wedding's off!"

My heart sped up as I continued to listen.

"Please leave your name and number, and I'll get back to you as soon as possible."

Oh thank goodness.

I was about to hang up when I heard something in the background; the very faint sound of a female voice. I smashed my ear into the phone, trying to make out what the voice was saying, but I couldn't quite tell. I ended the call and blinked, staring straight ahead, at nothing in particular.

Why was there a female voice in the background of Isaac's new outgoing message?

It's probably nothing, my brain said. *Someone probably walked by while he was recording the message.*

And I, being the reasonable gal that I am, agreed and put the phone away.

Oh wait, no I didn't.

I dialed again, this time turning my phone's volume all the way up.

"You've reached Isaac . . . I'll get back to you as soon . . ."

And there it was; the high feminine voice. I closed my eyes and listened to it say " . . . Riboflavin tacos."

What?

I dialed the number another three times, straining to make out the words, but I just couldn't do it. I'm usually pretty good at this kind of thing, but the ocean and crowds were too loud for me to hear properly.

I looked around to see if anyone was watching and then stuck my head under my beach towel, hoping it would muffle the sounds around me. I redialed the number.

"This is Isaac's phone." A live voice that absolutely, undoubtedly, 100 percent belonged to Chloe Payne answered.

Stunned, I quickly pushed the End Call button.

I removed the towel from my head and stared at the phone in my hand, an icy blanket seeming to cover me. And before I knew what was happening, I was throwing my phone into the ocean. I don't know what I was thinking. It ended up being a very expensive thing to do.

Tears stung my eyes as my mind raced with horrible thoughts. For some reason, Isaac didn't want to speak to me. And he was changing things in his life, like his out-going message. But worst of all, Chloe Payne was answering his phone—the phone I'd called so many times just to hear his voice.

"Did you just chuck your phone into the ocean?"

I forced back the tears, cleared my throat, and looked over my shoulder. There stood Alex, dressed in the pair of loose-fitting board shorts and T-shirt that had made Katrina grab me and whisper, "I thought you said George told you Alex wasn't coming. If I'd known I would have worn my red Missoni suit! He looks seriously hot."

"I was tired of dealing with bad reception," I said nonchalantly as I blocked the sound of Chloe's voice answering Isaac's phone out of my mind. I was not going to let Alex see me upset over Isaac.

Not again.

"Aha." Alex nodded, the sun bathing him like a special-effect.

"Aha, indeed."

Alex used a hand to shield his eyes. "Are you avoiding me?"

"Of course not," I said before returning my gaze forward.

It was a lie. I had been avoiding Alex and dodging his calls ever since he'd tried to . . . I don't even want to say it.

Alex sat down on the sand next to me, and I noticed a group of teenage girls looking at him as he leaned back into his tanned arms. "Well if you're not avoiding me, I guess you won't mind me sitting here."

"Nope," I said, staring straight ahead at a girl trying to teach her boyfriend how to surf.

"Why aren't you hanging out with the group?" Alex asked.

"Just felt like a little peace and quiet," I answered.

"Have a lot on your mind?"

"Not really," I said, channeling my inner ice queen.

Alex looked over at me, and I could feel his gaze on my cheek. "Well I'd be lying if I said I wasn't thinking about high school right now."

"Yep high school was cool." *And apparently my inner ice queen likes to speak in rhyme.*

"It was cool," Alex said. "And I have to admit, I've been thinking about it a lot lately."

With that my head snapped to the right, and I glared at Alex, all the despondence inside of me suddenly transferring to him. "What the heck is wrong with you? We're at a work party right now, *work* party. And you're over here hitting on me."

"Who says I'm hitting on you?" Alex asked, the left corner of his mouth curving upward so slightly someone who didn't know him probably wouldn't have noticed.

I rolled my eyes. "Please," I said. "Just . . . leave me alone. I was having a perfectly nice time before you came over here."

Alex moved like he was about to get up. "Okay. I'll leave if you want me to.

I nodded my head, and Alex began to stand. But before he left, five words flew out of my mouth. "Why did you do that?"

Alex sat back down. "Why did I do what?"

I looked to make sure no one from work was within earshot. "You know what. One second you were helping me like . . . almost like you were my friend and the next second you were trying to . . ." I lowered my voice to a whisper, glaring at Alex like I believed everything that was wrong in my life was his fault. " . . . kiss me."

My words hung in the air and Alex, the guy who had a quip for everything, was completely silent.

Suddenly uncomfortable, I was about to say something—anything—to change the subject like, "Hey, so this global warming thing sure stinks," when Alex looked over at me, his face sincere.

"The same reason I suggested we have the quarterly work party here," he said. "I wanted you to remember."

Alex's words made my skin kind of prickle, and I turned my gaze away from him to a breaking wave in the distance.

Alex cleared his throat. "I know you don't think I'm a very good guy, Annabelle. And I understand why. But I thought maybe if we came here . . . maybe you'd let me explain."

"Explain?" I said, my voice still agitated. "Explain what?"

"Explain what happened back then."

"I know what happened. You saw this cute new girl, and you decided you'd rather be with her." The words felt strange, like they were half eighteen-year-old me and half twenty-four-year-old me. "Apparently that's the story of my—" I stopped myself from finishing the awful sentence.

Alex's expression was almost pained. "That's still what you think? You're so far off."

"It's okay," I said, chancing a look in his direction. "We really don't need to talk about this now. It was a long time ago."

"It's not okay," Alex said. "I can't stand the thought of you not knowing the truth."

"What are you talking about?"

Alex's jaw clenched then unclenched. "I was scared, Annabelle. I was so unbelievably in love with you that it scared me to death. And I knew I wasn't going to college with you and you'd find someone else, and I just didn't want to deal with that. I never told you this, but my parents told me if I went to Cal Poly they wouldn't help me at all. They basically said they'd completely cut me off. They wanted me to go somewhere with a nationally ranked business school."

I blinked my eyes. "Like Columbia."

Alex shook his head as if disturbed by the memory. "Yes."

I felt my mind reel at this revelation. His parents basically forced him to go to Columbia? Forced him to . . .

"Why in the world didn't you tell me this back then?" I asked. "It would have hurt. But not the way seeing you with Rona did."

Alex looked at me so deeply I was sure he could see every line on my face. "I just knew if I talked to you I would have done anything to be with you. I would have gone against my parents. You didn't deserve that kind of pressure. It just seemed easier to pretend I liked someone else. I took the dumb, cowardly way out, and I'm so sorry. So sorry you didn't know the truth all this time."

"So you never . . . with Rona you . . ."

"I never had feelings for her."

"Why are you telling me this now?" I asked. "What do you think this is going to accomplish?"

Alex rubbed his chin with one hand. "Do you think everything happens for a reason?"

Yes. But I had a feeling I shouldn't say so.

"I do," Alex said. "I've been thinking a lot about you and about how stupid I was to let you go. Back in New York, I thought I saw you all the time. In restaurants. At plays. One time, I chased down this poor lady, thinking it was you, and she mistook me for a mugger. She beat me with her purse. What do you people put in those things, bricks?

"Anyway . . . what I'm getting at is . . . obviously I don't know the specifics of what happened with you and Isaac. But I can't help but think that the way everything has worked out, is more than just a coincidence."

I gulped, suddenly afraid of where this was headed.

"Does he know the story about how you got that?" Alex pointed to a tiny, nearly invisible scar on my ankle that I'd gotten when I somehow managed to paper mache my leg to the huge chicken-wire otter on the senior float.

"I'm not sure I've mentioned it."

"Does he know that you got so sick with a fever that April that you heard the song 'MMMBop' on KDON 102.5 and asked me if aliens had invaded America and taken over the radio?"

I pressed my lips tightly closed, as if to signify to Alex that I wasn't going to answer the question.

"And he obviously doesn't know how much you love Monterey. If he did, he'd know you'd never want to leave it. Everything is here: your family, your friends, your chance to be editor-in-chief of a bridal magazine, your whole life."

The words made my neck hot. I stared out at the Pacific Ocean and thought about how similar, but very different, the view was in Southern California. And before I knew what was happening, I felt tears welling up in my eyes again. I tried to fight them with everything in me, but there was no use. I stared straight ahead as the warm drops fell down my face.

"Why doesn't he know?" I said in a tiny voice, almost as if I were asking myself the question. "Why doesn't he know me?"

"I don't know," Alex said in a gentle voice.

I rested my face in my hands. "Why doesn't he call me? Why does it seem like I have been completely forgotten after just one week? Why is Chloe answering his phone?"

"I don't know," Alex said again. And I noticed something strange in his voice, like he was suddenly uncomfortable.

"Maybe he doesn't love me," I said, my voice choked by the

tears. "Maybe he never did."

Alex gazed at my profile and moved a strand of hair off my face. I sat there, frozen, completely shocked by the gesture. "I don't know if he did or if he didn't. But I do know this: He could never and will never love you the way I do."

Alex's words pounded in my ears, and I suddenly found it hard to breathe, like I had been swallowed up in one of the waves of the ocean. The colors and sounds around me all seemed to blend together, like when you're almost but not quite asleep.

After a beat of stunned silence, I opened my mouth to speak. But no words came out.

"You don't have to say anything," Alex said. "I know you're dealing with a lot right now and have a lot to work out. But I really believe with a little bit of time, you'll find the truth. You'll realize we belong together."

Alex gazed at me for what seemed like an eternal minute. Then he stood up and without another word jogged away on the sand, up toward the boardwalk.

Completely and utterly gobsmockunned—a combination of gobsmacked, shocked, and stunned, which is the only way I can think to describe how I felt—I lay back on my towel and looked up at the gulls in the partly cloudy sky, trying to wrap my mind around what had just happened.

As I stared heavenward, memories of Alex and me flooded my brain. All of those memories I'd worked so hard to forget. The memories I honestly thought I had been making with the first and last love of my life.

And as those memories peeked out of the crevices of my mind, Alex's words mingled with them, like subtitles to a movie. "You'll find the truth. You'll realize we belong together."

Chapter 34

"I hate you," Katrina said.

It was Monday afternoon, and Alex's assistant Kim had stopped by my desk to ask me if I wanted to take a look at "my future office." Kat had insisted on coming with me.

And the second I swung the cherrywood and glass door open, both of our jaws dropped. The place looked like something out of a movie. Like an office a high-powered New York editor would have.

"I still don't know if I'm taking the job," I said as we stepped inside. "No need to hate me yet."

"Oh, please," Katrina said. "You're so taking the job. Isaac's going to call you—within the next twenty-four hours I'm betting—and tell you he's been in the hospital or something and that's why he's been MIA, and then you'll work things out and he'll tell you to take the job and you two will get back to being disgustingly adorable again."

I would have been more bothered by Kat's suggestion that something may have happened to Isaac if I hadn't already wondered the same thing the night before the work party and called Isaac's family so I could allay my fears.

Yep. I'm not proud of it, but I called Malette, posing as a researcher conducting a survey about the quality of medical care in America, and asked her a few questions—including if she had any family members who had recently experienced an accident, illness, or hospitalization.

She'd said no, and told me she thinks the American medical system is worse than that reality show where people do dance routines with their pets.

So, no matter how I came upon the information, I knew nothing terrible had happened to Isaac.

"This place is insane," Katrina said as she slid her hand across the chic, modern desk and gazed out at the panoramic view of the Monterey Bay.

"It is . . . pretty amazing." I shoved aside my feelings about the whole Isaac situation—and the *other situation* I was currently dealing with by pretending it hadn't happened—and tried to take everything in. It wasn't every day I got to walk into a sleek amazing office that could possibly be mine.

I lowered myself into the supple leather chair behind the desk and noticed there were controls on the right armrest. Apparently, I could warm the chair or even set it to massage my back. Wow.

I spun like a kid on a merry-go-round and looked out at the ocean. I imagined myself spinning around and looking out to the sea for inspiration when I was working on a big project. The inspiration-view from my current desk is the back of a podiatrist's office.

I was lost in the scenery when I heard Katrina gasp from the other side of the room. "You have got to be kidding me!"

I looked over my shoulder. "What?"

"Get over here."

I joined Katrina outside what appeared to be a simple coat closet. But the closet did not contain hangers for coats. No. It contained everything a girl needs at work but never has with her. A chenille blanket for when it gets cold. A pair of slippers for those "Why did I wear these five inch stilettos?" days. A basket filled with lotions, creams, serums, and mists with a note attached that said: "Annabelle, give these a try to see what your future holds."

"Is this stuff La Mer?" Katrina asked, her voice almost reverent as she pulled a jar of face cream from the basket. "Oh, I so hate you!"

I lifted my eyebrows. "Keep it."

Katrina looked like I'd just given her a jar of gold and patted some onto her cheeks. Then she moved away from the closet and plopped down in the office's sitting area—which was complete with an overstuffed couch, two art deco chairs, a gourmet cocoa maker, and a spread of pastries that were displayed neatly on a lucite table. Katrina nibbled on a cookie. "I'm so hanging out with you up here all the time."

I plopped down in another chair across from her. "If I take the—"

"Yeah, yeah," Katrina cut me off, "if you take the job. So did you hear the latest gossip?" she asked, focusing one eye on the door.

I didn't answer. No matter how I answered, she was going to tell me anyway.

"Apparently our new publisher has eyes for someone in the office."

I felt my heart jump at the words. "Oh, really?" I said, my voice all high and squeaky.

Katrina nodded. "Uh huh. Josephine, that new girl in advertising, said he was all over a girl at the work party on Saturday. She saw him with her down on the beach."

I gulped. "Oh, uh, I'm sure he was just trying to be nice to, you know, everyone. Boost office morale and all that."

"Well he was trying to boost something all right," Kat said. "Josephine said she saw him kiss the girl."

"What?" My head shot up in shock, and suddenly I found myself flying backward in my chair until I made a loud clunk on the floor. "I'm sure they didn't kiss," I said from my spot on the ground.

"Oh my goodness! Are you okay?" Katrina hopped up from her seat and came to my side, holding out her hand.

"Oh, yes, totally," I said as I let her help me up. I smoothed my hair as if it were nothing that I had just toppled over. "So . . . about this girl. Did Josephine get a good look at her? You know . . . did she see who it was?" I rested my hip against the couch and looked at Katrina.

"Look at you," she said. "My evil gossipy ways have rubbed off."

"No. It's not that. I'm just . . . curious." I shrugged as if to say I didn't care at all about this gossip, which was a surefire way to get Katrina to spill any details she hadn't yet disclosed.

Katrina rubbed her hands together, cleansing them of cookie crumbs. "She didn't see much, but she did say the girl isn't as pretty as someone you would expect Alex Pearson to pick. Josephine said she looks a little bit like a gopher."

"I do not!"

Katrina frowned at me.

I cleared my throat and laughed uncomfortably. "Sorry. I thought you said Josephine said *I* look like a gopher and I was like . . . *What?!*"

"No," Katrina said slowly. Then I swear I saw her eyes scan my face as if she were checking to see if I did in fact resemble one.

"Oh thank goodness," I sighed a little too dramatically. "But still . . . I have to say I don't really think it's very nice for *Josephine* to be going around saying mean things about people. I mean first of all, how close was she to this girl? Maybe she couldn't see her very well. Plus, a lot of things could have affected how the girl looked. Like the sun. And . . . you know . . . plate tectonics."

"Plate tectonics," Katrina said, her face blank.

Knock. Knock.

I jumped at the sound and looked at the half-ajar door.

"Annabelle." Kim poked her blonde head inside. "Alex would like to see you in the conference room."

A feeling of dread instantly gripped me. "Okay. I'll be right there."

Katrina raised her perfect eyebrows and grabbed a few more cookies. "Maybe you can ask him who the girl was."

I took a long, deep breath as I walked to the conference room. This would be my first contact with Alex since our conversation on the beach. And I had no idea what I was going to say to him about what had happened. None. But, luckily, for now, all I had to worry about discussing with him was business. And I was immensely grateful for that. Still, my hand was sweaty as I turned the doorknob and stepped inside the room.

Alex was sitting at the middle of the table, dressed in the kind of suit you'd see on a slick and handsome businessman in a movie. "Hello, Annabelle."

"Hello." I walked toward Alex with a little swagger in my step that I hoped made me look completely nonchalant.

Alex watched me, a wrinkle in his brow. "Why are you walking like a rapper?'

"I'm not." I sat down in the nearest seat and looked three chairs to my left at Alex. "Kim told me you wanted to talk to me?"

"Yes. I wanted to know how you like your new office."

"It's not my office yet," I said, staring at my lap. "But I like it fine. Thank you."

Alex moved like he was going to stand. "Great. So are you ready?"

"For . . . ?"

"I'm taking you to lunch."

Lunch with Alex? No way. The last time I was alone with him something very, very bad happened.

Make that the last two times.

"That's very nice of you. But I actually have plans." *To sit at my desk and eat stale Triscuts.*

"Cancel them," Alex said. "I have something important to discuss with you."

I looked at Alex warily. "About the magazine?"

"Of course."

Chapter 35

"I didn't know this place was up here." I looked around the classy-yet-comfy restaurant hidden on the top floor of the Monterey Beach Hotel.

"You're going to love the lobster pizza," Alex said. "It doesn't sound like much, but it's amazing."

"Well thank you for the suggestion." I sipped my Shirley Temple and gazed down at the beach, where a woman was running with her dog.

"Thank *you* for joining me."

I turned away from the window and straightened the napkin on my lap. "No problem," I said, my voice curt. "I guess we should get down to business."

Alex nodded. "Yes, we should. So it seems you have a big decision to make over the next couple days."

"I do."

"Well. I was hoping I could ask you a few questions about your plans for the launch of *Central Coast Weddings*. That is, presuming you accept the job."

I crossed my arms. "Okay."

"First question: I was thinking a 'how they met' column might be good for the magazine. Do you remember the first time we met?"

I felt my chest turn hot and then cold. "What kind of question is that?"

"It's going somewhere," Alex said, gesturing with his hands.

"Well then, yes," I said, my jaw tight. "I remember the first time we met."

Alex leaned forward in his chair and fixed his eyes on me. "I do too. I remember your perfect smile. And your adorable laugh. I remember how I wanted to know everything about you."

"Alex," I said, my eyes darting to the diners at the tables near ours, "I don't know what you're trying to do. But this is not the time or the place."

Alex smiled a pleading smile that would make a lesser woman melt. "Come on, Annabelle, just bear with me."

I shook my head vehemently. "I can't—"

Alex cut me off. "The first time I saw you after I came back to Monterey and you were dressed in that great yellow dress, your hair all wavy and gorgeous around your face, I knew that everything I felt back then was real. And that it couldn't be erased with time or distance."

"Alex. Please. Not now."

"I've been in love with you for seven years, Annabelle. It has to be now. I know maybe this isn't the best time for you. That you have other stuff going on. That you're confused. That it's too soon. But I really think everything that's happened is because we are meant to be together. And we've both known it since we were eighteen years old. I made the mistake of letting you go seven years ago, and I will not make that mistake again.

"So: next question." Alex paused to remove a robin's egg blue ring box from his suit pocket and set it on the table. "Will you . . ."

He slowly opened the box, giving me the perfect view of what was inside. And what was inside was a platinum band bearing the hugest marquise-cut diamond I have ever seen. I'm talking HUGE. I'm talking borrow it and wear it to the Oscars big. "Marry me," he said, his expression somehow intense and soft at the same time.

Suddenly my body felt like it was covered in pins, and my heart seemed on the verge of cardiac arrest.

"I want to give you the perfect life, Annabelle. I want to make you so incredibly happy that you wake up each morning with that perfect smile on your face. And I want you to wake up . . . next to me."

I felt myself shoot up from my chair, my legs dangerously wobbly. "I . . . I have to go!"

And before I knew what was happening, I was jogging through the restaurant, toward the nearest exit.

"Annabelle, wait!" Alex called, jogging after me.

Ignoring him, I burst through the restaurant's front entrance and landed on the sidewalk where I took a sharp left and ran as fast as my little feet would carry me. I didn't know where I was running to, only that it needed to be far, far away.

I hadn't run far when, like a lighthouse appearing in the fog, I saw a cab pulling away from the curb in the distance. I sprinted for that cab, waving my arms. "Taxi!" I screamed.

The cabbie slammed on his brakes and I jumped in, hollering, "Go! Go! Go!"

The cab driver didn't hesitate, putting his foot heavy on the gas just in time for me to see Alex standing on the sidewalk in front of the restaurant, looking broken in a way I'd never seen before.

⚜

"Turn right up there," I said pointing to the street I grew up on.

The driver nodded.

I rubbed my hands together, anxious to talk to Mom. She'd help me figure this all out. Most likely with the help of something freshly baked and chocolate.

We were almost to my street when the driver stopped at the crosswalk in front of the neighborhood church. I looked with interest at the clump of dressed-up people on the church lawn and the stretch-limo parked along the curb.

Must be a quinceañera, I thought.

But then the church doors opened and a bride and groom emerged.

Apparently Monday *was* the new Saturday in weddings.

The cab driver waited at the crosswalk as wedding-goers crossed to get to their cars, obviously to go on to the wedding reception.

I stared out the window at the bride and groom on the church steps. The bride looked beautiful in a white chiffon gown and waist-length veil. And the groom was just staring at her, completely enthralled. He held onto her hand like he was lucky just to be touching her.

And then, as the couple walked to the waiting limo, I saw him help her with her veil. It was a tiny gesture, almost unremarkable, but there was just something in the way he did it that sent an ache into my chest.

"Excuse me sir," I said to the driver. "Could you please take me to the *Central Coast Living* Offices: 1805 Cypress Drive?"

"Of course, Miss."

Chapter 36

"Alex we need to talk!" I threw open Alex's office door and there sat Kim, in his leather chair, shoving the gourmet biscotti he kept in his bottom drawer into her mouth. Her legs were up on the desk, crinkling a pile of papers.

I blinked my eyes in shock. "Oh. Oops. I was looking for Alex."

Kim's face turned a deep red. "He's not here," she said, her words almost impossible to make out due to the cookies. She covered her mouth and chewed swiftly. "He just went to the conference room with the hiring committee."

"Okay. Thanks." I turned to leave.

"I . . . um . . . just realized the biscotti were about to expire," Kim said to my back. "I didn't want them to go to waste . . ."

I waved a you-don't-have-to-explain-to-me wave over my shoulder and took off.

I was just around the corner from the conference room when I heard the sound of a group talking. I thought nothing of it until I heard Jarvis, the intimidating English guy from the hiring committee, say my name. " . . . Miss Pleasanton simply . . ." His voice disappeared behind the closing conference room door.

My pulse was racing, urging me to go into the room after

Alex so I could say what I came to the office to say—but I didn't.

Something just wasn't right about the way Jarvis had said my name.

So, suddenly feeling very Nancy Drew, I slowly moved to the corner and eyed the conference room door. I could just make out four large fuzzy figures through the frosted window panel. Must have been the men from the hiring committee—Jarvis, Patrick, Tim, and Alex—since Helen, the lone female on the committee, had already gone home to New York.

Something was up. I could just feel it.

And before I knew it, I was looking to see if anyone was coming down the hall and pressing my ear to the conference room door.

"I appreciate the hard work you all have put into getting *CCW* off the ground," Alex was saying. "And since a number of you have voiced your concerns about the editor-in-chief position, I thought it best to meet before you all head back to New York."

Well, Alex was quite the compartmentalizer wasn't he? An hour ago he was proposing to me and chasing me down the streets of Monterey, and now he was all business.

And what was he talking about, "concerns about the editor-in-chief position?"

I pressed my ear even harder to the door and heard Alex clear his throat. "Why don't we start with you, Jarvis?" he said.

"Thank you, Alex. My main concern is—"

My eavesdropping on Jarvis's response was interrupted by the sound of footsteps coming down the hallway. I moved my head away from the door just in time to see one of the temps walking by with a stack of papers in one hand and an iPhone in the other.

"Hi," I said, with a weird wave. "I was just . . . polishing this door." I pulled the sleeve of my cardigan over my hand and pretended to, well, polish the door. Then I gave the wood a little knock and stood frozen, terrified that someone inside had heard.

Luckily no one did.

The temp looked up from her phone just long enough to shoot me a glare that said she had no time for me or my shenanigans.

I kept up my polishing charade until she was gone and then returned to my listening position.

" . . . You know we all trust your judgment," Jarvis was saying in his scratchy, made-me-want-to-offer-him-a-cough-drop voice. "But we want this magazine to be of the same caliber as the others under Pearson's umbrella. We would hope someone who understands the business would be in charge. I know our decision was split and that you ultimately made the choice, but Annabelle Pleasanton?"

Chuckles masked as coughs sounded in the room. I hadn't heard laughs like that in the conference room since one of the guys in tech support patched into one of George's PowerPoint presentations and replaced it with a Star Wars dub video from YouTube.

What was making them laugh? And why had the laughter come right after the mention of my name?

"I know Miss Pleasanton was an unorthodox choice," Alex said.

"Yes," I heard Patrick respond. "We're just voicing our concerns now because we don't want to see this magazine fail because we didn't speak up."

Wait just one second.

The committee thought I would fail? And that I would take the new magazine with me?

"I, for one, thought we had many promising applicants to choose from," Tim said, his deep voice easy to recognize. "And since Miss Pleasanton has not yet accepted the job, I think if we were to rescind the offer now, we would be fine. Much better off, in my opinion, than if we do nothing."

He wanted to rescind the offer? He thought I was that bad?

I suddenly felt like someone had taken a fire poker and hit me right in the gut with it. I moved away from the door. I didn't want to hear another word.

But . . . it was like I had to. Like when I was in the bathroom stall in eighth grade and heard the popular girls spraying their hair with Salon Selectives in front of the mirror, talking about the hairstyle I'd decided to copy from *Fab* magazine, and I just had to know what they were going to say . . .

"You really think our advertisers will want to be associated with this kind of ridiculous sap?" Jarvis was saying when I pressed my ear to the door again. "'Brides Who Give Back'?" He said the title of my proposed theme for our premier issue in an incredulous tone. "Listen to this rubbish from her sample article: 'Food Fight catering company not only offers brides and grooms the opportunity to select delicious fare for their wedding celebrations but also to give to a worthy cause while doing so.' We're trying to put together a modern bridal magazine, not start a non-profit organization!"

"I have to agree," Tim added. "I just got married on Valentine's Day, and I have to say, my wife would definitely tell you, a wedding isn't about changing the world, it's about a pretty dress and cake and flowers. And that's what readers will want to read about."

It is now! I heard myself cry inside. *Because no one will take a step out of that box! But if someone just tried I know it could be amazing!*

"I know Annabelle's writing is pretty bad," I heard Alex say.

My eyes went wide.

"But I have my reasons for hiring her for this job. And I assure you, once we start work on the premier issue, I'll steer her in the right direction."

What???

Alex continued. "And if she can't get it right, we'll just move her around. Give her a nice little office in a corner and a job title where she can't make waves. I'll have no problem getting her to take whatever job we want her to take. I'm good at convincing her of things. Two days ago, I convinced her that the reason I cheated on her in High School was because my parents made me."

The room of men chuckled in frat-boy fashion.

Alex joined in the laughter. "And she bought it hook, line, and sinker."

I moved away from the door as if it had stung me, and my ears and mouth burned, like I'd eaten a whole box of Hot Tamales.

Suddenly, I was eighteen again, staring through the window of that Italian restaurant, seeing Alex's arm around Rona Bircheck.

Without thinking, I threw the conference room door open, and the four men inside looked up at me, Alex's face registering that he knew he was caught, and that he was already coming up with ways to charm his way out of it.

And there it was again, that overwhelming urge to throw something.

Anything.

Now, this is not to say you should give into overwhelming urges but . . .

I reached into my handbag and retrieved a few of the products that had been in the closet of my "future office." I pelted Alex with the face mist, the hand cream, the sea algae foot lotion.

The other guys at the table moved out of the way, looking at me like I belonged on that cable TV show *Snapped*, as the foot lotion exploded on contact, sending the greenish goo all over Alex's suit.

"We, uh, we'll leave you two alone," Jarvis said, looking at me as if I had just confirmed all of his concerns about me.

The men all booked it for the exit.

And then, there I was, alone with Alex, the room so quiet I could actually hear my heart pounding in my chest.

"Annabelle," Alex said, standing. "So . . . I take it you . . .

heard some of that . . ."

I didn't respond. I was currently putting all my power into not lunging at him.

"I had to say those things," Alex claimed, turning up the charm as expected. "I can't always just pull rank around here."

"You are such a liar," I said, telling myself that no matter what, I would not cry.

Alex looked down at the goo on his suit.

"Just tell me the truth," I demanded. "Why did you offer me the job?"

Alex leaned against the table behind him and lowered his head. "I thought you were right for it, Annabelle. That's the truth. And, yeah, sure, if I'm being completely honest, maybe part of the reason I think you're so right for it is because I want to be with you. To see you everyday. And when I found out your fiancé was offered a job with Pilar Sanchez I—" Alex stopped abruptly, like he knew he'd just let too much slip.

I felt my eyes narrow. "What did you just say?"

Alex shifted uncomfortably. "I wanted to be with you. I—"

"I never told anyone in this office that Isaac's job offer was with Pilar Sanchez." I looked up to the ceiling, everything hitting me at once. "That's why you offered me the editor-in-chief position. That's what it all boils down to, isn't it? You wanted to win."

"Annabelle—"

"It was a trick," I said, cutting Alex off. "You pretend to help me with my portfolio and offer me my dream job and a mansion so I won't leave Monterey. And then you build me up, pretending my writing is great, and then humiliate me in front of a room full of executives. I cannot believe how manipulative you are! I put my engagement on hold, Alex! I told the man I love that I wanted to stay in Monterey and yeah, part of it was that I'm not a huge fan of L.A., but another part, a big part of my reason was this . . . lie! How could you do this to me?!"

"Because *I* want to be the man you love," Alex said, coming toward me.

"Don't you even," I said, putting a hand up. "Don't you come near me!" The words came out in a shout that physically hurt.

"I had to do what I had to do," Alex said. "I love you. More than you know. And when you love someone, you'll do anything to be with them."

"No," I said, snapping my head toward him. "When you love someone you tell them the truth. You tell them the truth even if it means they go to L.A. and decide you're not worth it and get together with perfect-ballerina/pageant-girl Chloe and you lose them forever. You do not love me. You never have."

"I do, Annabelle. And I want—"

"You know, Alex," I said, interrupting him. "Today at the restaurant there was a moment when I thought maybe you were right, maybe there was something between us, maybe this did all happen for a reason. But then I saw this bride and groom on the steps of the church by my house, and I knew. I knew there was nothing real between you and me. And then I came here and found out the only reason any of this *happened* is that you made it happen.

"I spent seven years wondering what it would be like for you to come back and say you were wrong, say that you still loved me. But now I realize I don't want what you think is love."

Alex winced at my words, looking defeated.

I opened the conference room door. "I'll be out of my office by tomorrow at noon, and I'll be out of the house by ten tonight," I said.

And then I stepped into the hall and left Alex Mikels behind me for the last time.

Chapter 37

The drive home was not a pretty picture.

I was so mad at Alex, so mad at myself for ever believing a word he said. And, I'm ashamed to say, I may have been taking the anger out on my fellow motorists. I was cutting people off, merging without manners, and honking at slow drivers only to pass them and see little old tourist couples with their Monterey baseball caps, Oklahoma state plates, and bobble head dogs on the dash.

When I finally reached the house, I got out of the car and an unbelievable sadness overcame me. For once, I had honestly thought all the pieces of my life were fitting together: amazing man, great work, lovely home. And when Isaac proposed in front of Sleeping Beauty's Castle, it was like some kind of sign that a fairytale life really was possible.

Well I should have known. Fairytales don't happen to me.

Even when I played Snow White in the tenth grade play— because I had the whitest skin, not because I was the best Snow White (so Kendra Shaw, the fake-tanned cheerleader, pointed out)—I managed to hit the prince, who was the pitcher on the baseball team and Kendra's boyfriend, in the head with my fiber-glass coffin when he came in to kiss me, sending him to the hospital with a gash that required fifteen stitches.

I should've learned my lesson back then.

It didn't take long to pack my belongings—and a few other things I gave to myself as parting gifts: all the beauty products from the guest suite bathroom, a bit of gourmet food from the kitchen, and all the fancy toilet paper in the house (hey, I'd gotten a bit used to it)—since I hadn't brought much.

With two rolling suitcases behind me, I was soon in the front hall, feeling like I was checking out of a really fancy hotel. I turned off the lights and was about to leave when I remembered my Fresh Food Fanatics T-shirt. The maid had left me a note saying she had put it in Alex's office because she wasn't sure if it was mine or his.

I ran back upstairs and flipped on the office light. I grabbed my shirt from the desk and underneath it saw a large brown envelope. And, I'm telling you, there was just something about that envelope. Something about the fact that the maid had left my shirt right on top of it, like she was telling me something.

So I opened it.

Inside I found a stack of papers. The top one was a letter on Alex's personal stationery.

Bridgett,

If any phone messages, packages, or mail come for Miss Pleasanton while she is away, please put them in this envelope. I will deliver them to her personally.

Alex

An uncomfortable prickle grazed the hairs on the back of my neck. Why was Alex keeping my messages?

I read the next note in the stack, this one written in the maid's handwriting, on the yellow paper she used when taking phone messages.

10:16 a.m. Saturday, February 28

Isaac called for you, Annabelle. He wants you to know he's thinking about you.

Also, he's using a new cell phone with an L.A. number. The number is: 555-209-7653. He will try your cell.

Oh no! I remembered getting calls from a strange number all that weekend, but I'd rejected them and then set my cell phone to automatically block the number!

I read the next message.

7:30 a.m. Monday, March 2

Isaac called for you, Annabelle. He said he's sorry for calling so early. He's been having a hard time getting a hold of you, so he tried to catch you before you left for work.

I thought back to last Monday. I was at work all day. Why hadn't he just called me there?

My mouth dropped open as the answer came to mind. The day after Isaac and I put the wedding plans on hold, Alex moved me to that new office and told me my voicemail would automatically be forwarded. Another lie, for sure.

I flipped furiously through the messages, my heart racing as I read the stack. There were at least three for every day I'd thought Isaac was avoiding me. These added to the ones I'd surely missed at work . . . the poor guy must have tried to call me a hundred times!

How could Alex do this to me? What a cruel, conniving little creep!! I mean, making me believe he thought I was good at my job and offering me one he didn't believe I was qualified for was one thing. But this . . . this was the kind of thing you see people on 20/20 listing as "signs we should have seen that told us Tommy was headed for a life of crime."

I read through the rest of the messages. Everything Isaac wanted me to know. Everything I needed to know. And to think I had convinced myself he didn't care. Convinced myself he had forgotten me, moved on.

A horrible feeling of dread caught in my throat. What if Isaac was thinking all those exact same things about me?! What if Chloe had pulled an Alex and confessed her obvious love for him and . . . Frantically, I picked up my cell and dialed the L.A. number on the paper in my hand.

Voicemail.

I hung up. I didn't want to talk to voicemail. I needed to talk to Isaac. I drummed my fingers on nothing in the air, trying to formulate some kind of plan. As I thought, my eyes caught on a few items protruding from the top of the brown envelope. I dumped them out to find a box of Milk Duds, a Cold Stone gift card, and a blue notebook.

I furrowed my brow as I opened the notebook. Inside was a folded paper with my name on the front. I unfolded the page.

Hello Love of my Life,

I'm not exactly sure what's going on with you right now. And I guess I understand that. It wasn't right of me to ask you to give up everything that's important to you. But I want you to know I'd do anything, give anything to be with you. I need you in my life always. I've tried everything to let you know what you mean to me, but since you seem to be avoiding me, I guess it hasn't been clear. I think this will be clear.

I love you,

Isaac

I opened the notebook and read the first page, which was sort of a handwritten title page. There, in Isaac's adorably guyish writing was:

Isaac's Blue Notes

What? Isaac's Blue Notes?

I flipped to the next page.

Blue Note #1: Annabelle Pleasanton

Why She's Noteworthy: Annabelle was actually the person who inspired me to do this. I've never been much of a journal keeper, but I thought this would be a good place to start. Annabelle has this pink notebook she carries around with her. She writes in it when she meets someone who inspires her. It's such an Annabelle thing to do. She's the kindest, sweetest woman I've ever met, and she sees people in such an incredible way. So I thought it would be a good thing for me to do. Of course, pink is kind of girly, so I decided on blue.

Blue Note #2: Arthur Naylor

Why He's Noteworthy: Arthur's been cutting my hair for about two years now. He has this tiny, hidden barber shop in Seaside. He's a disabled war veteran, and his right leg and arm are pretty badly crippled, but despite any setbacks, he takes great pride in giving a good haircut. I spend probably three times as long at Arthur's as I would at another shop, but I really can't imagine going anywhere else. Arthur's stories, his reverence about what it means to be an American, just really astound me.

Blue Note #3: Katie Northington

Why She's Noteworthy: Katie is an adorable little ten-year-old girl who I met today when taking her family's portrait. Katie's been battling leukemia for the past year. When I met her family on Carmel Beach, where they wanted to have the photo taken, Katie gave me a handshake, and told me, "You better not get any of me blinking!" I was floored by her spunk, her wisdom, and the optimism that just radiated from her. I knew I had met someone remarkable. I have to say, of all the photo shoots I've ever done, that one was *by far* my favorite. There was just something about being behind the camera, seeing that angelic little fighter through the lens. I was pretty much floored by how much that ten-year-old girl taught me in the short time I was around her.

Blue Note #4: Annabelle Pleasanton

Why She's Noteworthy: I just have to write about Annabelle again. It's almost Christmas and Annabelle decided we needed to be "Santa's Elves"—her words, not mine—for a family. She asked me to look for someone and she would too and then we would choose. We ended up picking Katie's family, the Northingtons. We talked about them and, I admit it, we both got choked up thinking about what they all must be going through. Annabelle couldn't wait to start getting things together for the family. So you know those stores that have huge deals the day after Thanksgiving, starting at 4:00 in the morning? Annabelle went. She got in line the night before and even brought cocoa to give to people. That's just the kind of thing she does. She said once she got inside, a lady tried to fight her for a Barbie bike that was 75 percent off, but Annabelle won by pretending to see Dr. Phil. You wouldn't believe how much stuff she came back with. Stuff she paid for out of her own pocket, because, of course, she completely blew the budget we set. She's such an example to me of giving and kindness. I feel blessed to know such a wonderful woman. I think she would make an incredible wife.

Tears filled my eyes and fell onto the page. Isaac had said a lot of beautiful things to me in the time we'd been together, but this was beyond anything I could have ever imagined. For years, I had been filling my notebook with Pink Notes. But now I had made it into someone's Pink Notes. Okay, Blue Notes, but still. Someone felt I was noteworthy.

And I realized that was the most important thing I could be. I thought over the past while. In all of the time I'd spent engulfed in wedding-planning, job-applying, huge-house-enjoying madness I hadn't written a single Pink Note. In fact, the last one I'd written had been the day after Isaac proposed. In L.A.

Suddenly I knew exactly what I had to do.

Chapter 38

"You're sure about this?"

"Absolutely sure."

"You're crazy, you know."

I touched the condensation on the glass of water Jenna had given me when I came into her office at 5:50 pm for the emergency appointment. "Maybe. But I know this is right. Now, you only need my signature, right? Not mine and Isaac's."

Jenna nodded. "According to the Dream Wedding contract, you, the prize winner, get to call the shots."

"Great. Where do I sign?"

Jenna slid the papers across her desk, but stopped short of handing me the Waterman pen. "Why don't you take some time to think this over? I mean, once you sign these papers there's no going back. You're taking the cash instead of the wedding. And the amount is significantly less. One-third of the prize value."

"I know."

"You'll be giving up the dress, Love at First Bite—everything." Jenna's words came out the way someone would say, "You'll be giving up water and air."

"That's okay."

Jenna shook her head from side to side, eyes closed. "I

would really discourage making any pasty decisions."

I blinked. "Huh?"

"You know, like doing things too fast."

I couldn't help but smile. "I'm going to miss you Jenna. Thank you for everything. I'm sorry you didn't get to see your vision realized."

Jenna handed me the pen and waved a hand in the air. "I get paid no matter what. Maybe I'll use the cash to go to the Caribbean or something."

"That sounds like a great idea."

After I signed the papers, Jenna had me fill out a bank draft form and told me the money would be deposited into my account by eight the next morning.

"Thanks again Jenna," I said as I rose from my seat and went to the other side of the desk to hug her.

"Get out of here you crazy girl," she said, kissing my cheek.

My heart beating fast, I left the office and headed for my car.

Okay. Here goes nothing. This plan had better work.

It's not working!

I kicked the "easy to assemble" desk with a frustrated grumble. I have no idea in what universe the thing could have been considered "easy" to put together. I guess the same universe where little stick-figure men with circular hands as big as their heads can levitate screwdrivers—which the man on the inside of the instruction book was doing.

I took a sip of my fourth bottle of water and wiped the sweat from my face. I had no clue it would be this hard.

Oh wait, I can see you staring at the page in confusion. You have no idea what I'm doing, do you?

Well. Okay. I'll fill you in. I was in L.A.—turning the spare room in the house Isaac loved into a photography studio he'd adore.

I flew into LAX at about 7:00 pm. Then I got in my teeny, tiny, manual-doors-and-windows rental car and drove to a condo belonging to one Rona Bircheck. Yep.

From the comfort of Rona's immaculate living room, I filled her in on what had happened with me and Isaac. She obviously knew a lot of it, because it had gone from Isaac to Ethan to her, but she pretended it was the first time she'd heard it all. Then I dropped a wad of money on her coffee table, like I was in a Mafia movie or something, and asked her if she could let me into the Santa Monica house Isaac had showed me.

She said yes.

And then she told me something I never knew.

"I guess what Alex did shouldn't surprise me too much," she said, taking a sip from her mug of low-carb hot cocoa. (Honestly, low-carb cocoa, what's the point?) "He ditched me at the prom, and I found him in the parking lot kissing Christy Barber. He told me she had a dentist appointment on Monday and he was checking her mouth for loose fillings."

"Are you kidding me?" I asked, eyes wide with shock.

Rona nodded. "But I made up for it at school on Monday by starting the rumor that he wasn't eighteen, but twenty—because he'd been held back in kindergarten *twice*—and that it was illegal for him to date anyone at our school."

My jaw dropped. "No! *You* started that rumor?"

Rona raised her eyebrows and grinned into her cocoa mug.

I couldn't help thinking how weird it was the way life came full circle like that. No way would eighteen-year-old me ever think I would be in cahoots with Rona Bircheck.

Or saying the word *cahoots*.

So now I was in the house, having spent all night and morning working on the studio, sleeping for short bouts on the floor. (Rona had insisted on letting me sleep in her guest room, but I'd just asked to borrow a sleeping bag and pillow—I needed to work fast.)

And I have to admit, the studio looked pretty amazing. Well, besides the current lack of a desk.

I finished off my bottle of water—Mom had loaded me up with enough food and fluids for a week when I filled her in on my plan—and picked my handbag up off the floor.

It was time to do the craziest thing the plan required.

I flipped my phone open and dialed Isaac's old number, hoping to get Chloe.

As planned, she answered, and I felt my entire body tense at the sound of her voice. I repeated a Dr. Harmony mantra in my mind until I found the ability to speak.

"Hello mate," I said, for some reason deciding on the spot to disguise my voice by using an Australian accent. Not a very good one either. "I'm calling for Isaac Matthews."

"I'm sorry," Chloe said. "This is no longer Mr. Matthews's number. This is his agent, Chloe Payne. Is there something I can help you with?"

"You can start by moving to Mexico," I muttered.

"Excuse me?"

"Uh . . . Texaco. I just drove past one. Anyway, the reason I'm calling is I'm hoping to set up a meeting with Isaac, uh, Mr. Matthews, to talk about possibly photographing my . . ." I paused. I hadn't thought about what I was going to say at this part. "You know . . . scarferblarb," I mumbled into my hand. "Will he be available today?

"He has an opening this evening," Chloe said.

My jaw clenched at the words. It hurt to hear Chloe sound so . . . knowledgeable about Isaac. But I had to set the hurt aside—I was a woman on a mission.

"He has a shoot at the Santa Monica pier from six to eight tonight," Chloe continued. "Would you like to set something up for after that?"

I couldn't help the mix of hope and anxiety that bubbled up inside of me. "Okay. How about I meet him at the restaurant at the end of the pier after his shoot, say eight o'clock?"

"That should work," Chloe agreed. "I just need your name."

Um...

I quickly tried to think of a good Aussie name. *Wallaby...* *Boomerang...* "Uhh... Bloomin."

"Bloomin? That's ... unusual. And your last name?"

"Onion."

"Bloomin Onion?"

"That's right, mate."

"Do I know you?" Chloe asked, her voice suspicious. "Your voice sounds familiar."

"You're probably thinking of Nicole Kidman," I said quickly. "She and I are both from down under. Anyway, please tell Mr. Matthews that, uh, Bloomin will see him tonight. Thanks for your help."

I hung up and stared at the phone. The plan was in motion. Just one last thing to do. Well, make that two.

"Hello."

Linda, the woman I met during my last trip to Caring Blooms adjusted her bandana and smiled. "Hey there!" she said, obviously remembering me. "It's good to see you again. How's the story coming along?"

I bit my lip. "Well ... I'm no longer with the magazine."

"Oh, dear. I'm sorry."

"Don't be. It's actually a really good thing. So ... I'm here because I was hoping to get a bouquet of flowers. Something that will look good in a photography studio."

Linda nodded. "All right. We can do that. Let's see ... For a photography studio I'd probably suggest something white and simple that won't compete with all the color around. Maybe calla lilies."

"That sounds great."

"All right." Linda handed me a book filled with photos of bouquets and helped me pick out a modestly priced one in a pretty, square vase.

"I was also hoping to order 100 additional bouquets," I said.

Linda nodded. "We can do that. What type of event are they for?"

"No event. I just . . . the last time I was in here I heard you talking about the Crestview Care Center and how some of the residents didn't get Valentine's Day visitors. Well, I called the center and got a head count and thought, why not send them all bouquets—just because."

Linda gave me a sideways look. "You're serious."

"Yes. And the rest of the bouquets I'd like to have sent to the nurses stations at Saint John's Health Center in Santa Monica."

"You are my kind of lady," Linda said, pointing at me. "We can definitely do that. Did you just win the lotto or something?"

"Not exactly. It's just . . . something I need to do."

I filled out my flower order form and waited while Linda and another florist quickly put together the bouquet for Isaac's photography studio.

After a minute, she returned to the front. "Annabelle, this is ready for you. And we'll deliver the other bouquets by 5:00 pm tomorrow."

"Thanks so much." I got out my checkbook, ready to pay for my order with my second chunk of Dream Wedding payout money, the first chunk having gone to the good people at Home Depot.

"Thank *you*," Linda said. "I sometimes get used to all these celebrities who come in here and throw money at me for lavish parties and weddings to people they stay with for three months. But to have a young lady like yourself come in here and do something like this—that's what this place is really about."

I smiled as I took my flowers, gave Linda a wave, and left the shop. She was a Pink Note in every sense of the word, and I would do well to be more like her.

At least I was a little bit on my way.

My next stop, the Food Fight in Pacific Palisades was only a short drive away. The second I stepped inside, I was greeted by the incredible smell of freshly baked bread. My stomach growled at me, mad that I had neglected to fill it in hours.

No one was behind the shop's counter when I approached it, so I looked at the large menu on the wall and laughed at the clever names of the shop's goodies: "Frosting Face Sugar Cookies," "Black Eye Blueberry Tarts."

After just a few minutes, Hope, the woman I had met at the bridal fair, appeared behind the counter, wearing a white apron decorated with bright yellow, orange, and pink polka dots that coordinated with the shop's bright, cool, old-meets-new décor. I couldn't help but grin. I hadn't expected at all to see her, but it made what I was about to do so much cooler.

"Hello." Hope greeted me with a pleasant yet weary smile. "Can I help you?"

"Yes you can, actually. I met you at a bridal fair in Monterey and fell in love with your food and your cause. So . . . I decided to come in."

"That's absolutely wonderful! Are you looking to order your wedding cake?"

The question made a whole mess of thoughts and emotions rush through me. But I pushed them aside, focused on the task at hand. "Not this time. I'm actually here for . . . a bit of a gift."

"Okay, great. What can I get you?" Hope reached for a dull pencil that was conveniently placed behind her ear.

"I'd like half a dozen of your 'Chocolate on My Pants Cupcakes' please?"

"Okay. Perfect. I'll be right back with those."

Hope disappeared, and I looked around a bit, enjoying the humorous Groucho Marx-esque black-and-white photos of food fights on the walls. Judging by how cool the place was, I was surprised it wasn't completely full of people. In fact, it was completely empty besides me and a group of teens lounging at one of the tables as if they were in there own living room.

"Here you go."

I spun around as Hope returned, placing a clear cupcake-holder on the counter.

I reached for my wallet. "I hope you take checks."

"Sure do."

"Great." With a giddy little I-have-a-secret smile on my face, I filled out the check, put it on the counter, and quickly began to spin around, ready to run out the door.

The idea was to make a quick, good-bandit escape and for Hope to see the check once I was gone and be in total happy shock.

But of course, my attempt at a smooth 180 in my tennis shoes didn't go exactly as planned—my ankles got tangled together, and I stumbled in a very non-bandit-y manner—and by the time I was solidly on my feet, Hope had picked up the check.

"Wait a minute," she said, her eyes narrow as she examined it. "I think you made a mistake on here."

"Nope. Don't think so. Bye." I waved over my shoulder as I darted toward the door.

"Wait!" Hope cried. "I can't cash this. You put three extra zeroes on here." She waved the rectangular paper in the air.

"It's not a mistake," I said with a defeated sigh. "It was supposed to be a surprise."

"What?"

I moved back to the counter. "Well . . . it's a long story. But . . . I was on your website about a week ago, and I saw the cute little surfboard filled in with color to show how much more money you needed to raise to send the kids to the Surfers Healing camp in Cabo San Lucas. And I wished I could do something to help. And then, again another long story . . . I was presented with the opportunity to help. And that's why I'm here."

I looked across the counter at Hope and saw she was getting a little misty-eyed. "I can't . . . I don't know what to say. You have no idea what this means. You really don't." Hope let out a half-laugh. "The travel agent called today and said she could only hold the special package deals she reserved for us until midnight tonight. I told her we didn't have nearly enough money yet and that we may just have to wait until next year.

"It was heartbreaking. This trip is just what the kids need. And the parents, too—we planned some surprises for them: massages; room service meals. They are such courageous, amazing people. But, I thought, maybe it was all too much. Too big of an idea. Still, I hung up that phone and prayed for a miracle. And now . . . They get to go to Cabo!"

At that moment Hope leaned over the counter and hugged me like I was Ed McMahon, and I'd just presented her with a fat check from The Publishers Clearinghouse. "How did you know?"

I couldn't help shaking my head. Because the thing was—I didn't know. I had no idea my donation would come exactly when it was needed. All I knew was I had to make it.

All I knew was big, fancy dream weddings come to an end, and there isn't much more than pictures to show for it. But giving, caring, doing something for someone else—these are the kind of things that have an actual, even sizeable, impact for good. The kind of things that make it onto the pages of pink and blue notebooks.

And that was all I needed to know.

"I hope everyone has an amazing time," I said to Hope.

"I know they will. I can't . . . There's no way I can thank you."

"You don't need to." I smiled at Hope and turned around to leave.

"Call us when you need a wedding cake," she said when I was by the door. "Any one you want, on the house. Or if you already have a cake baker, maybe you'd like to try our kids' cupcake station! Seriously, you'd better call!"

I smiled, suddenly so hopeful and sure about what was to come. "Thanks, Hope. I will."

I stepped out the door and onto the sidewalk.

Okay. Now it was time to go find Isaac and re-groom him.

In the make-him-my-groom-again way, not in the he's-unkempt-so-I-need-to-take-a-nose-hair-trimmer-to-him kind of way. Just to be clear.

Chapter 39

Okay. If this were a movie, I would have thought to bring the suitcase packed with my clothes, shoes, makeup, and deodorant, to the house with me—instead of leaving it at Rona's place—in the event that I worked to the last minute and didn't have time to retrieve said suitcase.

Or a woman with a wand would appear to whip me up some Acne jeans, a great black top, a pair of Manolos, and a hairstyle worthy of the VH1 awards.

But alas, neither occurred.

So I was running across the Santa Monica pier's wooden parking lot in: Jeans caked with dirt. A Hard Rock café T-shirt I had borrowed from Dad to work in—which had five not-exactly-small holes in it and smelled a little strange due to the entire bottle of hand-sanitizer I had rubbed on it to try to make up for the above-mentioned lack of deodorant. And hair covered in the paint that got there when I flung it all over the place because I thought I felt something crawling on me—which turned out to be an errant strand of my own hair.

I was panting when I reached the seafood restaurant at the end of the pier. I bent my knees and took a few breaths of the clean sea air before opening the door and going inside.

"Hi," I said to the host, the word coming out in a gulp. "I'm meeting my party here."

The young man looked at me as if he suspected I was there to redo the roof or something. "What is your party's name?"

"Isaac Matthews."

"Oh, yes." The guy looked at a stack of papers on the podium in front of him.

My heart sped up even faster. This was it.

"Mr. Matthews had to leave a bit early."

Okay. This wasn't it.

"Excuse me?"

"Yes. He left this note for you." The host handed me a piece of paper.

"But—" I began to protest, but the guy was already looking behind me at a lovey-dovey, nicely dressed couple waiting to be seated.

Deflated, I went out the door and opened the note. It was in Isaac's own handwriting and seeing it did things to me. My arms got all achy and my chest burned.

Dear Bloomin,

I apologize that I will miss our dinner meeting. I had an emergency shoot come up. However, if you still would like to meet, you're free to come speak with me at the shoot. I will be down on the waterfront on the south side of the pier.

Thank you.

Isaac Matthews

I read the note about five times, just so I could look at Isaac's handwriting and imagine what pen he had written it with, and if he had that cute little frown mark between his eyes because he was concentrating. Then I stared at Isaac's name at the bottom of the page.

And I might have given it a little peck.

Note still in hand, I booked it back down the pier, passing

the crowds, shops, rides and carnival games where people were paying five dollars a pop for a chance to win a 99 cent basketball.

I was at the top of the wooden stairs that led down to the beach when I saw him.

He was down near the water, assisting another photographer who was taking photos of what appeared to be an engaged couple. His shoes were off, his khaki pants rolled to his knees, and his white dress shirt was blowing around him. My heart literally stopped at the sight of him.

I smiled and took the first four steps down, but when I got to the fourth step, I stopped cold. The photographer Isaac was helping was now at such an angle that I could see her. And who do you think it was?

I'll give you one guess.

Uh huh. It was Chloe.

I tiptoed down the remainder of the steps, as if Isaac and Chloe could hear me coming, and watched the two of them. Something about the whole scene struck me as wrong, and a bunch of questions raced through my brain. Like: Since when was Chloe a photographer? And: Why did she pick this moment, when Isaac had an appointment with a very cool Aussie named Bloomin, to ask for his help?

Without thinking, I picked up a discarded basketball in UCLA colors that was lying on the sand. I held the ball in front of my face as I slowly moved closer to Chloe and Isaac, watching their every move as if I were waiting for something horrible to happen.

And then something did.

During some kind of break in the shoot, the engaged couple took a stroll down the beach. Isaac and Chloe semi-packed-up the equipment and stood there talking, laughing. Then all of the sudden, the two of them were racing down the shore, Chloe running like a duck and cackling like a banshee the whole way.

Oops. Did I just write that? Sorry, that wasn't very nice.

I'll come back and edit it out later.

Then, just before crossing the imaginary finish line, Chloe took a spill on the sand. Isaac stopped dead in his tracks, but did not kick sand in her face like a lesser person might have— not anyone I know or anything, but you know, a lesser person. No, instead he helped Chloe up. He offered her his hand so gallantly, it sent a horrible, flu-like feeling all over me

After Chloe was up on her feet, she smiled at Isaac, and there was something in her smile, something . . . not quite right. Then, as if she did it every day, she took him into a hug of the type I was sure violated the agent/photographer code of ethics. Isaac's arms touched her back ever-so-slightly, and I felt like I was going to throw up. This was obviously a scene they didn't know I was watching.

And it was not one I wanted to watch for a second more.

I threw the UCLA ball in the direction of the two of them and ran across the sand and up the stairs to the boardwalk. I collapsed in a heap on the ground, next to a pack of seagulls feasting on a dropped pretzel, and leaned against the wooden railing, kicking my sand-filled shoes off my feet.

Get back down there, my brain commanded. *Get down there and do what you came here to do!*

I fumbled with my right shoe, pouring the sand out of it. *It's over,* I argued with my brain. *I can't compete with Chloe. I messed things up, and now it's over.*

How can you just give up like that? my brain persisted. *You love him. This can't be your life; thinking you can't compete with people who have some kind of superficial one-up on you.*

"Would you just leave me alone!" The words flew out of my mouth before I could stop them, and I punctuated them by swatting a bug buzzing in front of my face.

A mom who was pushing a baby girl in a stroller and had a little boy holding an ice cream cone standing at her side, watched uncomfortably as I shouted to no one and waved my hand in the air.

"Mommy," the boy said, pointing in my direction.

"Stay close, cookie," the mom said. "That's a crazy homeless lady."

I looked around. I didn't see a crazy homeless lady.

And then it dawned on me. "Hey!" I hollered at the woman. "I'm not homeless! Well . . . maybe *technically* I am. But I can get an apartment. As soon as I find a job. Maybe I'll bottle sand. Or work at a carnival where I can get people to spend ten dollars trying to win a cheapo basketball. I could be a carnie!"

The woman looked over at me, a protective arm around her son. "Let's go. It's not safe over here."

"Hey! Just because I'm homeless, doesn't mean I'm deaf!" I added, watching as the woman corralled her kids away from me.

If you're not deaf, then why are you completely ignoring me? my brain chimed in. *You need to get down there and talk to Isaac!*

Nope. I'd like to keep my pride, my dignity, my—

Um, hello, homeless lady! my brain jabbed.

I looked down at my disaster of a T-shirt and my one shoeless foot, and for some reason felt a surge of courage fill my chest.

And before I knew it, I was throwing off my left shoe and my socks and running down to where Isaac stood on the beach. (Chloe was further down the shore, directing the couple, and I was glad for this fact.)

The moment Isaac saw me rushing across the sand, my shoes in hand, he almost dropped the light reflector thingy he was holding.

It was so cute.

I jogged to his side. "Surprise."

"Annabelle." Isaac fidgeted, like he didn't know if he should hug me or what.

"I flew down here last night," I said. "I have so much to tell you. And it just couldn't be said over the phone."

"How did you know I was here?" Isaac asked.

"I called Chloe and made an appointment to see you."

"So you're . . ."

"Bloomin Onion," I answered with a nod.

Isaac grinned slightly and took a quick glance over at Chloe, who still hadn't seen me. He scratched his head. "Where have you been? I've been trying . . . I mean, we decided to put the wedding plans on hold, and then you practically fell off the face of the earth."

He looked so hurt I felt my heart break a little. "I know," I said, my voice full of apology. "I thought *you* were avoiding *me*. I didn't know you—"

"Annabelle?"

I looked up and saw Chloe, her perfect, shiny hair flowing around her face like a stinking shampoo ad.

"Hey," I said, jaw tight.

Chloe looked over my outfit and straightened her perfect linen dress. "What are you doing here?"

"Talking to Isaac," I said, resisting the urge to add a "My man whom you better stay away from and P.S. I took that sweater you gave me and turned it into a Turtle Wax rag."

"Oh." Chloe did this weird thing with her lips, and I'm telling you, I could see her eyes say, "I thought you were out of the picture."

I turned to Isaac and looked at him almost pleadingly. "Could we . . . go somewhere?"

Isaac looked unbelievably relieved. "Yeah, that would be—"

"Actually," Chloe said, clipping him off, "we won't be done for quite a while."

"That's okay," I said, turning toward Isaac. "I can wait until you're finished."

Isaac looked at Chloe, a slightly confused expression on his face. "We only have ten frames left."

"I just decided I'm going to throw in an extra hundred for free," Chloe said, a look that very much resembled a smirk on her face.

Isaac glared at her. "A hundred free frames? Are you crazy?"

"Yes," I said.

Chloe and Isaac both looked at me.

"Oh, sorry. I thought you were talking to me." I put my hands in my pockets innocently.

"Let's just finish the ten," Isaac said to Chloe in a take-charge tone that was really gorgeous.

Chloe shook her head almost defiantly. "I want to do more."

"Well then, I'm sure you can do them on your own," Isaac said. "No one needs an assistant for engagement photos anyway."

"*I* do." Chloe looked behind her at the couple. They were so busy hugging each other they didn't seem too concerned that she was gone. "And you're being extremely unprofessional standing over here chatting with your ex and talking about leaving the shoot before its over."

Excuse me? I am not his ex!

"I'll finish the shoot as planned," Isaac said. "Ten more frames."

Chloe shot Isaac a warning scowl. "If you don't help me with this, as a professional should, maybe I won't help you when jobs come up."

He looked completely unfazed by the threat. "I was actually planning on letting you know after this job that I've found other representation. I think we both know you're the one who's been crossing the bounds of professionalism lately."

What? My mouth dropped open so far I think a little bit of sand blew into it.

I knew it! She made a move on him!!! I knew she didn't deserve clouds of white!

She wasn't just Chloe, old-family-friend. She was Chloe, wanted-to-steal-my-man, and she jumped the second she could. A hundred different scenarios filled my mind.

Had she asked him to look through a camera lens to see if it was blurry and then let the camera slip and tried to kiss him?

Had she dressed up like a roll of film and told him she's liked him since he took her high school cheerleading photo?

Before I could stop myself, I found myself lunging at Chloe, grabbing her by those fake highlights of hers. She tried to claw at me, but missed as I backed her into the water. I pushed her, a wild look in my eye that I'm pretty sure had never been there before. I smacked the water with my free hand, splashing it all over her perfectly made-up face, watching as mascara-dyed crocodile tears dripped down her cheeks. And then . . .

Well, and then I woke up from the fantasy.

You didn't think I'd actually do that, did you?

When I came back to reality, Chloe was looking at Isaac like she couldn't believe he would choose to run off with the paint-in-her-hair, holey-T-shirt girl rather than stay with her.

"Let's get out of here," he said, taking hold of my hand.

My heart beat fast as he pulled me in the direction of the stairs that led up to the boardwalk.

"Isaac!" Chloe called. "If you walk away, it will be the biggest mistake of your professional career!"

"I think I'll be all right," Isaac called over his shoulder, with a meaningful look in my direction. "Good-bye, Chloe."

"Yeah," I added before I could stop myself. "See ya, *Chlo.*"

What? I didn't push her into the ocean, did I?

Chapter 40

"Ouch. What the heck was that?"

"Oh. Sorry." I bit my lip and moved the candle-topped Food Fight cupcake away from Isaac's arm, rubbing the spot where it had touched.

Oops. Accidentally singed off a little of his arm hair.

"Can I take off the blindfold now?" Isaac asked. "Before I get seriously injured?"

"Just one more second." I helped Isaac maneuver down the hall to the room I had transformed, and planted him in the very center. "Okay. You can look now."

Isaac removed the blindfold and peered around. "What . . . did you do?"

I grabbed onto his hand and gave him a walking tour of the room, pointing out everything I had done. "Welcome to your new state-of-the-art photography studio," I said with a huge smile.

Isaac took in the scene. The cozy rugs on the took-way-too-long-to-polish wood floor. The huge bean bag chair, mini-fridge, and plasma TV in the corner for when he needed a break. The desk and shelves I had put together, filled with fancy leather photo albums and boxes. The newly painted walls—one entire wall covered with chalkboard paint so he could take notes without using paper.

He looked completely floored. "Annabelle . . . this is—"

"I built those," I said, pointing to the shelves and desk. "You can sit there and print off photos while I watch TV over there." I gestured toward the break nook.

"While you watch TV?" Isaac said, sounding confused. "But I thought you hated it here and, how did you put it, 'would rather live in a cardboard box with seagulls pecking at your feet than live in L.A.'?"

I looked into Isaac's amazing hazel eyes. "I know I said I have every reason to stay in Monterey. But that was before I realized I have much more important reasons to move here."

Isaac raised his eyebrows as if to ask, "What?"

"I have something to tell you," I said softly.

Isaac nodded. "Okay."

"I quit my job."

"You what?"

"Apparently I'm the laughing stock of *Central Coast Weddings*. I thought I earned the editor-in-chief position. That they offered it to me because I was good. But yo ho ho, how stupid I was!"

Hmm. That wasn't supposed to come out quite so pirate-y.

Isaac frowned. "What are you talking about?"

"The entire hiring committee thinks my writing is stupid and lame and that no one wants to read the kind of magazine I believe in. They think I'm a total idiot. And Alex, who I honestly thought was a professional, had this . . . plan to get me to take the job and then convince me I had it all wrong. And the worst part is: I overheard every bit of it." I paused for a moment, remembering the awful scene. "And then I walked into the room and quit."

Okay, reader, you and I know I didn't exactly *walk* into the room. But now didn't really seem like the time to tell Isaac about how I stormed in and started chucking beauty products. All in due time my friend; all in due time.

I sighed. "Maybe it was an impulsive thing to do, but at

the very root of it, I think it was because I love what I do. I love finding the deep story behind the one that usually gets reported. Rather than just say a bride is wearing a Lisa Wong wedding gown, I want to talk about how the woman who made the silk uses all her proceeds to fund a program that provides games and toys for orphanages in Asia."

Isaac touched my cheek with his hand, and I suddenly found it hard to breathe. And not just because of the paint fumes.

"That's what makes your writing so powerful," he said. "And if those people don't realize what a talented, incredible writer you are, then they're the idiots."

I blinked, my eyes resting on Isaac's incredible lips. "How is it that you see me in a way that's so . . ." I couldn't finish the sentence, I didn't have the words.

"I just do," Isaac answered, his voice all low and gorgeous.

I stared at him for a moment and then slid open the top drawer of the desk, retrieving his blue notebook.

"I found this when I was packing," I said. "I had no idea you left it for me. In fact, I had no idea you left anything for me at all."

Isaac shook his head, as if some suspicion was just confirmed. "It was that creep Alex, wasn't it?"

I emptied my lungs with a deep, long breath. "Yes. He came up with this whole . . . plan to make me think you'd forgotten me. And then, well . . . he told me he had feelings for me and asked me to choose him. It was all a game to him, and meant absolutely nothing, but I thought you should know. I hate that—"

"It's okay," Isaac interrupted. "Chloe told me she's liked me since High School and said I needed to stop denying that we were a perfect match."

"I knew it!" I couldn't help shouting. "I knew she wasn't my Earth Sister! I knew she was going to try someth—"

Isaac put a finger to my lips, and my pulse quickened at the touch. "She didn't stand a chance, Annabelle. She's not you.

She's not this." He pointed to the notebook in my hand.

"Thank you for seeing the Blue Note in me," I said. "I want so much to never be too far from that. And to do so, I need to never be too far from you."

Isaac looked at me hopefully. "Are you saying—"

"I'm saying I no longer believe we need to have everything in perfect order before we move forward with wedding plans, because we can work anything out as long as we do it together. I can learn to live with traffic and smog as long as I'm doing it all with you. I'm saying I'm sorry. I'm saying I love you."

Isaac touched my chin, gently moving my face upward until our eyes met. "I love you too."

Feeling almost lightheaded, I wrapped my arms around him and took in all the layers of his warmth.

I still wanted to hold on when Isaac pulled away. "So, uh, why didn't you turn the master bedroom into my studio?"

I froze, my hands suddenly feeling like they had tiny needles poking into them.

He hated the studio. It wasn't big enough. Or nice enough.

"Um, oh, well . . ." I stammered. "I was going to use the master, actually . . . but it was locked . . . and, uh . . ."

Isaac grinned at me strangely and then tugged on my hand, guiding the way across the hall to the master bedroom. He stretched a bit over his head and retrieved a key from the top of the door frame and unlocked the door.

Darn. I didn't know that key was there.

Isaac swung the door open, and what I saw inside made me almost stop breathing.

The room had been turned into a writing studio for me.

There was a gorgeous modern desk with a MacBook Air— oh my goodness, I had wanted one of those so bad!—on the top, and a chair that looked like it would be so comfortable to sit in all day. There was a hot cocoa machine in a little sitting area with— guess what, a giant bean bag chair—and a phone with a stack of long distance calling cards next to it.

And then there were the photos.

Bright, brilliant photos of me and Carrie; me and Mom; me and Dad; me and Cammie; and an adorable one of me and my precious niece and nephew that I recognized as having been taken at Christmas.

It was the most beautiful room I had ever seen.

I looked at Isaac. "I can't . . . When did . . ."

Apparently I wasn't going to be able to finish a sentence, so I just threw my arms around him, resting my head on his shoulder, completely overcome by his love for me.

"This is what you mean to me," Isaac said. "Your comfort is my first priority. I was hoping this might bring a little of Monterey, and the things that are important to you, here. But I want you to know, if you still don't think this is a place you want to be, then that's it. Because I want you to be completely happy. And I would follow you across the earth if it meant you would be. Because I need you. You make me better than I ever could be without you."

"I'm going to be happy here," I said. "Living in this house with the man who makes *me* better than *I* ever could be without *him*."

Isaac looked at me, obviously feeling the rightness of what was happening. "That's great," he said, reaching his arms around my waist. "Except we aren't going to have anywhere to sleep."

I smiled. "We'll work it out."

"Yes, we will." Isaac stared into my eyes so intensely I think I stopped breathing for a moment. Then he traced the line of my jaw with his finger and tucked a strand of paint-splattered hair behind my ear. I felt my breath return for only a second before he took my face into both hands and kissed me like a man who had been away at war.

I felt like it was my very first kiss.

Afterward, my legs like Jell-O beneath me, I blinked up at Isaac. "If I ask you a funny request do you promise not to think I'm crazy?"

Isaac shrugged. "No promises," he said, cracking a smile.

I rolled my eyes, but quickly refocused on Isaac. "I want to say yes again."

Isaac wrinkled his brow. "What?"

"When you asked me to marry you at Disneyland it was so perfect, like a fairytale. And then all of these things started happening that made me think maybe I was going to have a fairytale life, and I almost believed I wanted to. But I don't. I want the good and the bad. The ups and the downs. The things that will help us be the kind of people who make it onto the pages of the notebooks that really matter.

"And so I want to say yes again. Right here. In this place where life won't always be a fairytale, but it will always be us, doing the best we can. So could you do it again, maybe? Ask me?"

Isaac frowned slightly. "But I already gave you the ring."

"It's not important."

"Okay." Isaac got down on one knee, and I felt goose-bumps cover my entire body. "Let me just start by saying you are absolutely adorable. I would have crumbled if you just came down here and said, 'Hey, buddy, let's make this work.' But no, you slaved away making a studio for me. You scrubbed and painted and built. I can't tell you enough how incredible I think you are. How sweet, and beautiful, and bright. You are the most amazing woman I have ever met, and I will spend forever trying to make you as happy as you make me. So let me just ask you one more time Annabelle, will you—"

Isaac's words were interrupted by a horribly loud crash coming from across the hall.

"The desk!" I shouted.

I spun around just in time to see my "easy to assemble" desk crash right to the ground in Isaac's studio. But what was worse, somehow in my spinning frenzy I managed to send my right arm/hand right into poor, kneeling Isaac's face.

"Ah, man," he said, grabbing his nose in pain.

I put my hand over my mouth, looking down at Isaac with

apology. "I'm so sorry. Oh no! It's bleeding!"

I watched in a panic as a tiny bit of red came from Isaac's left nostril. Man. I didn't know I was strong enough to give a guy a bloody nose. I guess those self-defense classes at the gym really were working.

"Tilt your head back!" I shouted.

"I don't think that's right," Isaac said, pinching the bridge of his nose. "In Scouts we learned to tilt it forward."

"Well, do whatever!" I kneeled down beside Isaac and, suddenly feeling very Florence Nightengale, ripped off a portion of my T-shirt at the bottom. I handed it to Isaac to use as a makeshift handkerchief, and hoped he wasn't breathing too deeply, because bottle of hand sanitizer notwithstanding, the thing kind of smelled.

Isaac held the rag against his nose and looked over at me.

I stared at him, the amazing man who I had just clocked while he was trying to propose, and shook my head, laughter escaping from my lips.

Isaac's mouth cracked into a huge smile as he cradled my head with his free hand and kissed me on the forehead, the feeling of his laughter amazing against my skin.

"Yes," I said to Isaac, my laughter in perfect sync with his. "Yes I will!"

Chapter 41

"You ready?"

"We're ready."

Mom smiled and squeezed my shoulder, my elbow-length veil shifting ever so slightly. "Okay, I'll make the announcement."

I watched Mom walk toward the stage in the Monterey church-gymnasium-turned-reception-hall, weaving her way through the maze of round, people-crowded, lime-green decorated tables.

Uh huh. Lime green.

I don't even want to get into it.

Isaac and I waited behind the cake table, standing so close it was as if we were one person. Isaac had an arm around me and was tracing the words, "You are lovely" into my back with his finger.

At least I think that's what he was writing. It could have been, "You old lady." He was going pretty fast, so I couldn't be sure.

I smiled over at the deliciousness that was Isaac and felt my insides dance. I couldn't believe this moment, this day, was real.

As Mom got on the mic and announced the cake-cutting,

Carrie came to my side, looking lovely in her simple cream Maid of Honor dress. "Here. I'll hold your bouquet."

I handed over the daisy bouquet Hope from Caring Blooms had made for me. It and all the wedding flowers were going to the Monterey Bay Women's Shelter after the reception. "Thanks," I said, smiling at my best friend.

"That's what I'm here for," she said, her eyes glistening. "I'm so happy for you, Annabelle. And you look beautiful."

I blinked, peering down at the satin A-line wedding dress I'd bought at a place called Cinderella's Closet. The shop sells gently used bridal and special occasion dresses and uses the proceeds to fund trips to Disneyland and Disneyworld for families who've been through natural disasters. I'd found the place by accident one day and bought the gown for ten times the ticket price.

The dress wasn't fancy. It had a simple square neckline and cap sleeves and a bit of beading on the empire waist. But it was beautiful. And you know what, I felt better in it than I ever did in the dress at Monique's.

The guests quickly gathered around the cake table with Dad, Cammie, and Isaac's family in the front.

Mom came behind the table and slid a large rectangular box toward Isaac. "Here you go," she said, raising her eyebrows.

I bit my lip. Isaac didn't know about this yet. And I was kind of looking forward to the look on his face when he first saw our cake-cutting sword.

Yes, that's right. I said cake-cutting sword. As in . . . normally used to cut off knight appendages.

I could see Isaac struggling not to show how puzzled he was as he opened the box and surveyed the two foot long mini-replica of Excalibur with, what else, lime green flowers tied to it.

"Um, Annabelle," he whispered into my ear as he lifted the sword from the box, "where did we get this thing?"

"Ginny picked it out," I whispered back. "She said all the celebs are using cake-cutting swords."

Isaac grinned, kissing my ear, the warm tickle of his breath feeling beyond amazing. "Well, if I have to defend your honor after this reception is over, I guess we're set."

Isaac and I cut the first piece of our cake, a huge chunk with ragged edges—because, hey, when you're cutting with a sword, that's what you get—and put it onto the plate Mom had set on the table for us.

Isaac was the first to pick up the wedding cake chunk and feed it to me.

"Smash it in her face!" his sisters ribbed, sounding much too excited by the prospect.

"Yeah!" Dirk—who was snapping photos with Isaac's camera—added. "At least get some in her nose or something!"

Isaac ignored the chiders and fed me the cake in a civilized manner. There would be no in-the-face cake-smashing going on here. We were mature, well-mannered adults.

Plus I told Isaac he'd spend the honeymoon on the floor of our cabin in Lake Tahoe if he tried anything funny.

Hey, a girl's gotta do what a girl's gotta do.

I swallowed my cake—it was even more delicious than the sample Mom had given me when she was testing out recipes in her quest to find the perfect one—and gave Isaac his first bite. He enjoyed the treat and kissed me, his mouth still sweet, and the room clapped, photo flashes going off everywhere.

The DJ—which was Cameron and his iPod—put on a song by the Old 97's, and I kind of felt like I was floating as Isaac and I made our way to our seats at the head table, cake in hand.

We were about to sit when someone I didn't recognize came up beside us.

"Excuse me?" the thirty-something woman said, her greenish-blue eyes fixed on me. "Annabelle Pleasanton?"

"Yes."

"My name is Kiersten Bailey."

"Oh," I said, trying to hide my blank face. "Hi."

I stared at Kiersten, struggling to figure out who she was. I looked over to Isaac for help, but he just stood there with a strange expression on his face.

"Kiersten," I bluffed, "so glad you could make it. I'm glad you . . . got your invitation."

"Actually," Kiersten said, holding up a spiral notebook. "I'm here on assignment."

Assignment? I wondered. And then an awful possibility gripped me: *Dirk.*

"Listen," I said to the woman. "I don't know what Dirk told you, but please ignore whatever it is. Are you supposed to sing some kind of weird song to us or something?"

"Pardon?"

I eyed the notebook in the woman's hand. "Some kind of skit?"

Kiersten frowned. "No . . . I work for *Benevolent Bride.* You sent us an article about a month ago."

I felt lines immediately form on my forehead. I'd never heard of *Benevolent Bride.* And I certainly never sent them anything.

But wait a minute . . .

I looked over at Isaac who was fake-whistling, putting his hands in his pockets, and pretending to look at the ceiling.

What did he do?

Kiersten reached into her oversize tote and retrieved something that looked very familiar. It only took me a second to recognize it as my sample article. "I have to tell you how much we at *Benevolent Bride* loved this," she explained. "As a brand-new online not-for-profit publication, we've found it a bit hard to find quality writers who understand our vision. But when we received this, we knew you were a perfect fit.

"Needless to say, there's an offer for the staff writing position you applied for coming your way. Obviously we can't compete with the salaries offered by other L.A.-based magazines, but we are hoping you will still consider."

"Oh my goodness!" My mouth dropped open so far, anyone

in the room could have counted my fillings, and I threw my arms around Isaac.

I knew he didn't want me to give him a bound copy of the article plus a cover letter for his own personal journal! "I heard about the magazine from Pilar's assistant," he whispered in my ear. "The wedding world needs you, Annabelle."

I squeezed Isaac tightly and then turned to Kiersten. "But . . . I don't understand. You came all the way up here to deliver this news to me?"

"Oh no," Kiersten said. "That has all been done through email. I'm here to cover your wedding."

"Huh?"

Kiersten nodded. "Your article idea was great, but the only thing it lacked was firsthand coverage of a wedding that exclusively features vendors with philanthropic causes. And since you are a bride who decided to have just such a wedding, I'm here to get your story."

So, wait a minute? I was the subject of the article?

I stared at Kiersten as she clicked her pen. "What motivated you as a bride to choose a caterer, dressmaker, and florist that, to use your words, 'give back'?"

"Well . . ." I squeezed Isaac's hand and looked over at him. "It's kind of a long story . . ."

With Isaac's help, I told Kiersten that story. The story of the Dream Wedding I'd won. The couture dress, imported flowers, and five-star cuisine I traded in for a secondhand gown, recyclable bouquets, and a dinner of burgers and green salad. And with tears filling my eyes, I told her why. I told her about Food Fight and Caring Blooms and Cinderella's Closet.

"And how do you feel about the way things turned out?" Kiersten asked.

I paused for a moment, looking over at Isaac who was smiling beside me. "You know, when I won the Dream Wedding and we started planning it, I thought nothing could be better. But I was wrong."

Kiersten scribbled in her notepad and Isaac squeezed my hand, "I love you," he said, looking at me like I was everything in the world to him.

I turned to kiss my new husband. The man I couldn't wait to live life with.

And as the bass boomed beneath our feet and the lights shone above our heads, I was so completely grateful for the simple dress, the lime green tables, and the flower-decorated mini-sword.

Because in the end, the reality was so much better than the dream.

The End

Book Club Questions

1. Can you think of anything Annabelle should have added to her WDPC?

2. Annabelle is excited by the prospect of a "Dream Wedding." Is this something you can relate to? What do you think about the fact that weddings are a billion-dollar industry?

3. Dr. Harmony's *Guide to Sisterly Harmony* discusses female relationships. Do you think women feel the need to have the "upper hand" on each other rather than to "join hands" with one another? Which category does Annabelle fit into? Does this change during the story?

4. Annabelle and Cammie get into a brawl in their parents' kitchen. Think like Cammie: Is there more going on here than just a pair of ruined pants?

5. Annabelle doesn't really feel accepted by Isaac's family. Do you believe when you marry a person you marry the family? What would you do if you loved the person but couldn't stand the family?

6. Compare Annabelle's relationship with Alex to her relationship with Isaac. How do they differ? Are they at all similar?

7. Did you suspect that Alex was not all he seemed? How could you tell?

8. Why do you think the author had Annabelle find Isaac's "Blue Notes" when she did?

9. What do the lime green tablecloths in the closing scene of the book symbolize?

10. Annabelle ends up choosing philanthropic wedding vendors. What is the significance of this in relation to her "Pink Notes"?

Elodia Strain

Elodia Strain grew up in California and left home at seventeen to attend Brigham Young University where she majored in advertising and English and learned how to study, make soup, and paint her nails at the same time.

After dabbling in everything from advertising copywriting to Spanish translation to music composition, Elodia published her first novel, *The Icing on the Cake*, and was named CFI's Best New Fiction Author.

When she's not writing or scribbling book ideas onto whatever paper is in sight, Elodia enjoys dancing, dreaming of a day when H&M will sell clothes online, and spending time with her family.

Her wedding to her husband, Jacob, was a very simple affair, and she never once forced him to try on a frilly designer suit.

Visit her website at www.elodiastrain.com or her blog at www.theinkladies.blogspot.com